THE GODLY SERIES

Sebastian's STORY

GODLY BEGINNING

Written by:

CHARLES D. RAYFORD

BOOK SERIES READING ORDER:

GODLY BEGINNING: SEBASTIAN'S STORY

TRINITY

Paperback: 978-1-963883-13-8
eBook: 978-1-963883-14-5
Library of Congress Control Number: 2024903889

Ordering Information:

Prime Seven Media
518 Landmann St.
Tomah City, WI 54660

Printed in the United States of America

About the Author

Charles Rayford was born December 15, 1989. At a very young age, he had a fascination with mythology and religion. At the age of thirteen, he attempted to write his first book, but after some computer issues, lost all of his hard work. In 2018 he started writing a new series. This one was called The Godly Series. Charles continued working on this series for the next 5 years and was noticed by a media company and did a tv interview (Spotlight with Logan Crawford), and then started working with the media company to publish his books. Charles is still currently writing and working on new series and short stories.

Table of Contents

CHAPTER 1

The Story Of Sebastian's Reincarnation

What is the universe? It's a question that's asked quite often. What is God? Another question that gets asked. Most of us never think to ask the question, what kind of ability, or what kind of being can create a planet, or a star? Or even an entire solar system? Are they beings who look humanoid? Or, are they beings way beyond the comprehension of our minds? It is a scary notion. But let me present an idea. What if there are multiple gods? Much like ancient religion suggests. But what if these gods that I am referring to…they are beyond the understanding of creatures such as Vishnu, or Buddha, or even Jehovah? These creatures wouldn't call themselves gods, but would most likely call themselves something else. Something we can't understand. But these creatures would have had to come from somewhere as well. Everything has a creation process. Something cannot come from nothing. Life can be many things. As seen on Earth. Plants, animals, people, even machines. Yes, so much creation. But never would one imagine it to be a bad thing. Not at all. Not once. Because creation is beautiful. But, it depends on what is being created. Or does it? What do you do when you have the power to create? Well, of course, you create. But what do you do when your creation becomes what you have always feared it would? When it starts to destroy itself in horrible ways. Ways that make you cringe to the core. But through all the devastation, there are the ones that show love and compassion and everything you've come to value in your creation. You feel those are the ones that make it worthwhile. But what do you do with the other ones? There's so many variables when it comes to creation. But what do you do to make your life and theirs as well, simpler? Well, you move among them. Not an easy feat for the creationist to join his insects, but it's a sacrifice for what you feel are your children. You join them, and see all the suffering first hand. You claim to be the guy who brought them life. And how do they treat you? Some worship you without question. Others… They fear you. To the point where they are afraid you bring a much bigger threat. You will turn the sheep against them. You realize you don't know your insects as well as you think. They have separated the lesser people from those they consider having great prominence, and these people have the power to seize you from your lair, cut your throat, and end your campaign for peace. You realize, of course, you should have at least taken some of your abilities with you. To save yourself from your creation's madness. Of course, they can't really kill you. All that's happened is your soul has returned to its actual vessel. Now you revise your plan. You will try again. But this time you split a part of yourself to keep just enough of your strength to teach your children a lesson. But then, something unexpected happens. You didn't know what you were doing fully and have created another being. In a sense, it's another you. But this one has a different view. He feels your children don't deserve saving. He feels they should all pay for what they have done. Their arrogance has cost them their planet, their home, and everything else they care about. But you realize that the only way to stop this is to give up your power fully again, but this time you add a twist. A genetic one. You choose a devout worshipper and place yourself within the womb. You are born again. But as one of your insects. You don't remember who or what you really are. You know you were a miracle. Your mother couldn't have children, and your father was skeptical as to if you were his. But in the end, realized the love your mother had for him and never left you. You have no idea of the real reason you exist in this form. But one day you will remember. And then it will change the world. It will change everything. For the dark creator will awake and destroy us all.

CHAPTER 2

Sebastian's New Life

SEBASTIAN: "Son? Can you come help place the dishes?", I heard my mother call. I got up, looked around, and realized it was morning. I had been dreaming of a most terrible battle with a most terrible being who I felt could rip my world apart. "Sebastian!", my mother called again. I moved out of bed, and put on my clots; (shoes made of tuk, which is a sort of wood). I walked into the eating room. My dad walked in the door from outside, "I tell you, it's getting ridiculous out there. All these stupid, new, laws!". I often heard Father complain about the king but just didn't pay it any mind. There were four kingdoms in my land. We call it Plinth. The four kingdoms are Dasha, Kindy, Alexandria, and my home, Nasher. Dasha was known for being filled with villainous characters. They are always so put up on themselves, you can smell the shite in their nose. It was ruled by Queen Falsa. She had a son named Caprius, who was known for being cruel and abusive to his subjects. Kindy was more of a... Well it's in the name. These people are very polite and will shine your clots if you ask them. Everything about the king and queen suggest that they smoke a lot of their stress plants. Kindy was ruled by King Derek and Queen Shay. They have a daughter named Alisa. Alexandria is ruled by Queen Alexandria, or at least that is what I heard. My king is Oliver, and he is pretty much a dog, but he rules his people fairly. "Just waking up, Son?", "Yes, Father. I was having those dreams again.", "If you're having a nightmare, what did I tell you to do?", Father asked for the two-hundredth time. "You said, always remember when you go to sleep.", "Exactly. That way, you'll know you're sleeping.", Father replied. Mother placed food on the plate. It was ham and stony. Stony was a malleable rock that had a sweet flavor that sort of went with anything. As I took the first bite, there was a bang on the door. The house went stone silent. "OPEN UP, IN THE NAME OF THE KING, DAMN IT!". Father opened the door and the king himself was standing outside. His guards were standing on both of his sides, looking quite confused and menacing. "You've probably never seen me, but I am King Oliver. I have come to inform you, in my respectable manner and dignity, that we are unfortunately at war.". It almost sounded unreal. Mother embraced me, while father just stood there, trying to determine how to handle the situation. "I have tried unsuccessfully to keep peace, which is why we have had all these new laws. But now, we have reached a place in our relationship that I find deplorable. We are going to war with the kingdom of Dasha. And while I regret bringing such fear to our nation, I fear more what that evil queen and her spoiled son will do. Please bear with us at this time of trial.", King Oliver completed his speech, turned on his heel, and walked back to his wagon. The soldiers turned and followed. We all returned to breakfast. "What does this mean, Clad?", Mother asked. "It means we have to be on guard. We can't afford to lose. I'm thinking of joining....", "You can't! We need you! What do you expect me and Sebastian to do without you?", "What happens if we all die? We need to think! Queen Falsa isn't going to be kind to us! Hell, she doesn't even give a shit about her own people! I can't let her hurt you and Bastian...I just can't!",

Father shouted, as he fell to one knee. Mother rushed to his side and held him. I joined. We all just held each other. Bracing for what was coming. But I didn't know what was coming. I couldn't know just how involved I was. Because I didn't know. I didn't have a single fucking clue. It all happened so fast. I feel like all the dreams, all the fighting back then, all the craziness that came out of this… I had no idea what the hell I was in for.

CHAPTER 3

Alisa Meets Alex

ALISA: Kindy has always been a kingdom of…excuse my language, dope heads. A word we use to describe people who inhale the fumes of our native plant. The other kingdoms buy from us. We have lots of coins. So much coin. I've been a princess for seventeen years. I've watched my parents smoke and drink their rule away. I've been so humiliated to the point of straight insanity. Once, my mother was so high, and I had been such a spoiled brat, and my mother couldn't deal with me, so she immediately did something that was against all imagination. She tried to murder me. Literally put my fluff over my face and tried to smother me. I've never forgiven her. My dad saved me. My mother tries to act like it never happened. She still inhales. That's when I was three, now I'm seventeen, and practically running the kingdom. My parents are always passed out, or too disoriented to make decisions, or deal with serious shit. Which is why I'm so focused on this situation with this crap war between Dasha and Nasher. Fact of the matter is, it will get crazy after a while. It will come here. My parents are over here smoking and lazing around, when they should be here to help me strategize on what the hell we should do if the war comes HERE! And then there's this queen who's coming here from

Alexandria. I have no idea what she wants, but being the diplomat that I am, I've got to meet with her. Funny thing is, I know all about the other two kingdoms, but I don't know about Alexandria. Like at all. Except for its name. "Uhh...Your Highness? You said to tell you when that queen is here...", "Yes. Has she arrived?", "Well, that's the thing. We've had to detain her.", "Soldier, you had better not be inhaling.", I said, as I watched his demeanor cower immediately. I passed a law that strictly prohibited soldiers from inhaling on duty. Couldn't stop them all together, but I was at least able to get them clear headed before their shifts with a little concoction I came up with in our castle's lab. And before each shift they must drink it. But I've had soldiers who inhale right after. Now them, I suspend. Most of these guys got families, so I must do things this way. But at the thought of detaining a queen... "Do you realize this could start a war? Are you a special kind dumb, or were your parents inhaling when your mum was giving birth?", "Mam, believe me, I know the situation, but she became upset with one of the guards and threatened to kill the man, then she attacked him and none of us were a match for her.". I made my way down to the dungeons. I walked past the guard standing outside after he saluted me only to hear chatter, "So, you are the queen of that ridiculous hidden kingdom? Why did you travel by yourself? And most importantly, how are you, how you are?". I made my way towards the cell and realized the one asking questions was my father. "Father! What are you doing down here? Don't you have some leaves to burn?", "I'm here because I was witness to what this young lady did.", "What exactly is that?". My father had a strange look on his face. He looked at the girl one more time, then said, "Ask her yourself.". My father turned and walked out. I faced the girl in the cage. She was glowing. Either she was decorated this way, or this was something else...something more sinister. I stared at her and waited for her to speak. But she didn't say anything. She just sat there staring at me. Aside from the glow, she was quite beautiful. If Kindy was not a peaceful kingdom, I'm sure my soldiers would have their way with this one. Of course, there's no telling what she is made of and if it's a threat. But she looked like she was my age. Her hair was a very pale pink that matched her glowing skin as well as her lips. She had baby blue eyes that any man would kill for. This girl was beauty in physical form, and I hated her. But since I'm the responsible one here, I should handle this maturely. First thing I did was open the cell and stand aside. She walked out, "Thank you. Now perhaps you and I can talk business. Is there a more appropriate meeting place?". She was strange. Very strange indeed. But I obliged her, and we made our way to my meeting chambers. There was a desk and two chairs. I sat down on one side. She sat on the other. We looked hard at each other and I was jealous of her beauty. Finally, she spoke, "I am Queen Alexandria of the kingdom under the same name. I understand that there is a war right now. I have come to tell you, there is more to this war than you may think. To what Queen Falsa is trying to accomplish.", "And what exactly is she trying to accomplish?", "She is trying to find the god sword. Because with it, she could destroy all that is holy. All that lives. All that becomes of us will be dust. I just so happen to know where the sword is.". I was quite amused. I mean, the god sword doesn't exist. I know for a fact because there is no god. This is a crazy world filled with drunks, rapists and thieves. At the same time, I was intrigued to know what she was talking about. "So, if the sword is real, where the hell is it?". She swallowed, waved her beautifully pinkish arm and pointed at her chest, "The only way Falsa gets the sword is by killing me. I am the sword.". Shocked by what she said, I had to ask, "Why did you threaten my soldier?", "Honestly, it was just a misunderstanding. He attacked me, because he thought I was a monster, because of my skin.".

CHAPTER 4

Sebastian's Friend: The War Begins

SEBASTIAN: Mother was beside herself. She had been constantly checking outside. Father spent less time outdoors, and both wouldn't allow me to stray too far. It was scary. I felt this overwhelming feeling that something big was coming. There were rumors saying the king was aiding Falsa, because she promised him a stake in the new kingdom. But she betrayed him by threatening to invade Nasher. So now he was being stubborn about the fact that his people are in great danger. We are on the verge of death, and he didn't care. At least that was how Father was putting it. Most days I kept to myself. Hoping for the best. Other days, my parents were so afraid of the war, that just taking a walk to get apples from the fruit garden was ridiculously terrifying. I started to also hear other things. Like the fact that the other two kingdoms were intervening in the war. Part of me believed that because the other two kingdoms were getting involved, this was going to make it go away. I mean, wouldn't that be great? Unfortunately, all the signs that tensions were getting worse were getting more obvious as the days passed. Everyone was on edge. There was a girl who I would often see in the village. Her name was Micka. She was a very beautiful girl with purple hair and red eyes. Often, I would see her when I would head into the village with my father. Her father brought vegetables from my father. We of course were the only farm in Nasher, so wasn't really anyone else to go to anyway. When my father and I rode into the village today, it was very quiet. I saw Micka standing with her father. Guards were all over the place but were just observing. "Hey, Micka, what are you getting today?", "Just tomatoes, cabbage, and carrots. My father wants to conserve some coins so we can get out of here before Falsa arrives.", "Everybody is afraid of this war, huh?", I asked. "Well, what do you expect, Bastian? People can die. Anytime you have a situation like that, it's bound to be bad. Not to mention what I've heard.", "What have you heard?", I asked, stepping a bit closer, so the guards couldn't hear us. "Well, Bastian, do you believe in the God? They say he came down five-hundred years ago, and we killed him.". I wasn't too sure I believed in this story, but could hardly see what that had to do with the war. "Queen Falsa is trying to find the god sword and she wants to rule all the kingdoms with it.", Micka said. I still wasn't sure what I thought about that situation, but I knew that can't be what this war is about. It's such a silly thing. "I'm not sure I believe that, Micka. I mean, I know I don't really believe in this God, and I know my parents do, and they've always tried to force that belief on me, but come on. Falsa making all this noise over a fictional sword. Seriously?", "This isn't some joke, Bastian. There is something I never told you, but my father used to do business with Alexandria. And he says that kingdom is almost like visiting the home of the God. He says their princess is some kind of 'godly' weapon and is closely guarded. But I heard that Alexandria was first attacked, and now the princess is running. I heard she is somewhere in the wilderness. Waiting.", "Waiting for what exactly?", "For the God to come and take what's his.".

It was quiet all day. My father worked solemnly in the yard, while my mother cleaned and dusted the cottage. I sat in my room, wondering when this supposed war was coming. Every day that passed was the same. My mother waited outside every night for my father to come home because she was afraid he might not come. Instead, it will be a Dashin soldier, coming to kill my mother and me. I stopped going into the village, because Mother wouldn't allow me. She said that it was only a matter of time before the danger came. I was so bored. A seventeen year old boy shouldn't have to go through that. Being this bored. It wasn't scary to me for some reason. It was beautiful that life was going the way it was going. But this war just seemed like something that was going to go away soon. But the truth was, it was happening. Because you can literally feel the tension. My father would come home at night and be so tired and angry from all the soldiers hanging around. They, of course, were there for our safety, but it didn't seem much like something was coming. But the tension was there, it just felt like there was nothing to worry about.

I woke up in the middle of the night to hear yelling. I leaped out of my bed and ran out to see the most horrible scene taking place in Mother's kitchen. A guard had my father's head dangling in his hand, and a young man who looked maybe seventeen, and a woman who wore a green crown walked around my mother, "I'll ask one more time. WHERE IS THE BOY?!". My mother was stuck, watching my father's head dangle in the guard's hand. "So, I still get no answer? I suppose searching the house is the only option.", Falsa said, pointing for her men to check the house. I sat hidden in the darkness. I wanted to save my mother, but didn't know how. I looked around for any kind of weapon, but couldn't find a damn thing. Suddenly, they found me, and a soldier snatched me from behind the wall I was hiding behind, and roughly put me on my knees before the woman with the strange, green, crown. "Do you know who I am? Well? If not, I shall introduce myself. I am Queen Falsa, leader of Dasha. And I know exactly who and what you are. My boy…you are mine.".

CHAPTER 5

Sebastian's Mission

ALISA: When we arrived in Nasher, Alex and I became a bit sick to our stomachs. The first thing we encountered was a farm. It had been set ablaze, and the house that was nearby was positively devoid of life. We walked into the house and realized that the farmer and his wife had both been beheaded. There were signs that there was one more person in the house, but Falsa must have taken them. "So, now what do you think?", I asked Alex. "It's just like my kingdom. Falsa will truly stop at nothing. We must catch her and stop this soon.". Alex had informed me of how Falsa invaded her kingdom. Her men mercilessly slaughtered her people, who apparently weren't soldiers, but ancient monks, who guarded over the princess. Her parents were ripped apart by carriage, and now she was the queen by default. She told me Falsa needs her and the god's vessel to retrieve the sword. To me this was good news. Because there is no such thing as the god's vessel. Or at least that's what I believed, until Alex fell to the ground and her skin started changing from pink, to normal, then to pink again. I fell to one knee next to her and asked, “What’s wrong?”, “He was here. I can feel him. I can feel his energy. He doesn’t know who he is or why Falsa took him. We must rescue him!”, “Now hold your damn horses. We are not going after some imaginary boy. We need to stick to the plan. We come up from behind and wipe her out.”, “Alisa, you aren’t listening to me. She has half of what she needs. I can’t go with you to try and rescue him. It would be suicide to all the kingdoms.”. Part of me was starting to doubt my own misbelief. If there was any validity to this story, and if Alex really is connected somehow to the god, maybe I should start taking this whole god sword thing more openly. Just then, we heard shouts coming from the village. I ordered my men in that direction. Alex stayed rooted. “Alex, you wait here if you must, but I must ask, how does Falsa even know what she has?”, “She stole something very important from my castle. It tells her exactly who he is.”, Alex answered. “And what is this object?”, I asked. “The shield.”.

My men and I rode into the village. It was immediate pandemonium. Blood was flying everywhere. My men were slashing and clashing they’re blades and at the same time, I was stabbing every Dashin I could. I heard a girl screaming and I rushed in that direction. A Dashin had cornered this poor young girl and was attempting to rip her clothes. I stabbed him from behind with my blade and the blood splattered onto the girl’s face. She fell to the ground crying. Upon looking around, I realized there was a man lying in the dirt. The girl fell to him and placed her face in his chest. I realized this must be her father. “What is your name?”, I asked, placing my hand on her shoulder. “Micka.”. I helped Micka up, “We can’t stay here Micka, it’s way too dangerous.”, “PLEASE! You must help my friend! His name is Sebastian, and the queen has him. I saw she had him chained to her. Please help him!”, Micka pleaded with me. I started making my way towards the castle because I figured that’s where Falsa was headed. Micka had joined me, even though I told her to go to the farm with Alex. I was intrigued by the fact that the queen would have a villager chained to her personally. Then I remembered what Alex told me. How she had a shield that would reveal the identity of the god. Is this Sebastian kid the god? If he is, should I let Falsa keep him and go all out protecting Alex? I didn't know what to do, but the castle was finally right in front. I passed the gate. The battle was mostly happening in the village. You could smell the blood and hear the screams of the villagers. Micka walked beside me as I approached the main hall of the castle. As we fully entered, there were Dashin soldiers standing guard. Lucky for us, there were only three. I quickly eliminated them and made my way up the stairs. When I approached the King's Chamber, you could hear voices, "I never intended to share my power with you, Oliver. I always intended for you to fall in line with everyone else.", "But you can't just do this! There are laws that must be followed! Things that must happen! You can't just eliminate the kingdoms!", King Oliver was shouting. As I watched the scene, I saw Prince Caprius sitting in a corner with blood stains on his face that I was sure wasn't his. Falsa was walking around the room, pulling a young man along as she moved. "Sebastian….", Micka whispered. I took in the sight of the boy. No doubt he was handsome. He looked like he was the same age as me. You could tell he was a farmer from the look of his hands and the way his wavy brown hair was unkempt. "Do you realize who I have here?", asked Falsa, pulling Sebastian towards Oliver as she spoke. "This is the god in his Plinthinian vessel. Surely you had no clue, because if you did, then you would have known that you held all the cards. Now I do.". Prince Caprius stood up and started to beat Oliver. He continued hitting him until his face was just a mass of blood and pus. "STOP THIS! I'm not going to let you do this!", Sebastian shouted, as the king turned his mangled head towards him. "Well I don't see you doing anything to stop me exactly. Now, I must find this troublesome princess, then, my son, we'll rule over Plinth.". I had seen enough. I rushed out, urging Micka to stay hidden, "Enough! Release the boy, leave this kingdom alone!", "Well…this is certainly unexpected. Princess Alisa. Here to try and save this piece-of-shit. Well if you can beat my son, no problem.". Caprius tried to sucker punch me, but I deflected. And immediately slashed his neck. Blood splattered. Falsa screamed. Micka came out of hiding and tried to help Sebastian, but Falsa slapped her and she fell. I rushed over and slashed at the chain with my blade. The chain snapped and Sebastian, who was now free, took a soldier's helmet, and knocked Falsa across the face. "We have to go! Nasher is lost!", I found myself shouting, as I led the two out of the kingdom. After fighting our way back through the carnage in the village, we made it back to the farm. Alex was sitting in the house. She wasn't glowing. When she saw us, she immediately looked towards Sebastian, and there was a quiet chill. Sebastian stared at this beautiful girl, and she was staring back at him.

SEBASTIAN: I knew something was different right away. She had the most beautiful face I'd ever seen. She said she is the Queen of Alexandria. She had survived a holocaust like mine and Micka's. As I listened to her story, especially the part about how we are connected, I couldn't help feeling this strange feeling. Not that I was just attracted to her, but that we somehow belonged. Being on the run wasn't so bad. We had an army, so we weren't totally helpless. Alisa doesn't seem to buy the whole 'god story'. Honestly, I don't, either. But another part of me knew that there must be some truth. After all that's happened, to believe my parents died for some crazy queen's imaginary fantasy of ruling the planet with some mystical kind of weapon they're son possesses, was just too much to bear. Alisa had scouts that were going around and, of course, gathering as much info as they could. Apparently, Caprius was still alive. Alive, but barely. His mother was beside herself with this recent defeat. She's claiming vengeance on Kindy for getting involved. Caprius has said he will personally ruin Alisa. Now, either she is extremely brave or maybe just that stupid, but she seems to show no signs of caring. All through the day, she's plotting and planning with her soldiers. Micka and I were trying to stay from getting too involved. She was angry over the loss of her father, her mother having died when she was very young. "Your stalker is trying to hide again, but she isn't very good at it.", said Micka, as I was fooling around with a bush. I looked up to see Alex, hiding behind a tree and staring at me. Watching me. "What the hell is her problem?", asked Micka. "Well she believes we have some sort of connection.", "And what do you think?", "I think she's got some of that kind plant.", "Maybe I should do something to make her go away.". Micka grabbed my face and planted her lips on me. Alex stormed away afterwards. As she did, a faint pink glow started to set on her skin. "Why did you do THAT?!", I asked Micka, as she was still holding me. "Because I knew you first.", she said, planting another kiss on me. I liked it, but I found myself thinking of Alex. She was beautiful. So is Micka. Micka, with her lovely, wide, smile, vibrant purple hair, red eyes, and a perfect fair complexion. But I couldn't stop thinking about Alex.

As time moved forward, it had been a month since our escape from Nasher. Alisa was taking us in circles around her kingdom. She wanted the soldiers to stay prepared. I would often spot her staring at me. Basically, trying to understand how I fit into all this, which I must admit, I still have no clue. I still had the marks on my wrists from Falsa's shackles, still remembered as the blade came down and took off my mother's head. I wanted to kill Falsa, but Alisa had soldiers watching me, and making sure I didn't leave camp. It was getting harder and harder to find privacy. Micka wanted to kiss some more, while Alex had been avoiding me, and Alisa didn't want to be bothered. Every time I tried to speak with Alisa, she would ignore me and change the subject. I was very confused about what was happening. Then one day out of the blue, Alisa popped up in my tent I had been sharing with Micka, who now was asleep. "Put some clothes on and come with me. Now.". I threw on some pants and made my way outside with Alisa. I kept wondering what she could possibly want after ignoring me all these weeks. We finally stopped.

I could see the Kindy Castle in the background. "I need you to tell me your thoughts.", Alisa said to me. I was confused, though, because why did she want to hear what I had to say now? "I don't understand what you mean.", I replied, screwing up my face. "I get it. I haven't exactly spoken to you. And I get that you're experiencing extreme pain because of your parent's death. But there are some things I seriously need to discuss with you.". She reached into her pants pocket and pulled out a bracelet. "Do you know who this belongs to?", "Alex?", "She isn't in the camp and I don't know where she is. She was really upset with you and that's the last I heard of her.", "Well if you expect me to know where she is, I don't...she's been really weird.", "Whenever you are around her, do you FEEL anything?". Now I was even more confused. "What are you asking me...?". Alisa's face flashed a nasty bit of irritation, then she puffed her chest out. "Alex, believes that you are our creator in a vessel. She thinks you just don't remember, and if you get your sword and shield it will all come back to you. Now what do you think about that?". I danced around with different answers in my head. They pretty much all came back the same. "I'm nobody special.", "Falsa didn't take you for no reason...", Alisa said, rubbing her thumb and index finger on her chin, "Sebastian, I need you to be more open to what Alex is talking about. I know it sounds a bit insane, but I'm starting to think there might be some truth to it.", "Do you realize what you're saying? Do I look, godly, to you?", "Honestly, no. But what if? What if?", she said, more to herself it seemed, "Alright, listen to me, Falsa wants you and Alex. So, here's what we are going to do. You are going to get that shield. Then we will get the sword, then we'll kick that bitch's ass.", "Um, how do you expect me to get that shield?", I asked. "If Alex is right, then it's inevitable. You'll get the shield anyway. And the sword. But I'm going to need you to stop messing around with Micka.". In the background, in between the trees, I could make out Alex's silhouette, watching closely. "Did Alex put you up to this? Because if she did...", Alisa put her hand up, "I've been running my kingdom since I was seven. I'm a queen, technically speaking, and I just gave you a command. I need you to get close to Falsa. And I need you to keep your mission a secret. Especially from Micka, she cannot know any of this.", "Why me?", "Because I didn't see anybody else shackled to Falsa. It's time you start understanding your place in this war. Because, soon, things are going to get complicated. My scouts tell me, Caprius is finally able to move about and swing his sword. He's got a sketch of me pinned to some dummy and he's slashing at it every day. As for his mother, she is yelling bloody murder. She wants you back, and she wants my head. So, you listen to the plan. Or else they are going to hit us hard.". I considered everything she said. With most of my life back in Nasher, I felt there was nothing for me here. Not even Micka had soothed over what I was feeling. Lost, confused, and terribly missing my parents. I looked Alisa hard in the eyes. She was set on this idea. "So, you want me to sacrifice myself?", I asked sadly. "She isn't going to kill you. She needs you and Alex together. Look, this might be our only chance. She has already destroyed your kingdom, Alexandria couldn't have helped anyway. So, this is it. You go with Falsa, get that shield, and win half this war for us.", "I'm not who Alex thinks I am!". Suddenly, Alex came from out of the woods. Alisa turned, surprised. "Where the hell have you been?!", Alisa asked her. Alex stared into my eyes and said, "I know you are afraid. But you don't need to be. She can't hurt you.". Then she grabbed me and kissed me. It felt like my lips were burning. Alex must have felt it as well because she pushed me a part from her but smiled as she did. Alisa just looked annoyed, "Are you done making out with him? We have a serious battle strategy going on.". In my body, I felt a warmness creeping up. Alex kissed me again. And I felt it even more. "What did you do to me?", "I gave you some of your strength. You feel it now, don't you?". I felt like I could take on a million men. This feeling I was feeling felt like a completely new me. I wished I had this power to save my parents. "Only I can give you this strength.", she added as if to tell me something. I knew what she was referring to, so I decided it best not to say anything. "I accept the mission.", I looked at Alisa as I said this, with a cocky smile on my face. "You're sure?". I became annoyed. First, she tells me she wants me to do this, then asks me if I'm sure. "Look, I just want to be sure that you are okay with this. Because I know I'm asking a lot. And you didn't seem that excited before. Maybe I should have Alex kiss you until you kill Falsa.", Alisa said. I did not appreciate the sarcasm. Neither did Alex, who replied, "I told you about my connection to him! I told you we are the keys to winning this war!", "Well if you ask me, you just seem obsessed with him.", Alisa said. "OBSESSED?! SINCE I WAS BORN, I'VE WAITED TO MEET HIM!", "Yeah, and since you have, you've acted like a jealous cow...". Alex took a swing at Alisa, who dodged and retaliated, only to miss and take a sharp punch in the face. "Hey, stop! We're on the same side!", I said, trying to break them apart. The commotion attracted an audience, and once the girls were done rolling around, they realized this and immediately broke up. Alex stood up, looked at me longingly, then stormed off. "EVERYONE, BACK TO YOUR POSTS!", Alisa yelled, as she straightened herself out. "Why did you pick that fight with her?", I asked. "Because she is a stuck up bitch, that thinks everything revolves around you two being together. She needs to get knocked down a peg. Anyhow, forget about that, so you are taking the mission?". I could still feel that power that Alex's kiss gave me. I couldn't understand how, but she made me stronger. Micka came out of the trees, looking confused and angry. "Why'd you disappear, Bastian?", she asked, approaching me and Alisa. "I needed to have a discussion with him. Don't worry. I'm not trying to steal him from you.", Alisa said. It was almost like she was trying to pick another fight. Micka wasn't supposed to know about me going to Falsa, so I came up with a lie on the spot. "I'm just trying to find out what our next move is and how we can help.", "Okay...but I was worried Falsa took you!", Micka replied. "Look, it's none of your business. So why don't you just scurry off, wench?", Alisa said, with a hard look on her face. "I can handle talking to her, thank you.", I said, hurrying Micka away, before another fight could break out. "What the hell is her issue?", Micka asked me, as we were walking towards our tent. I didn't know if I should tell Micka about the mission she assigned me, but I decided it was for the best to tell the truth, "She's sending me into Falsa's camp.". Micka's reaction was just about what I thought it would be, "IM GOING TO GO CONVINCE HER OTHERWISE!", Micka shouted. I grabbed her before she could storm off towards Alisa. "Look, Alisa is not in the mood, and I just wanted to be honest with you.", "Okay, and while we're being honest, are you even going to mention Alex kissing you?". I didn't think she had seen that. "That kind of just happened.", "Kind of just happened twice! I saw the whole thing. You didn't even try to stop her!". Considering I'd never had a girlfriend before, I could see why it was really difficult to know how to handle this. One thing I knew I should not do, is tell Micka about the connection I feel with Alex. "It was just really fast! I wasn't expecting it, that's all! Please don't be mad at me!", "I just feel like since our parents are dead, all we have is each other, Bastian. We can't just abandon one another.", Micka wrapped her arms around my neck and kissed me, "Do you understand, Bastian? I need you.". I felt immediate guilt. Not only was something going on with Alex, but at the same time, I knew I had to go on this mission that Alisa wanted me to go on. Micka and I made our way back to the tent. She started to pull at my pants. "I've never done this before. But I feel like we should.", Micka said, as I laid down and she climbed on top of me. It was also my first time. I kissed her and slowly entered into her. She moaned and I slowly started moving. As we began to have sex, I was still thinking of Alex. I was confused, but then I climaxed, which was awesome. Then, we fell asleep.

When next I awoke, it was to the sounds of what sounded like battle. I rushed out of the tent, and sure enough, Falsa had found us. I spotted Alisa slashing her way through the crowd. We looked at each other, and I knew what I had to do. I went back into the tent and woke Micka. "Come with me.". Micka woke up and was alerted by the sounds outside the tent. She grabbed some clothes, and as she was dressing, a soldier entered the tent. I punched him, and he went flying out of the tent. Shocked by my sudden strength, Micka stood rooted to the spot, "How…?", Micka started to say. "NO time, let's get moving.". We made our way across the field. I spotted Alex, who was taking men out with her bare hands. She really was a skilled fighter, I thought. She saw me leading Micka across the field. She nodded and continued fighting. As I continued moving, Micka asked, "Where are we going?". I replied, "We're looking for Falsa. I'm going to get close to her and steal the god shield.", "ARE YOU CRAZY?! SHE'LL KILL ME!", Micka shouted. "Not if we both come to her willingly. I just couldn't leave you here.". We ran for what felt like hours. Then finally through the tree lines, I saw Caprius. He was just sitting amongst what I had to guess were his personal guard. They turned and looked in our direction. Caprius stood up. He had an ugly scar on his neck from where Alisa had slashed him. He looked angry. "It seems like my mother's pet has come to us. And look! He's brought us a gift!", Caprius shouted, looking Micka's way. He started to walk towards us. He walked up and reached for Micka and I grabbed his wrist. "Ahh!", he yelled as I released him, he cowered away, "KILL THEM!", "I do not think so, my son.", Falsa said, coming from out of the trees. She smiled when she saw me, "I see the Alexandrian has given you some of your strength. Interesting… Well, it matters not. If you think you will easily kill me…", "No, actually I decided to come with you. I just ask that you keep Micka safe.". Falsa looked at Micka and determined what I was asking. It almost seemed like she was going to say no, but then, "Okay. I will ensure her safety, if you come with me. She'll be sent back to my kingdom. There she will receive nearly royal care from my maids. And will remain untouched.", she said, looking towards Caprius. Caprius, who was still holding his wrist, nodded that he understood. "We will travel to Dasha now.", "But, Mother, what about the Alexandrian bitch?", asked Caprius. "Don't worry, Son. All in good time.".

CHAPTER 6

Alisa And Alex's Journey

ALISA: The soldiers were retreating. Alex had fought her way towards me. I had half a mind to not let a single Dashin soldier escape. But that was going to have to be the case. If they are retreating, that means Sebastian is with Falsa. My plan is going well so far. Alex grabbed my arm, "I apologize for my behavior earlier. Something comes over me whenever I'm around Sebastian.", "Well don't worry about it, I'm over it. Now that Bastian is doing his part, it's time we do ours.", "What do you mean?", "I mean it's time to get reinforcements.". Unbeknownst to my parents, there was another kingdom. One that lay in secret in what all of Plinth referred to as the Dark Wood. It basically covered half the planet as far as our ancestors knew and was the most dangerous place on Plinth. There were two known explorers who had journeyed into the woods. Only one is known for coming back out alive. His name is Wilson Sheen, and lucky for us, I knew where his cottage was. "Oh, I know what you're speaking of. Sheen, if I'm not mistaken...", Alex said. "You know about the kingdom in the woods?", I asked, surprised. "Well, of course. Who did you think taught me to fight? Remember, my kingdom was built on peace. So, someone had to know how to protect it.". I was blown away. Ever since Wilson came to my kingdom when I was little, he told stories of these people that lived in the woods. They supposedly wielded magic and could tear through all the kingdoms if they desired. But to learn that's where Alex learned to fight was too much, even for me, to take in. Especially because from what I understand about these people, they don't like the outside very much. I remember Wilson saying they are very closed off people, who take their culture and solidity very seriously. They have been practicing magic for over four-hundred and fifty years, and it's said that they started when the God first came to Plinth. They even learned it from him. But they are the most powerful force on the planet and they are hidden within a deep jungle, filled with all sorts of creatures that can poison, maim, or straight kill you by tearing you apart. "I need a little more explanation, Alex. How is it that you ended up traveling into the Dark Wood?", I asked Alex, as we made our way through the dead bodies of both my soldiers and Dasha's. "Well, I told you what I am. The people of the wood came to my kingdom and sought me out. They told my parents they wanted to teach me their ways so that I may protect myself. They predicted this war.". This shocked me even more. Slowly but surely, I was buying into this story of the god coming here. It just seemed like I was so out of the loop. Here are these kingdoms, who not only were aware there was a war coming, but they also worship the god. And they realized Alex's connection, which after seeing Sebastian destroy a man with one punch, I must believe there is some validity. Since Alex kissed Sebastian, I noticed her skin was slightly different. It was sort of normal, but with that same faint pink glow. We entered my tent, where I sat down, exhausted. Alex was standing before me, arms crossed, "So, your plan is to ask them for help with this conflict? Well I should tell you, that most likely won't happen.", "Why the hell not?", I asked and started to feel let down. After all, I had never been in the Dark Wood, but I knew these people were there. Wilson had brought back items from their kingdom. One item I wore on my wrist. A bracelet that was for great protection. I never really thought it worked for real. I just assumed it was more like a charm. But I remember that time when this young man, who used to be my guard, tried to assault me. Somehow, I managed not only to escape unscathed, but it cost him his life. As I was fleeing from him, he tripped and fell on a large thorn. It stuck through his stomach and he died slowly. I always chalked that up to dumb luck. But then I can remember all the other times I had close calls since I started wearing this bracelet. With everything that's happening now, it was no wonder I was starting to change my mind. But I wondered if Falsa had Bastian shackled to her again, or if he had come up with a master plan within my plan. Not just that, but he took Micka with him. Which either was a bad idea, or maybe genius. But I had secretly planted one of Wilson's protective charms on her. I did it when I entered their tent. I gave her a tattoo that immediately sticks to your skin and has the same properties as the bracelet. At least I did it hoping it would protect her. And in truth, I don't know why I did it. Alex answered my question, "Well, they don't want any kind of outside contact. That's why they trained me. It's my duty to protect the godly sword and shield.", "Well, you did an excellent job of that. They'd be proud.", "Why are you constantly looking to fight your friends?", Alex asked. "I'm not, I was just trying to lighten the mood. Sorry. Look, how about we just march right in there, and tell them we will lose if they don't help?", I said. "Prince Lab would not be happy with that. But I can see what you mean. We are in a losing battle. Falsa has Bastian. And if she gets a hold of me, then we really lose.", "So...we should go to the Dark Wood, right?", "I fear you will lose a good amount of your men in the endeavor.". I realized she was right. Not while in the woods, my men won't even go in there. "So, it'll just be me and you. You know the wood. And it won't be disrespectful if it's just the two of us compared to showing up with my army.", "Okay, it's settled, then. Just, we may need to stop in

Alexandria.", "For what, might I ask?", I said, a little confused. I'd never been to Alexandria. Nobody in Kindy has. It was known as a sacred place. And the rumors I'd heard stating it was like visiting Heaven seemed impossible. But my first meeting with Alex, gave me the impression that perhaps it's real. "I'll need to leave somebody in charge while we are gone.". I looked out of my tent at my remaining soldiers. There were at least three-hundred-something left over. I knew some of my men, but not all of them. That's when I first saw HER. This girl with yellow hair, and a face stained by battle. But underneath the blood and dirt, a beautiful young woman was hidden. She had a group of men who had surrounded her, and she was giving a speech, "…do we really want to let that happen? We have the power here, all we have to do is say no more!". It seemed like her speech was about ending the war. I stepped out, so she could see me. "And look who decides to grace us with her benevolent presence. Our fearless princess. So, have you come to tell us how we are to die tomorrow? Or maybe, it's to leer at us while we battle tirelessly for you.". It was obvious she wasn't very happy about the situation. "And where has your little boyfriend scurried off to? By the way, you should know, I saw him with another wench.", as she said this, the men started laughing. I knew she must be talking about Sebastian. Alex must have guessed as well, because she was standing next to me with her fist clenched. "First off, you should watch who you're talking to. I know this war has us all frustrated…", I started speaking to the crowd, "…but we cannot allow ourselves to forget what we are fighting for!", "And what is that? The opportunity for your parents to keep getting high?". That was the final straw. I grabbed the girl and pulled her towards my face. "What the hell is your issue?", I asked. "My issue, Princess…", she said as she struggled in my closed fists, "…is that because of your parents, I don't have parents! Because of your parent's laziness, my sister was raped and killed by our own people! Now, you want us to follow your spoiled-ass into battle?!". I knew she was familiar. Sheena Kine. Five years ago, the man who had tried to assault me, succeeded with her parents and her sister.

The man was dead, but Sheena has always blamed the laziness of the king and queen. Not to mention their ungrateful daughter. But, of course, this was just how the kingdom perceived me. “I’m truly sorry. But I know how you feel. I am not the heartless bitch you think I am, Sheena.”, “You know my name? What a shock?!”, Sheena exclaimed, breaking free of my grasp. She straightened herself out and stared at me intently, “I hate you! I hate everything about Kindy. She started to unsheathe her blade, when I decided to say something, “Look, I understand your anger, but this is uncalled for and it is not the time for this. You do realize we are at war with an incredibly evil woman whose son would do far worse? This is just being stupid, selfish, and irresponsible.”. She looked at me, still angry, but starting to calm down. She looked at Alex, then the rest of the men who were wondering if they should stop this. “I…I’m sorry.”, she sputtered, then ran off. I decided to go after her. I found her in the woods, crying. She had perched herself on a tree branch and when she noticed I was coming, decided to jump down. “I know it isn’t your fault. It just has hurt for so long, and this is the closest I’ve ever been to you.”. Part of me could understand. While another part of me was highly annoyed. “You said a lot of messed up things about my parents. But I don’t disagree.”. When I said this, she looked up with a shocked look on her face, “Never thought I’d hear you of all people say that.”, she said, with a bit of awe in her voice. “I told you, I’m not the evil bitch you think I am. I care very deeply for my people, and spend a lot of time trying to make things better for my citizens. I know I’m not perfect. But the main thing is that what happened to your parents was an atrocity, committed by one person, who died, trying to do the same thing to me.”, “I never realized! And all this time, I was angry, thinking it was just the lazy rule of your parents.”, “No, unfortunately, it happened under my watch. And for that, I’m very sorry. But I can’t bring your parents back to you, and I can’t take your pain away. What you should do is use this pain in battle. That’s the best thing you can do. We can’t let Falsa win this war. We just can’t.”. Sheena was starting to lighten up. Since running off, she had cleaned her face. With the blood and dirt removed, she was even more beautiful. I felt a strange feeling with her. "Listen, I have to leave camp for a while, and I need someone to take charge while I'm gone. I was hoping maybe that could be you.". Sheena puffed out her chest, "I would love to take charge. I have a pretty good standing with the men and women.". So, with that settled, it was time for me and Alex to make our way to the Dark Wood. "Where are you going?", Sheena asked, as I started to walk away. I thought of telling her she didn't need to know, but decided against it, because I could tell that would only make her disloyal. "I'm going to the Dark Wood. I'm going to seek out reinforcements. Are you sure you can hold the fort?", I asked, wishing I had given her the protective tattoos instead of Micka. "Yes, I'm quite skilled at battle. My father used to train my sister and I before…", she broke off. "Don't worry, I trust you.". I suddenly realized what I was feeling. I was attracted to her. The thought came over me to kiss her, but I decided against it. I turned to leave and then, Sheena asked me another question, "Why are you choosing me? You just met me.". I didn't want to tell her that I think I like her, so I came up with a queenly answer, "Well, it's all about girl power, right?". Sheena smiled, as I turned to walk away. Sheena didn't call me back. I went to my tent where I was surprised to find Alex crying. "What the hell is wrong with you?", I asked, shocked by this sudden burst of sadness. "Sebastian hates me!", she screamed. "Why would you think that? He seemed to like it when you kissed him.". She looked at me, and all you could see was her pretty face, stained with tears. "I've waited my whole life to meet him, and he takes Micka with him. He's not even connected to her! I know he can feel what I offer!", she said, throwing a trinket across the room. I was confused. When I had left her, she was normal, gearing up for our mission. Now I return, and this is what I find. "I'm very confused right now… What the hell is wrong with you?", I asked. "Didn't you see him? Didn't you see the hate in his eyes?! I'm ugly. That's why he hates me!". This was too much. There was a name for people like her. But I couldn't think of it now. As I sat and pondered, Alex was working herself up even more, "I HATE MYSELF! I WANNA JUST DIE!", she screamed, as she reached for her blade. I immediately leaped on top of her and stopped her from grabbing the hilt. "Alex, you need to get a hold of yourself!", I found myself shouting, as I wrestled a struggling Alex down to the ground, "Alex, listen, Bastian does not hate you. He just met you, and if I might say, any man who doesn't fall in love with you right away is a fool.". Apparently, I said the wrong thing. Alex smacked me across my face. "HOW DARE YOU CALL HIM A FOOL?!", she shouted, standing up. Then almost as if she realized what she was doing, she started to apologize, "I'm sorry, Alisa. It's this stupid feeling. I can't control it. I didn't mean anything I just said.". I was in shock. How was I supposed to win this war with people like Alex flip flopping on if she wants to kill me or not. "You are going to have to explain how this feeling shit works, but for now, let's just get going.". As we started to leave, Sheena caught up with us, "I just wanted to let you know, I won't let you down. And I also wanted to do this...", Sheena grabbed me and kissed me before I could do anything. When she was done, I grabbed her and kissed her again. Then we looked at each other, and I turned with Alex and walked away. "I had a feeling you would like her...", Alex said, "...she has fire, and I sensed you're attracted to that.". I didn't know what to say. Being attracted to the same sex was never something I thought would happen to me. But to be fair, I liked it. As Alex and I walked towards her kingdom, she explained to me how she gets overwhelmed just being around Sebastian's energy, "He has a source within him that only I can pick up on. It affects me differently because I'm not like him. But he too feels a great attraction for me, even if he doesn't truly realize it.". Alex was complicated. Growing up, she was taught that she was not just the vessel that holds the god's greatest weapon, but also, she holds his heart. She also explained why her kingdom was peaceful and only she knew how to fight. Apparently, she is worshipped in her kingdom as a goddess. After all, she is meant to wed the god, who is supposedly, Sebastian. A lot of what she was telling me, I wasn't too sure I could understand. Specifically, the part about how she was born off planet but placed in the kingdom of Alexandria. Her parents, who Falsa had killed, weren't her real parents. They were just devout caretakers, who worshipped the god and knew that Alex was a gift from him. It all seemed like an incredible story, but the parts of the story that fit into this war was what got me thinking and realizing, everything she was telling me was the truth. And I had stupidly sent Sebastian to Falsa. And worse, he put an innocent girl near Falsa's perverted son. Caprius. But I remembered, I had given her the tattoo of protection that I got from Wilson. "So, what do you think about me sending Bastian to Falsa?", I felt compelled to ask. I was starting to feel like it might have been a mistake. "You made the right decision. Don't think that Falsa can hurt Bastian. Remember, I gave him power.", Alex replied. It was still too much, but I remembered Wilson telling me how I wouldn't understand everything, but just trust the war would end in my favor. As we continued, we finally came to a pond. There wasn't much water on Plinth. At least not on the surface. Most of Plinth was filled with underground waterways and ponds. The ones above ground were famous. There were three of them, the Jasmine, the Caper, and the Willet. The Willet being the biggest one. The Jasmine is the one we were stopped by, while the Caper and the Willet were both near Alexandria. As we settled in, we started to lay out our sleeping tents, when we heard a strange noise coming from the bushes. Alex and I slowly approached the bushes. Out jumped a strange looking creature that resembled a dog, but it was the size of a gopher. It had flappy, little ears, and even though it was growling at me and Alex, you couldn't help but notice its cuteness. Its fur was white covered with blue spots. "Aww, look at it!", Alex exclaimed, running to pick the creature up. The creature jumped into Alex's hands. "Have you been following me, you adorable, little, creature?". I was lost. "Um, Alex, does this thing belong to you?", I asked curiously. I had never seen a creature like this before. Near Kindy, we have horses, cows, and, of course, cats and dogs. But whatever this creature was, Alex was apparently familiar with it. "Alisa, this is Casian, my Dattur.". I had only read about Datturs. Basically, they are the most vicious creatures on Plinth. Very small, but can bite straight through the bone. What Alex was doing with one of these, I couldn't imagine. "When Alexandria was attacked, she must have followed me from the kingdom.". Casian leaped from Alex's arms and landed near me. She sniffed me and then jumped onto my shoulder. Surprised with the height this thing could jump, I started laughing, since it was the cutest thing I had ever seen. Casian licked my face, then jumped back onto Alex. "This is perfect. She can help us.", "Not to sound cruel, but how can Casian help us?", I felt compelled to ask, considering she was just a little thing. "Just trust me, Casian can help. She has amazing jaw strength and is very concealable. Nobody will ever see her coming. She can kill in an instant.", Alex finished saying as she started kissing Casian. "Okay, but will she be able to help us in the Dark Wood?", I demanded, remembering where I was headed. "Don't worry about the Dark Wood. That's why we're headed to my castle. There is something there that will protect us as we move through the woods.". With Casian, now we were a gang. And with our course clear, we went to sleep.

I was in a dark corridor. I could hear a sound that sounded a lot like crying. It was coming from further down. I began to walk down the corridor. I could hear somebody calling my name, "Alisa... please help.". I started to run, but no matter how hard I tried to run, I couldn't move as fast as I wanted. It was like I was running in water. Finally, the voice calling my name got louder, more desperate, "ALISA, PLEASE!", the voice shouted. Just then I could hear another voice, "The bitch can't help.". I recognized Caprius' voice, and tried to move faster. I still hadn't identified who was calling my name. "It's time.", "NO!". I started to feel tears running down my face, as I finally got towards the end of the corridor. In front of me stood a door made of what looked like flesh. I didn't want to touch the door, but I could hear shuffling and muffled crying on the other side. I dug as deep as I could for whatever courage I could find, and I pushed the door open. Inside, I saw Sheena, tied, with her arms over her head and Caprius was about to stab her his sword. I tried to move towards them to stop it from happening, but when I got close, there was an invisible barrier. Sheena was screaming my name. Calling for me to help her, but no matter what I did, the invisible barrier wouldn't come down. Then Caprius stabbed her. I knew I was screaming, but I couldn't hear myself. I couldn't move or do anything, then I felt a hand on my shoulder. I looked up, and Sebastian was standing there. He was wearing a white cape, with what looked like armor made of diamond. "I'm sorry, Alisa.", Sebastian said, as he helped me up. Suddenly, the barrier was gone and Caprius grabbed me by my throat. I could feel his breath on my neck and cheek as he pulled me towards him. "You're next, bitch.", he said, as he took out a dagger. I noticed at this point, I wasn't wearing my armor, but rather some rags. He took the dagger and started cutting off the rags. I started to cry, and Sebastian was still standing there. I looked at Sheena, who was dead, but her eyes were still staring at me the whole time. As Caprius laid me down, I felt like I was dead. If this is happening for real, then I am dead. I don't want to live. Then, Sebastian moved towards me and kneeled, "To save your kingdom, you must let Caprius live. Caprius is the key to winning this war.". I looked into Caprius' eyes and realized, Caprius wasn't Caprius. Somehow, he became Micka. Micka was now standing over me. I looked where Sheena's body was and saw Caprius hanging there in her place. Sheena was now standing next to Bastian. I just wanted this dream to end. Suddenly, Alex was here. "Hey, you need to wake up, NOW!". I woke up to bandits surrounding us. Alex had a not to worry look on her face, while the nearest bandit had already taken out his dagger. "Well, looks like we got a couple of tasty, little, girls.". I noticed Alex's skin wasn't glowing. I wished it were. "I am Princess Alisa, of Kindy, and I think you guys had better leave.". There were about six of them, and they were all dirty. Bandits weren't uncommon. They were usually made up of criminals who were exiled from the kingdoms. They lived in these wooded areas and some have camps in open land. I would say there are about over one-hundred total. They only pose a threat to those who are traveling outside of what was considered a safe road. From Nasher to Dasha, to Kindy, that's where the road usually runs. But going towards Alexandria is going off the beaten path. The fact that Alex had made it to Kindy was a huge surprise to me now. "We don't serve no kingdom, so you're not OUR princess.", said the biggest bandit, while a few of the others sniggered and shouted, "Yeah!", "Last warning to turn and leave bandits.", Alex said, still not worried. "Jake, let's just take them.", said another bandit, moving towards Alex, who, of course, was the most beautiful between the two of us. Just as the bandit grabbed Alex, Casian jumped out of Alex's tent, and leaped at the bandit's face. She sank her teeth into his face, and flew in the other direction. The man's body fell to the ground. The other bandits stared, then another one screamed and fell, grabbing his leg. Casian had bit through it. The other four bandits, including Jake, took off running and shouting, "It's a fucking Dattur!". I started to settle down some, and then I looked at Alex, who had already picked Casian back up and was kissing her again, "Good girl, Casian, good girl.", "Alex, I love Casian.", I said, heading to the creature and petting it. It purred and jumped on my shoulder and licked my face. "So, should we go back to sleep?", Alex asked calmly. "Yeah, but Casian is sleeping in my tent.".

CHAPTER 7

Micka's Choice

SEBASTIAN: Micka and I had been taken to what looked like a small getaway cabin. It was decorated in a sort of fine metal with tuk on the outside, giving it a sort of woodley look. We stepped inside of it, and it was luxurious. It had fine looking wood that had obviously been sanded down. The bed was humongous and had a rim around the top with a silken sheet to close around the bed. There was a fireplace, along with a chair that was near it that looked like you could sit in it and fall asleep. Micka had noted the bathroom, which was finely decorated with different colored crystals on the walls, and the toilet had a soft cushion. She looked at me, eyes wide. This was, without a doubt, the nicest place either one of us have ever been inside of. Falsa entered the cabin, looking us over. Obviously watching how impressed we were. "I had this built when I was carrying Caprius. I would often come here to escape my husband.", Falsa said, walking around Micka and myself. I hadn't thought about it with everything going on, but what happened to the King of Dasha? Now that I think about it, I don't even think I know his name. Micka voiced my thoughts, "What happened to the king?". Falsa tensed up some, then turned to look at Micka. Micka was afraid she may have said something wrong, but to both our surprise, Falsa answered, "He died at the hands of his own son.", "You mean Caprius killed his father? Why?", I demanded to know. After all, Falsa killed mine. "Let's just say, I'm not much different from you. I was once a child. But I made the mistake of being a beautiful woman. So, the king took me from my home and forced me to live in his castle. Wasn't too long after that I gave birth to Caprius, and from that point in my life, he was all that mattered.". I didn't know if I should feel sorry for her or tell her, who cares. "I became queen when my husband passed, and I have raised Caprius to be a complete and utter waste of my time.". This was a shocking thing to hear her say. "Why would you feel that way about your own son?", Micka asked, trying to sound nonchalant. "Enough questions, why don't you two get settled in while I go and make some other arrangements?". She turned and walked out. Part of me could understand her better now. She's angry at the fact her life isn't what she wants. She was forced to marry a man she didn't want to. Forced to sleep with him too. And even though I knew that about Falsa, it didn't change the anger I felt. She killed my parents, and basically destroyed my kingdom. Oliver was probably still alive. I'm not sure, since Alisa, Micka, and myself ran before we could know. Micka had jumped onto the bed, "Should we try it out…?", she said, in a sort of sexual tone. "Don't forget why we're really here, Micka. We need to find that shield.", "I honestly thought you would just forget about that.", Micka said, turning over and waving her hair. "I mean, didn't you hear what she said?", "Yes, I heard her, and it doesn't bring back your dad or my parents. Why are you so ready to forgive?", I asked. "I'm not, I'm just saying, why be miserable? We have this nice cottage, this nice bed, and in the corner over there, we have drinks.". I hadn't noticed, but I went to check out the drinks. This was all stuff my parents drank. "Do you think she wants us to stay here?", Micka asked. "I honestly don't know. I think that she just wants us to feel comfortable. Why? That, I really don't know. Makes me more nervous actually now that I think about it.". Why did Falsa bring us to this nice cabin? Was it to prep us before she tortured us?

Or maybe, she just figured we were stupid enough to buy into this nice situation. Get comfortable with it, then when we least expect it, would she take it from us? I watched Micka, who had become distracted with excitement. I thought of Alisa, and what she would say if she saw this cabin. Then I remembered, she grew up in a castle, so this probably looks like a normal room to her. Then I found myself thinking about Alex. Alex was so beautiful, and she was obsessed with me. But I chose to be with Micka. I wondered if I made the right choice, as I stared at Micka. She was beautiful, too, but not as beautiful as Alex. Suddenly, Micka was on top of me. "Make love to me, Bastian.", she said, kissing on my neck. I kissed her back, and I laid her down on the bed, we started making love, and strangely all I could think about was Alex. I kissed Micka, looked into her eyes, but in her place, was Alex. She reached up to kiss me and I vehemently wrapped my arms around her. As she was swaying on top of me, I called out, "Alex…". Micka immediately subsided from me and stared at me through hurt eyes. "Micka, I didn't mean…", but she was already putting her clothes back on. I got up to try and hold her, but she broke away from me, and without a word, stormed out. I chased after her, and when I got outside, she had disappeared. "MICKA!", I called out, hoping she would immediately answer, but nothing. Just as I was turning to go back in, Caprius caught my eye.

MICKA: As I ran through the village, I could hear my conscience telling me, "Told you so". Sebastian was in love with Alex. He had been since he saw her. I stopped to think about how much it hurt. Just then, I felt a hand on my shoulder. "What's wrong, little one?", Falsa asked me. She didn't seem so cold now, but rather genuinely concerned. "Sebastian lied to me, he's in love with Alex.", "Alex? You mean Alexandria the princess? My poor dear, I could have told you that. They are connected, dear. Can't you tell by the way they act around one another? They are meant to be, darling.", said Falsa. I thought of what my father would tell me. How he never truly liked Sebastian, and would have probably wrung his neck if he knew how he has now tossed his daughter to the side. "Listen, my child, you have great beauty, and you shouldn't waste that on someone who does not appreciate it. Come with me.", Falsa said, leading me into her village. The village of Dasha was a bit small, I noticed. I wondered how Falsa had such a big army. As we walked, Falsa continued to tell me things, "When I was about your age, I was taken from my parents. They refused to give me up, so the king had them executed publicly. This was the main event at our wedding. He shortly after, forced me to go into his castle, where he raped me and did unspeakable things to me. Not too long after, I found out I was pregnant. I didn't want my son to be raised by the king. So, I came up with a plan.". Falsa stopped and stood in front of me, "You...should never let a man control your actions. They will do nothing but want to keep you locked up in your room. Instead, be a QUEEN.". Falsa handed me a ring she had taken from inside of her armor. It was a beautiful ring, and where the rock would be, was a strange orb-like object that looked as if it had taken the whole night sky and put it into the sphere. "This, my child, is a very powerful object. It will provide you with a power you wouldn't have believed possible.", "Why would you give me this? I don't understand.", I replied, confused. I thought she was evil. But learning her story, gave me a whole new look at her. Things seemed different suddenly. I didn't care about the war, or the fact that I was alone. I felt suddenly, like I had a big place next to Falsa. I also thought about what that meant. "Listen, most don't realize, but my son has too much of his father in him, I hate it. I would much rather have a daughter. A strong girl who doesn't let a man dictate her actions. Most importantly, a daughter who wants to help rule this planet, so that when I'm gone, she may rule on her own.". I was blown away. Falsa wanted me to rule next to her. I honestly didn't know what to say. Even though I was angry at him, I still had feelings for Bastian. But at the same time, an offer like this hardly ever comes around. But it would be a betrayal. "I can't just join you. I'm sorry.", I said, as nice as I could, still slightly terrified. Falsa just laughed, "My dear, you don't seem to understand what I'm offering you. What I'm offering...is my kingdom. You will be Queen of Dasha. You will command my men. You will also have access to my vault.", "BUT WHY ARE YOU GIVING THIS TO ME?!", I demanded to know. It didn't make any sense to me. I was just a village girl from Nasher. This woman is the reason my father is dead, and so many other people I know. Now she just wants me to rule? Falsa let out a sigh, and looked me in my eyes and said, "I may be the one who started this war, but I won't be alive to see it's fruit.". I understood what she meant, but not why she said it. "I need an heir, Micka, and you are perfect. You're much better than my rapist son. I'm asking you, please do this? From this moment on you will be my daughter. I want you to be my daughter.". I felt lost for words. This terrible woman found favor with me. A favor I couldn't exactly understand. But then as I thought about it more, isn't this what I deserve? My father, dead, my kingdom, gone, and Sebastian forever lost to me, there was nothing for me. And Falsa is offering me the whole world. Still not feeling completely like I deserved it, I gave Falsa my answer, "Okay.".

SEBASTIAN: Caprius led me to the village of Dasha. It was small. I was wondering where Micka was, and if Caprius had done something to her. As we walked, I looked around at the villagers. They seemed frightened. Even more so, with Caprius walking among them. I noticed fathers rushing their daughters into they're cottages, no doubt because they were afraid of what Caprius would do. Finally, Caprius spoke, "Honestly, I don't know why my mother won't just kill you. I don't think she needs you, but who am I to say anything to her?". I didn't answer. My mind was still occupied with where Micka may have run off to. "Look around, Bastian...", Caprius said in a mocking voice, "...my mother wants to change all this. Personally, I love it. I love the fear felt through the streets. I love the pain I see on the villager's faces.", Caprius was saying with admiration and pride. "Why would you love any of that?", I asked him, having a hard time believing anyone could be so evil and uncaring. "Quite simple really, I just love the power.". I was already tired of talking to Caprius, and I just wanted to get away from him. "Ah, my favorite family to visit.", Caprius said, looking towards a rather beaten looking cottage. Outside was an older gentleman, who looked like he could barely hold the broom he was holding. He wore rags that sort of resembled a robe, and I immediately got the impression that he was fragile enough, that if you gave him one good push, he'd fall and break every bone in his body. Caprius was eyeing the poor man hungrily. I noticed a young woman looking out the window of the cottage. She was beautiful and looked like she may be my age. She had jet-black hair with a beautiful round face. Her lips were a certain pink that reminded me heavily of Alex, and I noticed the fear in her face. "PLEASE, JUST LEAVE US ALONE!", the old man shouted, as Caprius walked towards him, "HAVEN'T YOU TAKEN ENOUGH FROM US?!". I was watching the scene, the old man firmly standing ground, while Caprius circled him like a vulture. "Where is Tisiphone? Bring her out and we have no trouble.", "NO! You've stolen one daughter from me, and you won't be stealing another one!", the old man said, as he turned the broom upside down, as if he intended to use it as a weapon. Caprius grabbed it and snatched it from him, causing the man to fall on his back. "Uhh!", the old man yelled in pain. He clutched his back and rocked back and forth on the spot. "Last chance, old man. Where is Tisiphone? I told you I'd come for her one day. Today is the day. So, get her out here NOW!", Caprius shouted. "Never.", the old man said weakly, still holding his back. "Well, then I guess, Tisiphone doesn't care what happens to her father.", Caprius said, raising the broom, and facing the handle towards the old man's face. I was immediately reminded of King Oliver, and had the urge to stop this. Just then, the girl came running out of the house. "Tisiphone, no! Go back in the house!", "I'd rather he takes me like he took Chloe, than watch him kill you.", Tisiphone replied to her father. Caprius dropped the broom and grabbed her. "Well, it's about time, wench.". I had seen enough. I imagined what it would be like if Micka was in this girl's position. Micka, who was missing now, in a kingdom where this stuff happens often. "I think me and Tisiphone are going to go in the house for a bit. Would you like to join us, Bastian?". The old man looked up at me. In his eyes, I saw something. Something that when I had gazed into Oliver's eyes, I didn't see this. When Oliver looked at me, after Caprius finished beating him, I saw despair, all the hope that Oliver had gone. But this man was looking at me with hope. He saw somehow that I could save his daughter. And one look at Tisiphone, struggling in Caprius' arms, as he grabbed her and tousled her around, and I knew I really had had enough of Caprius. Suddenly, a plan came to me. One that would make me a hero to these people. I didn't know where Falsa was, but she was the only one who could ruin this plan. But I had to get Tisiphone on board with the plan. "Yeah, I want to head inside with you and the wench.". I watched as the last bit of hope drained from the old man's eyes and were replaced by tears. "Excellent.", said Caprius, pulling Tisiphone into the house, and closing the door behind them. As soon as I was sure Caprius would not see me, I bent on one knee next to the crying old man. "Don't worry. I'll stop him". The old man looked up, and was shocked to see the look of confidence on my face. I still had the strength I'd gotten from Alex, and was more than ready to end Caprius. I walked into the house, where Caprius was making short work of ripping off her coverings. She was half dressed and crying when I entered the cottage. "About time...", said Caprius, "...I was thinking I'll let you go first.". It was obvious that Caprius was testing me. He wanted to see if I was really going to do it. "Sure. But can I have some privacy here?". Caprius didn't find it strange that I was being his friend. As a matter of fact, he seemed excited. Maybe he was excited because he was tainting the image of me his mother had. Which I still had no idea what Falsa truly wanted with me. Aside from the god sword, what else could she want from me? I led Tisiphone to a room and closed the door. I threw her and watched her for a while. She just sat in the corner, crying, and waiting for me to do whatever I was going to do. "Listen, we don't have a lot of time...", I said, "...but if we are going to do something about Caprius, it has to be now. I have a plan, but are you willing to help me?". Tisiphone looked me in my eyes. The only time I saw eyes so beautiful was when I was talking to Alex. "Why...are you trying to help? Just get it over with!", she shouted at me. I, of course, partly understood. She wasn't going to trust me right away, but I knew how to make her trust me, "I'm on a secret mission for Queen Alisa. I'm not here to rape you, I'm here to save you, all of you.". She looked like someone just gave her the gift she'd been asking for her whole life. She stood up and rushed to the other side of the room. She pulled out a huge blade. She was surprisingly strong for her size, seeing as how the blade was at least half the size of her arm. She held it and faced me, "Come, try it now, you pervert.". She obviously still thought the worst of me. I started walking towards her and she swung the blade at me, which in turn bounced off me, causing her to stumble a bit. "What the hell are you?", she asked, more terrified now than before. "I told you, I'm here to help.". There was a knock on the door, "Having trouble in there? Do you need help?", Caprius said from the other side of the door. I gave her a sterner look. If Caprius came in now, the plan formulating in my head would be ruined. I stepped towards her with my hands up near my chest, and she slowly started to lower the blade. "What is it you're trying to do?", she asked with a slight tremble in her voice that told me I was somewhat finally convincing her. "I just need you to pretend. Pretend that we had sex, but when I let Caprius have his turn, I need you to keep him distracted long enough for me to subdue him.". She stared at me with wide eyes. She suddenly realized that I was telling her the truth. And with that she started making moaning sounds as if we were truly having sex. "Well, that's not what I was expecting.", Caprius said on the other side of the door. Tisiphone started to add a mixture of crying into her fake moaning, "Please stop it, you're hurting me.". She moved towards me and said under her breath, "…we need to make it seem like we just did it.". She grabbed me and forced my hands to grab her. She then screamed some more, giving me the hint to pretend that I'd finished with her. She laid on the floor in the most horrible fashion she could. To give the illusion that I had raped her. At that moment, Caprius had come into the room impatiently. "Are you finished yet or what?", he hissed, stepping into the room and observing the scene, "She looks all used up. I do hope you saved some of your energy for me, Tisiphone.". He kneeled over her and brushed her hair back off her face. She was looking distraught, but anxious. Caprius moved her body and turned her over. She looked at me with hopes that I was going to act. I nodded at her and mouthed the words, "Not yet.". Caprius was removing his armor and was about to remove his lower guard when I decided to come up from behind him and choke him. He struggled in my arms for what seemed like minutes. But it had been only a few seconds. Caprius passed out. "Quick, grab me some rope.", I told Tisiphone, as she gathered herself. "I don't know how to thank you…", Tisiphone started to say. "Thank me once we've got all of Dasha.", I said, taking the rope that Tisiphone handed me and tying a tight knot around Caprius' hands. "So, what are you planning now?", "I'm going to the castle. There's something I need from Falsa." "What about him?", Tisiphone asked, pointing an angry finger at Caprius. "Do whatever you like. Just don't kill him yet. I may need him alive.". Tisiphone picked up the blade she was brandishing at me earlier, and stabbed Caprius' leg. He wouldn't be able to walk anymore. This woke him up and he screamed in agony. "THAT'S FOR CHLOE, YOU SICK BASTARD!", shouted Tisiphone, who threw the blade down and started to cry. The old man came into the room and saw the scene. He came straight up to me and hugged me. "Thank you so much. You've done a great service by my family. This bastard is the reason my…first daughter took her own life. She was so miserable after what he did…", the old man sobbed into my chest. I wrapped both hands on his arms, "This terror ends now.", I said. Caprius was howling with pain. He turned to me, "YOU TRICKED

ME! YOU'LL PAY FOR THIS!", he shouted, trying to stand and immediately realizing he could not. Then he tried to pull his way across the floor, leaving a trail of blood. Tisiphone took the handle of the blade and hit him with it, knocking Caprius out cold. "I'll be back to help deal with him. I need to find my friend.". I turned to walk out of the house and Tisiphone grabbed my arm and kissed me on my lips. "Thank you. I never believed that this was possible. To be free of Caprius. But what if the soldiers come?", "Don't worry about them. Just keep quiet until further notice.". I walked out of the cottage and started towards the castle. I was going to go straight for Falsa. And with Caprius out of the way, nothing could stop me.

As I made my way up the path, the Dasha castle loomed in the distance. It held a very beautiful aura, even though it was surrounded by evil. There were three towers with red bricks at the top that shaped into a cone. The castle itself was a typical castle. It was a big square building with a moat around it and a bridge leading up to the gate, which was already open. I could see into the castle. I walked across the bridge and made my way inside. As I walked down the corridor, I looked at my surroundings. There were paintings of who I had to assume must have been the King of Dasha. Caprius looked a lot like his father. They both had short hair that looked like someone just threw a mop on his head. He had a sort of mousey nose and a very smug face. As I continued, I saw different paintings. These featured a young beautiful Falsa. In the painting, she looked hurt and angry. Another painting right next to this one, was of a pregnant Falsa and an exceptionally smug king standing next to her, holding her stomach. After this painting, there were no more paintings with the king. All the paintings now had Falsa and a young, smug, Caprius. I continued to admire the paintings, which I felt were very nice, even though it was Falsa and Caprius. I finally entered another corridor, which contained some more paintings. But these were a bit more of Falsa rather than Caprius. These were pictures of Falsa leering over the people of Dasha. One portrayed her as a goddess in the clouds. But the one that stuck out the most, was the one where she was holding a sword and shield. The shield was solid gold with intricate carvings and a language written around the edges that I didn't recognize. The sword was steel with a golden handle and the same kind of carvings with diamonds placed into the blade itself. I marveled at the painting, then read the inscription on the bottom, THE GOD SWORD AND SHIELD. So, this is what I'm looking for, I thought to myself. I wondered how I was going to find it, when a guard came from around the corner. He looked at me for a moment and considered. But I was too quick and punched him and he fell out cold. The noise attracted a few more guards, and I quickly fought them. Just then, another group of guards were passing by. I was going to hide, but then one shouted, "Oy! Boy!". I fought these other guards and took them out as well. I wasn't even remotely tired. Then I felt something hit me from behind. I turned and realized it was Falsa, holding the god shield. She uppercutted me with the shield, and that was the last thing I remembered.

When next I awoke, I was in a dungeon. Gold chains were wrapped around my wrists and I couldn't break free. I could feel my strength. It was still there. But it wouldn't let me break out of these shackles. "Well, here you are again. Chained up and looking pathetic.". Falsa was standing in the doorway. She had an, I've won this time, look on her face. "Where is Micka?!", I shouted. It was the first thing that popped in my head. Just then, I felt a kiss on the top of my head, then watched, as Micka walked around to face me. "Hello, Bastian.", she said, with a nasty tone in her voice, "I wonder what you must be thinking right now.". True, I was confused. "Micka, I was trying to find you. I thought Caprius had you. Thank goodness you're safe.". As I said this, I thought about the fact that I couldn't move. Micka had gone to stand next to Falsa. She was acting as if her and Falsa were working together. Which didn't make sense to me. "Micka, what's going on?", I asked incredulously. "I've moved on. You see, Falsa has adopted me as her daughter.". I didn't know what to think. This made no sense. Falsa is the reason her dad is dead. Not to mention my parents and our kingdom. Why in the world would she be happy about this? "Listen, you need to help me. You know why we are here.", "Yes, I know why Alisa sent you. But that doesn't mean that you will succeed.", Falsa said. I just stared in disbelief. Micka had betrayed me. She told Falsa about our mission. Falsa held up the shield. It started to glow. "This is a sign that you are near. It even shows me what you look like. To be honest, Sebastian, I'd have preferred the sword.". Falsa was smiling a nasty smile. She turned to Micka, "You go do what I asked of you now. I'll take care of him.". Micka gave me a last look, taking in my features, then she turned, and walked out. Falsa on the other hand was watching me maliciously. "This is everything I wanted. You here, under my control.". She came up close to me and then sat on me, wrapping her arms around my neck. "You see, this war was never truly about gaining your weapons. It was just about finding you.", "But, why? What do you want from me?", "Well, my dear, I want to know why. Why you felt it was okay for me to suffer. Why did you let King Killian take me from my home?". As she said all this, tears started to form in her eyes. "You don't even know who you are. It takes all the vengeance out of the situation.". Falsa was still sitting in my lap. My arms were hanging, while my torso was sitting on the floor of the cell. "You know, I got to thinking, and decided you should suffer all the indignities I had to, don't you agree?", "Please, just let me go.". I felt helpless. I couldn't move. It was something about these shackles. And as if she read my mind, "Yes, it's the gold. Gold immobilizes your power. Makes you weaker. Giving me all the power I need.". She started to undress me. "What are you doing?", "You're no longer a virgin, are you? Of course you aren't. Micka has already told me. She says that you are quite the beast. Not that she had been with anyone else. Shame what you did to that poor girl.". I laid there, helpless. Falsa was digging her nails into my chest. Blood started to trickle down my abdomen. Falsa leaned in and licked the blood off my chest and looked me in the eyes while she did so. "So, you're going to torture me?", I asked.

"Torture?", Falsa said, with a laugh that froze my insides. "No, my dear, you are going to give me something. Something that will make up for all the horrors in my life. You are going to give me a proper heir.".

CHAPTER 8

The Seer: Micka Meets Shay Tia

ALISA: If there was ever a time I felt completely lost, it wasn't anything compared to how lost me and Alex were now. Alex, who had already been to the secret kingdom in the Dark Wood, couldn't manage to find the place, either. We had been trekking for days at this point, and although she wasn't showing it much, I could tell she was worried about Bastian. The forest was cold. On the first day we arrived, Casian saved us from a creature I'm still not sure of what it was, but Casian was our savior from all the creepy things here. Most of the creatures seemed to know what Casian was and decided it wasn't worth tangling with a Dattur. While at the same time, there were plants that we had to be careful of. On our second day in the Dark Wood, while we were walking through thick bushes, one of the bushes turned out to be alive and immediately snatched me by my ankle. It took Alex and I a good forty-eight minutes to finally escape from its clutches, only to get caught in a field of dream sprouts. Dream sprouts were common, you see them all over Plinth. Just not in such a large abundance. With a field like this one, they have a certain effect on people. They put them into a dream state. Alex and I were passed out for eight hours. And if you can believe it, so was Casian. When we awoke, we had to fashion ourselves some face protectors to keep the pollen of the dream sprouts from entering our systems. When we had stopped in Alexandria, we gathered material to protect ourselves from these kinds of dangers. Alexandria was the most miraculous place I'd ever seen. Upon arriving, there was nothing. All I saw was a field that was lush, green, and clear of trees. Behind us, was the Willet, the largest pond on Plinth. I hadn't ever seen the Willet before. It was truly gorgeous. There were frogs jumping around, and fish jumping out of the water. I put my hand in the water, and it was cold to the touch. Alex was just watching my amazement. There were flowers that grew only in the water. "We call them aquatills.", said Alex, as I plucked one out and placed it to my nose. The smell was sweet and very strong, the whole pond smelled like the aquatills. We hung around the pond for a while, watching Casian chase down frogs, and catch unsuspecting fish that jumped out of the water. Standing in this field where Alex said her kingdom was supposed to be, was the strangest part of this trip so far. We stood there, and I wondered where it had disappeared to. After all, I knew Falsa attacked it, but she couldn't have completely wiped every existence of it from this field. But Alex crouched down, and picked up a stone that she breathed on. Suddenly, I found myself being lifted into the air. I was just about to scream, when I landed on solid ground. I turned, and before me loomed a castle the likes of which I'd never imagined. Its towers rose so high, I couldn't see the tips. It must be the biggest castle on Plinth. But what was really fascinating about it, was that it was a castle in the sky. It was no wonder no one had ever been to Alexandria. The rumors of the city being like visiting Heaven was not exaggerated. The castle was made of fine stone, a stone that was very close to diamond, but was breakable. The only thing on Plinth that could break diamond was gold. But all the gold seemed to only belong to Dasha. That was, of course, until I entered the castle. There was blood on the walls, and servants working to clean it all up. There was an older man with parchment in his hands, and he was frantically moving from spot to spot, yelling at the workers, "Do you think Queen Alexandria wants to come home to the memory of what happened? Clean all this blood, and please, can someone go and find out if the garden is done? They've been fixing it for days. Come on now! This is the last room that needs cleaning!". I noticed that all around, where the servants were wiping, were gold and white walls. When I walked up to the wall and touched it, I realized it was solid gold. At this point the middle aged man walking around giving orders, finally looked at me and Alex, "My Lord.", he said, bowing down so low, it looked like his nose would touch the floor. "Relax, Parnim, I know how hard it is to take in still.". Alex put her hand on Parnim's shoulder and Parnim winced and sobbed at her feet, "WE ARE ALL SO SORRY! WE TRIED TO PROTECT…!", "No… I don't want to hear any of this. Parnim, Alisa and I are here for the seatwine. We need it for our journey into the Dark Wood.". At these words, Parnim jumped to his feet and started shaking, "But, My Lord, you remember what Prince Lab said! He said you'd never leave if you ever came back!", "He also said to come in case of an emergency, and this is one of those moments.", Alex finished. Parnim gave her a look of worry but rushed off to go get the seatwine. The other servants were all staring at Alex in admiration. Most stopped what they were doing, just to watch Alex walk by. Casian had emerged from inside of her shirt, and had jumped down, and ran off. "Where is she going?", I asked, a bit worried she might not return in time before we leave. "Don't worry, I'm sure she's just going to see her friends.". We walked through the castle, while all the servants either worked harder or stopped what they were doing when Alex walked by. Soon, we entered a room that had a large bed, with red coverings, and a small indentation on the bed that told me Casian usually sleeps with Alex. Above was a painting of a pink glowing girl, with her arms wrapped around a figure in armor made of diamond. It took me a few moments to remember that Sebastian was wearing this armor in my dream. I didn't mention this to Alex, because I didn't know what it meant. Alex reached into a cabinet and pulled out a dagger. The entire dagger was diamond all the way down to the hilt. She placed it in her belt strap on her pants, and gave me a look that quite plainly stated, there was danger ahead. "So, this is your room, huh?", I asked. "When I first came to this castle, I was three years old. In truth, there is something I should have told you sooner.", Alex said, with a certain shakiness in her voice. Alex reached into a bag that was on the other side of the room, and pulled out a square paper looking object. When she handed it to me, I noticed it was sort of like a mirror reflection, but there was no movement. "This is called an Alexandrian memory sheet. It is a special technology developed here by the girl in this sheet.". I examined the sheet. There was a girl there. She was glowing, much like Alex does, but she wasn't Alex. I looked up at her. "I'm not the first of my kind. As a matter of fact, there is another one that you know. You see, every seventeen years, another, just like me, arrives on this planet. I'm meant to find the god, and bring him back to himself. But there have been others.", "What happened to these other women?". A thought was dawning on me. One I had hoped to high Heaven I was wrong about, "Who is this girl?". The picture was old. I couldn't guess its age, but the girl in the picture looked to be about sixteen or seventeen. That's when I recognized her. She was Falsa. Falsa was once what Alex is. I couldn't believe it. Alex stared at me. "WHY DID YOU WAIT TILL NOW TO TELL THIS TO ME?!", I demanded to know. This was a huge shock. Falsa has been Queen of Dasha for as long as I can remember. How could she have been connected at all to Alexandria? What about Caprius? Was he from here as well? Alex was watching me in my anger. Probably trying to think exactly what it was I was thinking about. "Well, I'm not too familiar with the story, but Falsa was taken from here, some time ago. I was the last goddess to arrive on this planet. Most of the other ones that arrived in the past didn't live very long. They had very short lives.". This didn't answer my question at all. "Alex, why are you just now telling me this?". Alex looked at me as if she had seen a ghost.

Just then, at that moment, a little girl burst into the room. She had green hair and was covered in what appeared to be a royal gown. She looked to be at least eleven and was crying out of her hazel colored eyes at the moment. "Oh, Alex! I missed you so much!". The little girl ran up, and threw her arms around Alex. I noticed Casian was on her shoulder. "Alisa, this little one is Alexa, my sister.". Now, I was totally lost. "I thought you were an only child?", "I am an only child. Alexa here is my adopted sister. Her parents were from Dasha and they were executed by Falsa. Alexa had been abandoned when she was six, that's when I found her. I was traveling back from the Dark Wood.". Alexa looked at me with hatred. She obviously thought I was only going to take Alex away again. She turned from me and stared Alex in the face, "Did you find him? Did you find the god?", "Yes. I found him. And he is as handsome as you imagined him to be.". At these words, Alexa blushed very heavily. "How about the war? Is it still happening? Did you get revenge for our parents? Did you…?". Alex held up a hand and smiled, "All in good time, love, but I must be preparing. Alisa and I are going to the Dark Wood.", "But, you said that you can never go there again! What if I never see you again?!". Alexa cried into Alex's chest, while Casian licked her face. "It's okay! You will see me again. Please don't be sad. I just need you to watch Alexandria a bit longer. Please, and stay safe, love.", "What about Casian? Will you be taking her with you, too?". It was clear that Alexa didn't want Alex or Casian to leave, and that she didn't fully understand what the situation was. Really, all I could think about was how when I was her age, I was fully immersed in pretty much all the political crap in my kingdom. I personally felt she was lucky, because she at least had Parnim to help her, whereas I had no one. Well, I guess I had Wilson, which I still didn't fully understand. Alexa looked at me, "Why does she have to go?", she asked me. "Well, because I need her help. She's been to the Dark Wood, I haven't.". Alexa looked like she might scream, but decided to give Alex another hug, "I love you so much.", she said, squeezing Alex's abdomen. "I love you, too. And try not to worry, this will all be over before you know it.". Casian jumped from Alexa's shoulder to Alex's, and as we were leaving, Parnim had caught up with us and gave us the seatwine. "Good luck, my goddess. I do hope everything works out, for all our sakes.". As we were leaving, I hadn't forgotten what Alex had just told me about Falsa but decided to sideline the conversation. We traveled for three days till we reached the edge of the Dark Wood. Now, here we are, wading through fields of dream sprouts. Finally, we made it out of the dream sprouts and into something worse.

The next day, Alex and I were exhausted. Alex kept muttering Sebastian's name in her sleep, while my mind had wandered back to Sheena. I wondered if she was okay. Then I remembered my dream, in which Caprius was raping her. I remembered how Sheena and Caprius switched, and it was Micka who was attacking me. I wondered if this meant something. I had heard a sound that sounded like a wounded beast. But I ignored it, and tried to go to sleep. As the noise continued and started to grow, I decided to investigate. I thought to take Casian with me, but she was sleeping on Alex's chest, and I didn't know if Datturs get angry when you wake them. I followed the sound deep into the wood. I knew I shouldn't be by myself, but something was compelling me. I tripped over many branches and was quite sure one of those had actually grabbed me. Finally, the noise was clear enough for me to see what it's source was. My jaw dropped. It was me. I was lying on the ground, naked and defeated. I was chained to a wall, which made no sense because I was in the... What was happening? I was in a dungeon all of a sudden, and in the dungeon, with me, were familiar faces. They were my men. They were standing around me, half dressed. I saw Caprius standing over me. He grabbed me by the back of my neck and pulled me up. Then I watched as he kissed me. I started screaming, "NO!". And as I did so, a man was coming from behind me. The scene was so frightening I turned from it. But when I turned to face the other way, the same scene was still visible. The men were having their way with me. I started to cry. Just then, I felt a hand on my shoulder, and realized where I was. I was still in the Dark Wood. There was no dungeon, or Caprius, or my men. I was fully clothed and wearing my armor. "Alex, what the hell happened?", "We have to leave this part of the wood. Now.". Alex helped me up. I was still sort of dizzy. When we made it back to camp, Casian had jumped on my shoulder and started licking my face. "That was the Den. In the Den, you will be forced to see your worst nightmares come to life.". I realized that's exactly what I was seeing. Because I was definitely afraid of Caprius doing something like that to me. And being surrounded by soldiers all the time, I definitely get afraid of that. Alex handed me a flask that contained some water. I drank deeply and handed it back, "Maybe we should get moving.". We started our journey again. I still had no idea where this castle in the woods was, and was starting to wonder if it was like Alexandria, and wasn't on the ground. As we moved from place to place, danger to danger, we became more aware of the fact that we were spending a lot of time in the woods. I was wondering if Sebastian had actually succeeded in getting the shield, when Alex put her hand in front of me. I looked up and realized we had made it to some kind of village. There was no castle, just little huts. The people were moving in a line up the middle of the path towards me and Alex. I was a bit worried, Alex was just smiling. A young man stepped out of the line. He had very blue hair and wore a talisman. "Prince Lab.", Alex said to me. Prince Lab walked up to Alex first, "I thought...we had an understanding, of you never returning here?". Alex looked Lab in the eyes, and said, "You said to come only if I've met him. Which I have. So now, everything is happening.". I was lost. Still trying to keep up with the fact that Falsa is a goddess. "Fine, fine, come this way." We followed Lab, until he led us to a bigger hut, located somewhat in the back of the village. Once we walked in, there was nobody else inside and Lab asked us to sit. There were five chairs inside of the hut, surrounding a round table. "You...", said Prince Lab, "...must be Princess Alisa of Kindy.". I wasn't expecting him to know me. Before I could ask, 'how?', Prince Lab was already giving me an answer, "We have had it written for centuries that you would come. You are both here because Falsa has started the war. Well I should tell you both, there is nothing that I'm going to tell you that Falsa doesn't already know.". As I was trying to work out what that meant, a man came into the hut. "She has arrived, My Prince. Would you like me to escort her in?", "Yes, that would be fine, please do.". The man ran off to go fetch whoever Lab was talking about. I was still trying to figure out what that crack about Falsa meant, when the man returned...with Falsa.

MICKA: Falsa's mission to me was to locate a certain person named Wilson. A man who had traveled all of Plinth and could be a great asset. Truth be told, I didn't fully understand the entire situation, and how he could be a great help to us. Part of me still felt bad over what happened with Bastian. I left him in Falsa's clutches, and I wasn't entirely sure what she wanted with him. What I did know was I betrayed him. At the time, I felt he had betrayed me by accidently calling me Alex. Now I realized that maybe it was an honest mistake. Falsa told me some amazing things, though. And after everything my father taught me, it seemed like it would be foolish not to act on what I was being given. Wilson was somewhere in the kingdom of Kindy. Alisa wouldn't be there. According to Falsa's scout, she had left for the Dark Wood with Queen Alexandria. How she planned on surviving, I did not know. The Dark Wood was the most dangerous place on Plinth, and death was all anyone had ever gotten from entering. At least it was believed those people died, they never did come back out after all. Except for Wilson, he was the only survivor. Falsa said he was a bandit, who had been kicked out of Dasha. He decided that instead of robbing travelers, he would just travel as well. He went to other kingdoms and had to make a false identity just to enter. He traveled to the edge of the Dark Wood, and wondered if he should go in. He went in, and quickly was attacked by all sorts of creatures and plants. But in the end, he had found a small village in the woods. They, at first, treated him as a threat, but then saw he just had an innocent thirst for knowledge, and shared with him the knowledge of the universe. They told him how Plinth is just one planet, but how we were favored by the god. That's why he sent his spirit to live among us. He wanted to understand us and see how we differed from his other creations. But the people back then were too narrow minded, and in the end, had surrounded him, and executed him. To prove who he was the next time, he had given himself some of his power. To do this, he had to make two of himself, but this is where he had made a mistake. Even the god wasn't completely, all knowing. He mistakenly made another half of himself. And it was this half of himself that the Dark Wood was designed to guard over. Prince Lab, and his ancestors before him, had guarded this sacred area for decades. At this point, it was inevitable that a much greater war, than the one we were fighting now was coming. I told myself in my head, Micka, you are now going to be a queen. You are no longer just a village girl. These were the words Falsa told me, right before I decided to betray a boy who I thought I loved. I had been traveling for four days and had finally started to see the kingdom of Kindy. When I arrived at the gate, the guards were very disoriented. I was wondering if maybe they were just exhausted, when a girl with bright yellow hair came out of the gate and started yelling at the guards, "ARE YOU SERIOUS?! YOU'VE BOTH INHALED?! WE ARE AT WAR! WE ARE NOT SUPPOSED TO BE INHALING KIND FLOWERS ON DUTY!". The girl took her blade out of her side holster, and with the handle, hit one of the guards on the side of his head. "You are now off duty until Princess Alisa returns, and you are to go find replacements. Now, MOVE!", the girl shouted. I was impressed by how fast she had made these men move. She was a better candidate to rule Dasha then me, I thought at the time. I noticed she had a beautiful face. And when she turned and started towards me, I became severely nervous. "Who are you and what is your business here?". I thought it best to tell the truth. Or at least some of the truth. "I'm Micka and I was with Sebastian. I've been sent back here to find a man by the name of Wilson. Do you think you could help me find him? It's really important.", "Sent back by whom?". I didn't know how to answer this. The answer was Falsa. So, I came up with the best story I could on the spot, "I ran into Princess Alisa, and she said that she needed me to fetch him.". It was a bit feeble, but it was the best story I could come up with. Just then, the girl grabbed my arm. "Where'd you get this tattoo?", I looked at my arm and realized there was a tattoo there that I didn't remember getting. It was writing, but no writing I had ever seen. As I tried to think of where the writing came from, a look of recognition came over the girl's face, "You must have gotten this from Alisa. She has stuff like this. I saw her wearing a bracelet with this kind of writing.". She released my arm and ticked off on a piece of paper. At this moment, two more guards had arrived, with the guard the girl had sent to fetch them. "Good, now you may go. And as for you...", she said, turning to me, "...I'll escort you.".

We walked through the gate, and the first thing that hit my nostrils was the strong pungent smell of the kingdom's native flower. They seemed to be planted all over. Villagers had gardens of them and some villagers were plucking the ones that had bloomed. I noticed there were entire fields of them beyond the village. And the castle, which wasn't even as big as Nasher's castle, was right on the other side of the field. "Wilson resides in the castle. He is our royal advisor. Funny, I never knew we had one until a week ago. Princess Alisa left me in charge of her army. I'm still a bit shocked.". Now I had a better understanding. "My name is Sheena. I grew up here. My sister and parents were murdered. For a long time, all I wanted was to make the king, the queen, and their spoiled daughter pay, but since meeting Alisa...". Sheena became very embarrassed and stopped talking for a time. She had started to blush, and my immediate thoughts were, "Ugh...". We started walking through the field of kind flowers. My father used to purchase these flowers. He also smoked them. He said they were good for his lifting. "Do the kind flowers ever kill anybody?", I asked, hoping just to make light conversation. "Well, no, it only closes you off for a bit. You still have control of your body, it just relaxes you. But nobody has ever died.". Sheena moved like a girl born to be a leader. Even the way she talked suggested that she was leading material. "So, have you ever met Wilson? I heard he's a very interesting man. Traveled all over Plinth he has.", I said to Sheena. "Oh yes, loads of times since our return. He's very kind. He told me that I shouldn't feel bad or alone. That Alisa will be there for me no matter what.". At these words, Sheena began to blush again. It was obvious she felt something for Alisa, like what I thought I felt with Bastian. She was smiling a kind of day dreaming smile when we finally walked through the castle gates. She looked forward and saluted. A woman wearing a crown made with kind flowers was walking towards us. The woman looked like an older version of Alisa. "I am Queen Shay. And who is this young woman, Sheena?". She wasn't even looking at me as she spoke, but rather looking past me and Sheena, as if looking for someone else. "This, Your Highness, is Micka. She's come here on Alisa's orders to fetch Wilson.". At these words, Queen Shay did look in my direction. She was watching me rather hard. "I wish to speak with this, Micka, privately, if that is fine with you, Sheena.". Sheena looked rather confused, but answered, "Of course, My Queen. She's all yours.". Sheena walked away and left me standing with Queen Shay. Shay watched me, and I just stood there, nervously. Finally, after what seemed like some long minutes, she spoke, "Do you truly expect me to believe my hard-assed daughter, sent YOU, on an important mission? Please, it's too early to be laughing.". I was lost. I hadn't expected the queen or the king to not believe me. It didn't take me long to come up with that story though, so it was easy to see how it could be seen through. Queen Shay eyed me, waiting for a response, but one didn't come. "My daughter doesn't trust me, or her father, given everything we've given her. She is very serious about stuff. Very serious indeed. Always making sure the soldiers are sober, always keeping all the political business in check when her father and I are incapable. So, you can see how I would look at you, and doubt my daughter sent you. You're nothing but a commoner from the looks of you. Nashin is my guess.". I was quite surprised with the knowledge Queen Shay had. I had believed her to be very out of the loop. At least that's how Alisa made her sound. "Sorry, mam. I wasn't expecting you to be so wise. Alisa gave me the impression her parents weren't bright enough to write on parchment.". At these words, a look of exasperation flashed across Shay's face, "My daughter stopped thinking the best of me, after I put her fluff over her face. I of course had my reasons for doing it, but she thinks it was sinister…", she trailed off. "Come now, I'll take you to Wilson.". I smiled and nodded, "Thank you, Your Highness.", "High? I haven't even had any flowers today.". I let out a soft laugh, as I followed the queen. She was leading me under the castle. We passed paintings of past rulers and of course past princesses. Alisa's painting was quite nice. She was a little girl, sitting atop of a purple maned pony, with a look of determination on her little face. I still greatly disliked Alisa, and something must have shown on my face. "So, how did my daughter entrust you of all people with a mission such as this?", "The last I saw Alisa, we were in the woods right outside of your kingdom. Falsa had attacked us and Alisa said she would need reinforcements. She asked if I could go to her kingdom and search for a man named Wilson.", "I see… And how did you become a part of my daughter's army?", "She found me in Nasher, while Falsa was attacking. She personally saved me.". Queen Shay looked as if she was over thinking my words. Finally, we reached the bottom. Just as I was thinking how odd it was that Wilson would live this far below, Shay directed me to a door. I opened it and realized it was a cell. Shay shoved me inside and quickly closed the door. "How foolish you are, girl. I knew you were lying to me this whole time. My daughter would never enlist the help of someone who's eyes AND ears are both closed.". I didn't know what she meant by that. "Please! I'm here to see Wilson. You must bring him to me. It's important. You don't realize what is at stake!". I thought if I could just confuse her enough, maybe she would believe me. I wasn't too sure, but something inside me told me that Shay is nothing like what her daughter sees her as. She is way more on top of stuff than Alisa had given her credit for. "My dear girl, you can't truly think me that stupid. I wish to know why you are really here. You had better start giving me an explanation, or things are going to get ugly here.". Now she was making threats. I didn't want to tell her that I was on a mission for Falsa, but I also didn't want to be tortured, seeing as how I've never been, and wasn't looking to start. "Do…you know Alex? The queen? She wants me to find him as well. He holds the key to defeating Falsa and ending this war. Please, I'm begging you to just let me go!", "Something…you may not realize about me, child, is that I'm gifted in knowing if I'm being lied to. So, let me give you a word of advice. The next words, out of your pretty, little, mouth, better be the truth.". Was this a test? Was she able to tell I wasn't being truthful? I didn't want to fail Falsa. After all, she was giving me her kingdom, so I proceeded, "Mam, please…", I threw in some fake tears, "…just let me see Wilson. I don't deserve this.". She considered me, then walked away. I sat alone in the cell. I put my face in my hands, believing my situation wasn't going to get any better. Little did I know, I was about to be rescued by the most unlikely person.

ALISA: Alex had to keep me from grabbing Falsa, and murdering her. Prince Lab just sat there like he was expecting this kind of reaction. "WHAT THE HELL IS SHE DOING HERE?!", I yelled, feeling the blood in my face, and pointing at Falsa. I was so angry. I felt betrayed, even though I hadn't met Prince Lab before now and hadn't been to this village. I turned to Alex, expecting support, but Alex just sat there, waiting for Lab's explanation. "Alex, don't you care? You're really just going to sit there?". Alex didn't move a muscle. Then I looked closer at her, and realized that one of her temples was pulsing. "Where is Sebastian?", Alex asked, staring Falsa right in the face. "He is alive and well back in Dasha. Oh, and I've left him his shield. I have no further use for it.". Falsa was holding her stomach preciously. As if she was carrying something in there. She gave Lab a look of mirth, and Lab returned the smile and stood up. "Perhaps, it would be prudent to give you ladies time to discuss things.". And with that, he turned and walked out. "What do you mean you've given him his shield?", I asked, keeping my hand on the hilt of my blade. Casian was hanging out of Alex's shirt, but had a rather confused look. She then leaped from Alex to Falsa and began purring on her shoulder. I just stood there transfixed. "I know I owe a huge explanation. You see, I am also a goddess. Much like you, Alex. But you see, I was never meant to be with Sebastian, because my job was just to help him realize who he truly is.", "So, what you are saying is that it was your job to kill innocent people. To start a war that would last…", Falsa raised a hand and cut me off. "You don't understand, Alisa. Sacrifices had to be made. It's important Sebastian realizes who he is. It's the only way Plinth will survive.". Falsa grabbed her stomach again, which seemed to be acting somewhat unlike a stomach. It would jump and force Falsa to move in directions she wasn't going. "What the hell is wrong with you?", I found myself asking. "She is pregnant. I can see it in her face.". I looked at Alex, unable to believe what I just heard. But that was nothing. "She's right. And the father is Sebastian.". Falsa said, with a look of triumph on her face. Alex jumped up and attacked her. "HOW DARE YOU?!", "ALEX, CALM YOURSELF!", I shouted, but it was too late. Alex was on top of Falsa, choking her. Falsa wasn't even trying to fight. I tried to grab Alex off of her, but she had that same look in her eye she had before we left for Alexandria. "HOW DARE YOU HAVE YOUR WAY WITH HIM, YOU BITCH?! I'LL KILL YOU!". Falsa finally managed to push her off and started for her. I stepped in between, "That is enough. Falsa, what did you do?", I asked, trying to keep Alex held back. Just then, I felt something hit my head and realized Alex had picked up a nearby object, and hit me with it. Before I could react, she hit me again. Next, I woke up to the sound of children's laughter and the rustle of trees. I looked around, as I slowly came to, and realized I was outside. A very strangely dressed woman with black paint on her face was moving around the area. She seemed to be fumbling with something. I looked to my right, and Prince Lab was sitting there. He had a fresh cut on his face that suggested he may have been in a fight. I tried to sit up, but my body felt drained. My armor had been removed and I was in my regular coverings. "You took quite the hit, you shouldn't be trying to stand. Just relax and let the moo water have its effect.", said Prince Lab. "I...don't understand, what happened? The last thing I remember is, Alex and Falsa trying to kill each other.", "Don't worry, that's all over now. Falsa is resting and Alex is taking a stroll around our moo pond. But you need to rest. Aye! Camacha, bring her more.". I could slightly feel my strength returning, as Camacha dumped the moo water over me. It smelled like shite. "I need to know what happened.", I blurted out to Lab, who in turn looked at me with amusement. "Well, two goddesses in the same room, who love the same man, well you can only imagine. Falsa was born a goddess and taught all the same things Alex was taught. She came here when she was thirteen to learn the ways of the gods. But unlike those before her, who waited patiently in vain, Falsa sought out the god, and forced him into his destiny. Of course, it was a selfish course, and now she pays the price for it.", Lab finished. I stared at him, amazed by what I just heard. "If that's true, then how did Falsa wind up in Dasha? No less, it's queen?", I asked incredulously. I mean, it made zero sense how a girl, who is supposedly a goddess, would just give up that role to be a queen. "Two of our people, Helion and Kappa, had grown very fond of Falsa. Falsa, who of course had no true parents, decided that she would accept them as her parents. When Falsa left here, she went to Dasha, along with Helion and Kappa. They quickly settled from what I understand. But, Dasha was always known for having corrupt royalty. And with Falsa being as beautiful as she was, it was only a matter of time until the king captured her and forced her to marry him. He murdered Helion and Kappa on the same day, and then forced Falsa to have his child.", "Caprius...", I said, with a note of realization in my voice. All this time, and now it finally made sense. Caprius was the son of the rapist king. I've heard my father and mother speak of him, but never associated the rapist king with Dasha. Part of me even felt sorry for Falsa. "So, Falsa took Dasha from the king somehow?". Lab laughed at me for asking this. "Do you truly think the king held all the power? Falsa played the king. Falsa's intentions were to infiltrate his castle and take the kingdom from him. That was always her plan. After all, how can she start a war without an army?". So, Falsa was always attempting to start this war. But there was so much confusion in what Lab was telling me. Up until now, Falsa has been the enemy. Now she was just this girl, who I realized was suffering. "Wait, so what you're telling me, is that Falsa killed the king? She actually killed the king just to...to take the kingdom from him? I can't believe it. But where does Alex fit into this?", "Alex, is what Falsa is. The only difference between the two, is that Alex is the one Sebastian will choose.", "WAIT! You know Sebastian?", I asked. How could he know Sebastian? He was from Nasher, and as far as I knew, wasn't anywhere near here, and had never been. But Lab just looked amused again, "I overheard the name. It sounds godly in a way, don't you think?". I just laid there, trying to tie it all together. So, Falsa is a goddess, who wanted to meet her god. But prophecy said that the god would only emerge when the great war begins. Falsa purposely started this war, just to find the god, and have him impregnate her. "But, doesn't this mean the war is over? I mean, I don't need reinforcements, right? Falsa's soldiers are going to stand down. They have to, right? I mean, she's here, and resting, and not leading an army. And I thought it takes much longer to experience pregnancy?". Falsa came into the area. She was still holding her stomach and looking like she was in agonizing pain. There was a huge part of me that was happy Falsa was in pain. She walked towards Lab and stood next to him. "Lab, I think I need to see your father. I know he won't be happy, but...", she trailed off, when she noticed me watching her, "So, you're awake? Well, Princess, what are you thinking now? Still want to kill me? If you did, you'd be killing Sebastian's child as well.". This time when I tried to sit up, I managed it. Prince Lab interjected before I could answer, "I don't think picking a fight is the best thing for you right now, Falsa. You need to rest. I'll go see Father about granting you an audience.". Lab left me with Falsa. I was starting to feel like Lab wasn't very aware. After all, even though I knew what I knew, Falsa was still the enemy. "Alisa, I know you hate me. Alex has every right to hate me, but I need you two to trust me. If I didn't start this war, Alex would have ended up dying. Just wasting her life, waiting for something that would have never come. Alisa, you're smart, you always have been. I've known, ever since I sent Wilson to your kingdom.", "What do you mean, SENT, Wilson to my kingdom?", I asked, turning an ashen face. "Wilson was a villager here. He left with me and two others. When we departed, the plan was for Wilson to find the seer, and guide her. My job was to gain a kingdom, and begin the war that would save Plinth.". Find the seer? What the hell did that mean? "And, did...Wilson ever find this seer?", "Of course he did. She's sitting right in front of me.".

CHAPTER 9

The End Of The War: Sebastian Gains The Shield

MICKA: I lost track of the days at this point. Queen Shay had locked me away, and I felt there was nothing I could do. I missed my father. I found myself calling for him, and then remembering, he was dead. I once again felt my hatred for Falsa starting to rise. It was her fault I was in this situation. Food would be brought to my cell. It was decent food at the least. Finally, after what felt like weeks, a man's voice spoke through the bars on the door, "Falsa sent you, didn't she?". I looked up with such hopes, that I couldn't even hide the gratefulness in my face. I had forgotten that I wasn't supposed to tell anyone that Falsa sent me, but I was so happy, I couldn't think straight. The man outside of my cell had a long white beard and was wearing a magenta colored robe. "Yes! Falsa sent me here to search for Wilson. She said I'd find him here.", "Foolish.", the old man muttered, "You shouldn't just blurt out stuff like that. Especially here of all places.". I stood there, holding the bars of the cell door, lost for words. Then the old man put a key into the door and turned it and opened it. "Come now, we don't have much time.". I stepped out of the cell. "What is your name, girl?", "My name is Micka, and I'm from Nasher.". The old man looked me over, considering me, then he said, "I am Wilson, and did Falsa tell you why she needed you to fetch me?", "She said that she's done it. She said you'd know what that means.". Wilson put his face in his hand and rubbed his face. He then stared sadly at me, "So, she has taken advantage of the boy? She now carries his child?". I couldn't believe it. "You mean, I left her with Sebastian, and she RAPED him?!". Wilson let out another sigh and nodded. I felt tears coming up. I hadn't expected that. She had played me. She gave me this mission, even said I could have her kingdom. But it was all just so she could have her way with my boyfriend. Anger such as I had never known was consuming me. The blood in my face was getting hot, and all I could think about was killing Falsa. "Please, do take pity on her. I know it's hard to understand now, but there is a much bigger game than you realize being played.", Wilson said, watching me with sorrow. He reached into his robe and took out a strangely shaped bottle filled with a green liquid. "Drink, my child. This will help you to understand.". As he handed me the bottle, I stretched out my arm and he noticed something. "Where did you get that tattoo?". Wilson was referring to the tattoo that Sheena noticed earlier. "I honestly don't know where that came from…", I said, staring at it in bewilderment. I never got a tattoo because Father would have browned my backside. Yet, there was a tattoo, plain as day. I know I really didn't get it, because I didn't even know what it said. The symbols looked like strange lines going in a circle, but somehow forming different sized circles. "This…is the language of the gods.", said Wilson. "But, that doesn't explain where it came from.". Wilson stared at it, and then realization spread across his face. "You must have gotten this from Alisa. I gave her protective charms when she was just a girl. The clever girl must have placed it on you when she knew you may be in danger.", "Alisa was trying to protect me with this? How can this possibly protect me? She should have given it to Bastian.". Anger was flowing through me again. Alisa gave me this tattoo. I was still slightly confused as to why. "You didn't think it odd that you have been surviving in a war most women who are as close as you are to, would have been dead? Or how about the fact that Falsa chose to give you the keys to Dasha?". I didn't tell Wilson about Falsa making me her adopted daughter. How could he know she was making me queen? Before I could ask, we heard noises moving towards us. "Quickly, we must leave.", Wilson said, grabbing my wrist and leading me the other direction. We turned a quick corner and ran into none other than Queen Shay. "Where do you think you are going? Where do you think you're taking her? She is a prisoner.". Wilson stared at the queen for a while, then took something from out of his robe. I couldn't see what it was, but whatever it was, the queen fell to the ground and was sleeping. "What...?", I started to ask. "No time, my dear, we must leave Kindy. If you wish to save your Sebastian, we must hurry and return to Dasha.". We rushed past soldiers who watched us, confused, not knowing if they should stop us. I was getting the feeling that Wilson was an important person to Kindy. When we had finally reached the gate, Wilson turned to me, "Are you ready to fulfill the destiny that's been given to you?". I thought about it, and realized he knew the real reason I'm here. I was scared, because what Falsa asked of me was rather hard. But I took the hidden dagger I had stashed by my leg out, and in a fast movement, cut Wilson's throat. He sputtered, and grabbed his neck, and fell to the ground, grabbing my shirt. I pushed him off and watched as he bled out. Falsa had told me that if I let him live, he would stop at nothing to make sure Falsa's plan fails. He was the last one who truly knew what she wanted. Now, nobody could stop her. The real question was, what do I do now? I took out the vial that

Wilson handed me. The green liquid inside was fizzing. I opened it up and wondered if maybe it's poison. Wilson couldn't have known my full plan, or else he wouldn't have gotten me this far. I drank from the vial and immediately felt a floating sensation. It felt like I was leaving my body. I saw shapes that resembled the tattoo on my arm. Suddenly, things were becoming clearer. What Falsa wanted, how Sebastian fit into it, Alex's role as well as Alisa's and the village in the Dark Wood as well. Having all this knowledge flow through me at once was almost unbearable. Just then I felt a heavy fist on my face. I was back at the front gate to Kindy. Wilson's blood was on my shirt. And standing over me, was Sheena. She grabbed my shirt and punched me again. "You'll be going back to the dungeon.", she said, picking me up with both hands by my shirt. I noticed there were men surrounding me as well, swords drawn. "HOW DARE YOU, YOU LITTLE BITCH?!". Queen Shay was walking towards me. She took one look at Wilson's body on the ground and then looked up at me in pure disgust. "Kill her.", said Queen Shay. The men started towards me. Sheena, being the closest, swung her sword at me, but I dodged it as if she was hurling a blade of grass. At that moment, the men chose to move in and start towards me. I suddenly felt like I was invincible. I realized at once that l was different somehow. These men stood no chance against me. I took one soldier's blade out of his hands and turned it into his gut. Blood spilled on my wrists as I turned and punched another soldier in the face. Then I saw Sheena coming towards me again. She blocked my first punch and I threw another one that knocked her out. Next, I rounded on the other men. I started taking them out one by one. Once I was finished, all the men either laid dead, or incapacitated. Queen Shay stared at me in horror. "Please, I just want you to know...you'll never win. No matter what.", said Shay, as I turned on her. I looked at Wilson's body again and decided my job was done. So, with that, I turned and walked away, leaving Queen Shay quaking in her heels.

ALISA: I sat and stared at Falsa with such a look of disbelief, that she had to explain to me at least seven more times, that I was the seer. Of course, this made zero sense. "Think of your dreams. Your dreams are telling you what to do. Don't you realize that yet?". Falsa's stomach was still twitching. "What is going on with your baby?", I felt compelled to ask, also thinking about the fact that I hadn't seen Alex since she knocked me out. "This…is my punishment for doing what I did. Of course, I'm not done yet. There is still so much more to be done.". I watched Falsa caress her stomach. "You know, when Caprius was born, I told myself he would be nothing like his father. How sadly disappointed I was. It was then that I told myself, if I do find the god, I'll have the child I was meant to have. I would take what I was owed. You and Alex can't understand because you two have had a sheltered life. Sure, there are a few bad seeds in Kindy, but ultimately, Kindy is nothing like Dasha. Why do you think I took it from the Rapist King?". Falsa wasn't exactly instilling in me anything different. I still didn't trust her. Plus, there was the fact that I didn't know what happened to Sebastian, or Micka. Falsa chose this moment to walk away. I got up and followed her. She led me through the village, which I was starting to realize was a lot bigger than I thought. It was mostly filled with huts. The people were all active, doing one thing or another. Children played, adults tended to the plants and animals. There were strange flowers I had never seen before. They were green and seemed to contain a liquid that was being processed into vials. "They're called revealers.", said Falsa, plucking one of the green flowers, and holding it to her nose. "You will only ever find these here. What this flower does to people, you wouldn't understand.", "I'm getting really tired of you telling me what I would and wouldn't understand, Falsa.", I said, feeling irritated. Falsa gave me a look that quite plainly said, "Child…". I finally saw Alex, who was sitting beside a pond. I left Falsa behind, who just stood there watching me, and approached Alex. Before I could say anything, "I'm sorry, for what I did. I feel I'm apologizing to you more and more.". When she turned her face to me, I noticed she had been crying again.

She looked back at Falsa, who was kind of just standing there in a sort of mocking position. "I'm going to kill her, Alisa. I really am. For what she did to Bastian.", "What? Show him a good time? Look at her. She's beautiful. You truly think Sebastian suffered?", I said, looking at Alex incredulously. "Not to mention the fact that you're both goddesses who are in love with him, so you should just get over it and move on.", "Alisa, if I had done the same to Sheena, would you be so calm?". This was a good question. I remembered my dream, and how I felt watching Caprius have his way with Sheena. It was a scary notion. At this point, I understood that Alex was pissed and wanted Falsa dead. But I felt that we needed to get back to Kindy and find out what was going on. If the war was over, or, if something more sinister had taken its place. Something about Falsa leaving Dasha and saying she's on our side just didn't feel right. "Alex, we have to leave. There aren't going to be reinforcements.". Alex just sat there. Then she put her face in her hands and said, "I CAN'T GO WITH YOU!". I stood there transfixed and confused. "Alex, what are you...?". Falsa cut me off, "She can't leave, until Sebastian comes for her. Which he will. So, I'm afraid you'll be traveling alone.", "Why can't she leave?", I asked, starting to get upset. "She must be here. Its prophecy.". I felt like I must have passed out in the Den again. I needed Alex to help guide me out of here. Now I was starting to feel frightened. "Alisa, I'm sorry, but I told you I wouldn't be able to leave. I have to wait for Sebastian.". Before I could say another word, Prince Lab had returned, looking ready for a journey. He was carrying a bag made of leaves and branches and had a sort of dreamy smile on his face. "She can't leave, but my father has asked me to join you.". Falsa looked a bit livid. "You aren't supposed to leave either, Lab, what is your father playing at?", she said, giving Lab a look of anger. I tried to understand what she was upset about, considering that Alex couldn't leave, someone had to escort me out. Lab gave Falsa a puzzled look, "I'm taking her out of the wood, that's all. I'll be returning right after she exits.". Casian had jumped onto my shoulder. "You can take Casian with you. She likes you.", Alex said. Casian licked my face and then leaped into the other bag that Lab had been carrying. "This bag contains provisions for your trip back through the woods. I've made you a tonic that you can take now. It'll keep the dream sprouts from affecting you.". I swallowed the tonic without question. "What about the Den?", I asked, afraid of running into that area again. "Do not worry. The tonic also fights the effects of the Den.". Feeling relieved I had someone to guide me out, I took one last look at Alex. She stood up and walked to me and hugged me, "Alisa, we may not have been together for long, but I feel I have found a sister in you.". I was very moved by this. I embarrassingly answered, "Thank you…I feel the same. Thanks for everything, Alex.". She released me and then walked away. Falsa looked at me. "So, till we meet again, Princess Alisa.". She walked away and did not look back. "So are you ready?", asked Prince Lab. I nodded, and then we began our journey to exit the Dark Wood.

SEBASTIAN: I awoke to the sounds of battle. I felt dazed and drained. My pants were lying next to me in a pool of sweat. I couldn't move, and when I tried to stand, my legs felt like my ankles would snap. I was used sexually and left to rot. Not too far from where my pants were, was my shield. Sitting there, just looking pretty and stainless. Why Falsa had left it, I didn't know. A voice was calling my name and asking where I was. I could hear it shouting and echoing throughout the dungeon. Finally, somebody appeared at the door and I noticed a beautiful girl, who was sticking her face in my cell, "Sebastian?! Oh, my word! I'm going to get you out of here, okay? Just wait.". I heard rummaging around outside. Then I heard scuffling. "Where is the key to this door? I want it now!", "Only Falsa had it, and we think she took it with her when she left.". I heard more noises, then my door opened, and there stood Tisiphone. The girl who I had saved from Caprius. She was looking somewhat battle worn now. She was covered in blood from her chest to her pants and was carrying the great blade I saw her use to stab Caprius' leg. "I'm sorry! I've been trying to find you. Falsa left a few weeks back, and with Caprius having been captive at my home, I knew the time to rebel had come.". She was undoing my chains. I fell to the floor in a heap. She quickly helped me put my pants on and heaved one arm over her shoulder. She carried me out of the dungeon. When we reached the sunlight, it burned my eyes. I slowly felt my strength returning now and was quickly starting to remember everything. Micka had betrayed me and left me with Falsa. "Falsa... She...", "Don't try to talk just yet, okay? Try and take it easy. You're weak and need sustenance.". She carried me to a mart, where the unmistakable signs of battle were present. Dasha was always a shit kingdom, but this was on a different level. Carts had been turned over and horses lay dead in the streets. Bodies were all over the place, heaped over carts or just face down or face up on the ground. Tisiphone barely seemed phased by this. She was casually looking for something that didn't have blood on it. "Ah, yes, here we are. This will help you.". She handed me a cup, which I drank from. It was the sweetest liquid I ever tasted, but it left a strange aftertaste. I felt a fast head rush and suddenly I was waking up in a bed. Standing over me with a towel and wiping my face was Micka. "Poor dear, if only I could do more for you.", she was saying, as I started to realize my surroundings. Micka was wearing a royal gown with a serpent on the front. I grabbed her hand, realizing we were back in the cabin that Falsa had left us in before. "What are you doing?", I asked. "I'm only cleaning you. You would think I'm killing you.", "YOU LEFT ME HERE, YOU BITCH! DO YOU KNOW WHAT FALSA HAS DONE TO ME?!", I shouted, now standing up. I was so angry, and Micka was just wearing this calm face. I noticed she was wearing Falsa's crown. "I know what she has done. And that is hardly my concern. I just thought it fair to ask you to leave my kingdom.". Leave HER kingdom? Obviously, a lot happened while I was passed out in that cell. "What do you mean, your kingdom?", "Falsa, gave me her kingdom, Sebastian. I am now Queen of Dasha. And I am no longer at war. So, you may leave.". I stood there, not knowing what the hell I should say. None of this made sense. "Oh, you should know, King Oliver is alive. I've already made peace with him. Now, don't keep your dear Alex waiting any longer.", "Why?", I asked. "Because, I imagine she is probably going crazy without…". I cut her off, "NOT THAT! WHY DID YOU LET FALSA RAPE ME?!". Micka just sat and stared at me, an evil smile spreading on her face, "You're going to tell me you didn't like it? Falsa is a goddess. Just like your precious Alex. Her cunt was just as good, I imagine. Or maybe it was too damaged after the Rapist King was through with her. Either way, isn't that what you like? Goddesses?". Micka was being very cold. It was almost like she lost the ability to care. I stared at her in disbelief. "When I left you here, I went on a journey…", she said, as if she was reading my mind, "…and I met a man named Wilson, who gave me a very interesting beverage.". She held up a vial that contained green liquid. The liquid was fizzing and somehow was calling to me. I couldn't make out what I was hearing at first, then it got incredibly clear, "SEBASTIAN! COME TO ME! JOIN ME! BECOME ONE WITH ME!". I grabbed my head, as it felt like it was going to burst. I looked at Micka, who was watching me with glee. She put the bottle down and out of sight. I felt my head starting to feel better, and I wondered what the hell that was. "You see, Bastian, I know things now. Things that I would never had known before. Honestly, it's all thanks to Alisa. She made it ALL possible.". Micka let out a cold laugh. It chilled me to think that this was the same girl I grew up with. The same girl who I escaped our kingdom with. The same girl that was making love to me, that was too afraid of losing me. She then walked towards me, "I do thank you for everything. Especially taking out Caprius. That made things so much easier. That girl who you saved, what was her name? Symphony?", Micka asked in a mocking tone. "Tisiphone.", I responded. "Oh yes. Tisiphone. Quite the brave girl. Way braver than I by a large scale. I've come to accept that I'm nothing but a cold-blooded killer. But her, oh man, is she something else. I think, if she had any kind of god blood in her, you'd fuck her too.". Micka was obviously lording over me. She was enjoying this beratement. She didn't care that I felt dead inside after what Falsa had done to me. She also didn't care that I was getting angrier with every word she spoke. "You think I wanted Falsa to rape me?", I said, trying my best to keep the anger out of my voice. "Maybe not the way you wanted it to go down, but I'd say you were pretty satisfied. According to my new general, she found you with your pants thrown to the side and oh yes, this.". She turned and revealed my shield. She handed it to me. At once, I could feel the power. It was incredible. It felt like I was being energized from inside of my body. Electrons were exploding and giving me even more power than when Alex kissed me. "Why are you giving me this?", I asked her, admiring the shield. "You really do not like to listen, do you? I told you, I have no problem with you and that the war is over. So, if you would like, you can leave and go wherever you want. Just please, leave Dasha and never come back.". I stared at my shield more and decided to take Micka up on her offer. Tisiphone greeted me outside the cabin, "Isn't she the best? She rode into the village saying Falsa is never coming back and that she is the queen now. She even has Falsa's crown, that's how I knew she wasn't lying. It truly is a new day in Dasha.". Tisiphone was overjoyed, but I felt like I had been hit with my shield two thousand times. How could Micka just take over Dasha? Where did this new knowledge derive from, and what happened to Caprius? I didn't really care, but once I had started thinking about it, I hadn't seen him. "Tisiphone, where is…?", before I finished my question, I saw Caprius. He had a cane, and his leg had been mended up to where he could stand on both. He was watching as I walked towards him. "About time. Now, perhaps we can leave?", "What? You're going, too? But…", "The bitch is exiling me from my own kingdom. My MOTHER apparently gave it to her.", "Yes, and if you ask me, it's the one right thing your mother did for us.", said Tisiphone, with malice in her voice, "You're lucky she is only exiling you and not killing you, because if it were up to me, you'd be hanging from the front post in my yard.". Caprius gave Tisiphone an angry look, but obviously thought it best not to say anything. “Sebastian, I don’t understand why Queen Micka wants you to leave, but I accept it, only because she wishes to do right by us. She is the best thing that ever happened here.”, Tisiphone said, it sounded like she was trying to convince herself. “It’s okay, Tisiphone, I don’t want to be here.”. Tisiphone hugged me and gave one last look of hatred towards Caprius and sent us on our way.

Caprius was limping with every step, all the while, staring at the shield I had now placed on my back by its straps. Caprius was not a very good travel companion. Many times, he would mention what he’d have done to Micka before his mother gave her all this power. How he would have killed me when he had the chance, and how he hates his mother for tricking him into this pointless war. Hearing his ranting took my mind off certain things. Hell, some parts I even agreed on. Like when Caprius said, “If Mother were here right now, I’d rip out her intestines.”. If I were a woman, I knew it would be worse, but just because I’m a boy, didn’t make the rape less heart wrenching. I felt so much anger towards Falsa but remembered what Micka said about her being a goddess. “Caprius, do you mind if I ask you a question?”, “What stupid question could you have for me?”, Caprius responded, with a look of irritation on his face. Trying to talk to Caprius was like trying to talk to a bowl full of stony. He was very secretive, unless he was talking about how he wanted to kill his mother and Micka. Micka had apparently embarrassed him more than Alisa had. She had paraded him around the city, forcing him to hobble on his cane and bad leg, while all the women who were afraid of him, spit on him as he hobbled by. Then she made him wait on the edge of town for someone else he hated even more. I could deal with the threats of how he wanted to kill Falsa and Micka, but whenever Caprius started talking about me, I just shut him out. All he would say is how he so wanted Tisiphone’s cunt, and I ruined that, costing him his entire kingdom in the process. Now he is being forced to travel with me to who knows where. “Caprius, did your mother ever say anything about...about being different?". Caprius eyed me for a moment, then finally answered, "Mother was always secretive, even towards me. She never explained all the details. She would always leave something out. Even this war was another one of my mother's hidden agendas. It was all a cover so she could impregnate herself.", "What did you think it was about?", I asked, wondering what reason Caprius could have for going to war. "I thought we were going to take over all of Plinth. Mother said, rule the four kingdoms, rule all of Plinth. But she never intended to rule all of Plinth. She just wanted to...", he stopped talking, realization dawning on his face. "...she... just wanted to replace me...", Caprius said, suddenly looking down trodden. In a kindred sort of way, I understood what he was feeling. My parents were dead. Caprius and his mother saw to that. But Falsa doesn't even love Caprius. I remembered Falsa telling Micka and I as much when she was giving us that cabin. Maybe that's why Caprius is the way he is. Because he was never properly loved by his mother. I felt sorry for Caprius, even though a part of me still loathed him. "But...that doesn't really answer me. Do you think that your mother has a connection with Alex?". Caprius stopped walking and stared at me for a moment, "What the hell are you asking me? Are you implying my mother is Alexandrian?". I didn't know how to answer this, because I didn't know the answer. I had the feeling that Micka knew, but now I can't go ask her. Just then, Caprius was hit with something and fell to the ground. A girl came running out of the trees with her blade in hand. She realized who I was and lowered the blade, staring at the shield on my back, "You got it!", the girl exclaimed, putting her sword back into her holster. Alisa had a strange creature on her shoulder that was eyeing me curiously. She stood over Caprius, who was waking up. "Why are you traveling with this shit?", Alisa asked me, with a hint of disgust in her voice. So, I told her what happened. How me and Micka arrived in Dasha, how Micka betrayed me, how Falsa used me to get pregnant, and how Micka came back and declared herself the queen, and exiled both me and Caprius. When I finished, Alisa didn't even look surprised, "Well, I can tell you, I already knew most of what you've told me.", she said, keeping her eyes on Caprius, who was just rubbing his head where Alisa had struck him. "What do you mean?", I responded. Alisa then went into her story about how her and Alex went to Alexandria, then traveled into the Dark Wood. She told me about the creature, Casian, who is apparently Alex's pet. She told me about the girl, Alexa, whose parents were executed by Falsa, and how she was adopted by Alex. She then told me about Prince Lab and the village in the Dark Wood. She told me about the amazing things she learned. Falsa is a goddess. Born off Plinth and sent here. Alex was born the same way. Where they truly come from, isn't known on Plinth. She told me Falsa's reasons for starting this war, which was just to get pregnant by me and start my destiny or something. Then she told me about the revealers. The flowers that had the green liquid. "I know what you're talking about. Micka said she got some from a guy named Wilson.", "In order for Wilson to have given her anything, she would have had to travel to…", Alisa stopped talking, dread spreading on her face, "HOW COULD I HAVE BEEN SO STUPID?!", Alisa shouted. I looked at her, wondering what she could mean. "Micka… You said she's Queen of Dasha now, right? Why didn't Falsa mention that. And Wilson wouldn't have let her take that vial. We need to get to Kindy, now.", Alisa looked at Caprius, "I guess, bring him as well.". We traveled past The Jasmine and straight into the kingdom of Kindy. When we arrived, you could feel the bad tension in the air. The guards at the gate made way for Alisa as she casually waved them aside. She stopped to greet no one while we basically flew past villagers, who from the looks of things, were in mourning. "Alisa, what do you think has happened here? Everybody is upset about something.", I asked. Alisa didn't answer, but rather instead pointed to a large gathering. From our viewpoint, you could see a man and a woman in the middle of the crowd. I assumed immediately that they were King Derek and Queen Shay. There were multiple mounds and what I finally noticed were dead bodies. As Caprius, Alisa, and I made our way towards the center, we realized the bodies were of soldiers and one elderly man in the middle. “No…”, Alisa said, as she moved forward towards the old man’s mound. Queen Shay tried to come to her and comfort her, but Alisa threw her arm off her shoulder. “How did you let this happen?”, she asked, with sadness and anger in her voice. “Wilson did this to himself. A girl, claiming you sent her, lured him to the front gate, then slashed his throat. She then turned and killed these poor men.”. I stared around and thought, I couldn’t believe Micka had done this. There was a young girl with yellow hair who came up to Alisa. Alisa turned to face this girl and then kissed her. So, Alisa preferred women, no surprise. I stood over Wilson’s mound, and looked at him. I stared into his eyes and something began to happen. I could hear that voice from before, calling out to me, “SEBASTIAN! LETS BE ONE!”. I started to freak out. I backed away, looking around at everyone. Caprius watched me as I ran off. I eventually came to a halt in a field of kind flowers. I laid there, still reeling from the voice in my head. The flowers were having a certain effect on me. I felt a bit dizzy, then I felt like I was floating. It wasn’t that nothing mattered, it just didn’t seem to be a big deal. I thought about my parents and laughed at the thought of my father’s head dangling from that Dashin soldier’s hand. I remembered when Micka kissed me on my forehead, before Falsa raped me, and thought, what was I so angry about? She was a good cunt. All these thoughts were just flowing through me at once. Then a cold, drawling voice from behind me said, “You shouldn’t put your face in a field of kind flowers like this, Sebastian, it’ll mess with your head.”, Caprius said, helping me to my feet. My head started to clear, and I suddenly remembered where I was. “Caprius…”. He had waved his arm and shook his head, “I saw you back there. Something happened to you and I want to know what.”, Caprius demanded. I stood for a while, looking back over towards the crowd, where smoke had started to rise. “They’re burning the bodies. Sending them to the heavens. A tradition my mom always kept in Dasha. I didn’t know they did that anywhere else.”. Caprius was watching the scene with a mixture of curiosity and confusion. I, on the other hand, was still worried about this voice. I had felt alone since Micka left me with Falsa, and one thought that had kept me going was that Alex was at least worried about me. Now that I was thinking of Alex, I realized she wasn't here. Alisa was the last one with her and could tell me where she was. I wanted nothing more than to be with her. The girl who had walked up and kissed Alisa was now walking towards me and Caprius. She was a beautiful girl, that eyed me suspiciously when she had gotten four feet away from me. "Well, you're the one who brought that girl into our midst. What do you have to say for yourself?", she asked me, with her hand on the hilt of her sword. She turned to Caprius, "And don't think I don't recognize YOU. You're the son of Falsa. The Rapist Prince. How dare you both show your faces here?!". It was obvious that she blamed us for all the bad that's happened here, on the fact that me and Caprius were connected to the evilest people in this war. Then I remembered that Micka said that the war was over, and that she would not be pursuing it any longer. But just because she wasn't, did that mean Falsa wasn't either? Just then, Alisa came running up. She placed her hand on the girl's shoulder, "Sheena, they are okay.". Sheena looked at Alisa as if she hadn't heard her clearly. "What are you talking about? This one is the Prince of Dasha, and this one…", "Succeeded in taking one of Falsa's greatest weapons. You dropped this, Bastian.". Alisa handed me my shield, which quickly rejuvenated me. "But that girl! I saw him with her! How do I know they aren't together?! I will NOT be tricked again!", Sheena yelled out. "Sheena, I'm ordering you to stand down.". Sheena looked at Alisa with a bit of pain and confusion in her eyes. "I need you to trust me, Sheena, there are things I've learned, and I need these two.". Sheena gave one last angry look towards Caprius and walked away. "This is just like my dream…", said Alisa. "What dream?", snarled Caprius. Alisa explained how Falsa had told her she was a seer, and how she was dreaming up the answers. "So, you told me that I should let Caprius live, and well, here he is. But I don't understand what reason I could have for wanting him alive.", Alisa eyed Caprius, and then continued, "Now, don't you see? It's all so obvious what's really happening. Falsa is playing us. Whatever her real goals are, we need to stop them before they happen. But I fear, we've already played perfectly into her plan.". I tried to process everything she was telling me, but part of me just kept thinking, where is Alex? "Alisa, where is Alex? Why isn't she with you?". Alisa turned to me and bit her lip, "She wasn't allowed to leave the Dark Wood, so she is still there.", "Isn't that where Falsa is as well?", "Yes, unfortunately. And I think this is all part of her plan. I just wish I understood better what the hell she was trying to do.", Alisa turned to Caprius, "What is your mother trying to do?", "I don't know, do I? She never told me anything.", "Did your mother send you here? Is this an elaborate plan to destroy my kingdom?". Caprius just sat there looking stupid and confused. He had never had this kind of treatment, and having been left out of the loop by his mother, he had no answers for these questions. "Micka kicked us both out of Dasha, Alisa. I honestly don't think Caprius has anybody now.", I said, trying to get Alisa to back off a bit. Caprius was looking hurt and scared. And besides from that time in Tisiphone's cottage, I had never seen him look like this. He realized he wasn't in his own world anymore. That he wasn't untouchable, but rather was now in Alisa's world, and would have to abide by her rules. At that moment, King Derek arrived on the scene, closely followed by the Queen and Sheena. "Alisa, what is this? What's going on? Who are these…?", King Derek stopped talking when he saw me and what I was holding. "Are you… are you…are you…?", he kept sputtering out. Apparently, all his nerves had left him. Queen Shay on the other hand eyed me with a look of interest and admiration, "I can't believe it. I never thought this would happen in my lifetime.", "You're…you're…you're…", the king had finally changed his sputtering. Alisa finally said what her father couldn't, "The god.", "Please, just call me Sebastian, I am getting tired of being called the god.". King Derek walked up and fell to his knees, kissing my feet, while Queen Shay bowed to me. "You two are embarrassing me! Stop this!", Alisa yelled at her parents. "Alisa…", said the king, "…this is who gave us all life. He gave us this planet to live on, food in our bellies, and a kingdom. Please, my good sir, I would have you come with us to the castle.". Having nothing else I could say to this except for yes, I followed the strange group up to the castle.

CHAPTER 10

The Great Sacrifice

ALISA: It had been a long journey. So much had taken place now that I was home with Sheena. We laid in my bed, just holding one another for some time, until Sheena broke the silence, "So, what are you going to do with our visitors?". She, of course, was referring to Sebastian and Caprius. It had been a month since we all turned up together. Since then, Caprius had taken on a whole new role. He was learning humility. He was helping the children in the village with their education and giving out life lessons about who he used to be and who he's becoming. My parents, of course, were all over Sebastian. They had given him servants to assist with whatever he asked. Once my parents learned the heartbreaking truth about Micka, they tried to make Sebastian feel better by getting a beautiful girl from the village to keep him company. But since Falsa had raped him, he didn't seem very interested in having sex. Sebastian spent most of his time training in our yard or trying his very best to avoid the gifts my parents kept sending him. Often, I would see him just sitting in the fields, thinking. My guess was that he had become accustomed to the kind flowers. It made sense that he would, considering the effects. I would also spot Caprius, who since learning how his mother abandoned him, had taken on a whole new approach towards women. He didn't see them as tools or objects, but rather, now saw them as equals. Spending time with my mother, Caprius learned more about his father. Apparently, Falsa had told him nothing. He learned how his father was nothing but an abuser to women and that many had tried to flee Dasha in the past, but soldiers had blocked their path and forced them to remain where they were. She had told him about her own encounter with his father, which even I didn't know about. The king had tried to convince my mother to choose him over my father. My father, who had been in love with my mother since he was a young boy, told the king he would never have her. The king, in his anger, had tried to kidnap my mother. But my mother was apparently smart enough to expect this, and, of course, my father, the Prince of Kindy at the time, was willing to go to war to protect my mother. Hearing this story made me question how my mother became such an uncaring person. Then, I noticed how she was with Caprius. She treated him very well, considering his crimes. She was always very kind to him, and was teaching him how to take care of the flowers. I noticed that caring for the flowers seemed to have a good effect on him, and he was even talking with a much kinder tone when you spoke to him. "Alisa, would you happen to have seen your father? He said he wanted to show me something.", Caprius had asked me one day, when I stepped out of my room. He was holding himself up with his cane and seemed to be in good spirits. "I haven't seen him this morning. Have you seen Sebastian?". Caprius smiled and answered, "Oh, you know where he is. Same place he always is every morning.". I left Caprius, who had hobbled off to go find my father, and made my way to the kind flower fields. Sure enough, Sebastian was sitting in the field, cross legged and motionless. His eyes were closed and his face relaxed. I almost felt bad disturbing him, but at the same time, I knew that things were too quiet. "Hey, Bastian, think you got time to talk?". Bastian looked up at me. His handsome features showed more than ever in the light, and so did his irritation. "What do you want?", he asked me flatly. "Well, honestly, I just wanted to know how you're doing. You haven't really spoken to me since we've been here.". Sebastian gave me a look that said that there was no reason to speak. He returned to his meditation, facing away from me. I took the hint and left him alone. I returned to the village, where I found Sheena. "How did it go?", she asked, as soon as I was near her. "Not good. He's upset about things. I don't blame him, but I'm quite afraid of what Falsa has planned.", "Falsa can't do anything without a kingdom.", said Sheena. While there was a lot to be worried about, Sheena was right about this. Falsa had given Dasha to Micka, who in turn had ended the war. But what wasn't clear was if this was her doing, or if Falsa had commanded her. Part of me knew that Micka had to be working with Falsa, because this was the only thing that made sense. Caprius had, of course, mentioned Micka, but was very different about his feelings towards her. "She was hurting. After all, my mother and I stormed into Nasher, and her father is dead because of it. And from what I heard, her mother had already died. I just wish I could take it back.". It scared me sometimes how different Caprius was. All the horror stories I had heard about him. And, of course, the scar I had given him was still visible on his neck. But even this didn't bother Caprius, "You did what you had to do. I was out of line. My mother had me brainwashed and I apologize for all the evil wrong doings.". Sheena wasn't so quick to trust him. "I don't care what the king and queen say…", she was telling me one night before we laid down, "…if you ask me, it's just a matter of time before he reverts back to his rapist ways.". I agreed with Sheena, but secretly had remembered what Sebastian said in my dream. That I should let Caprius live. There were times I thought about my dreams, and other times I thought about Sheena. But what seemed more important than Sheena, or my dreams, was Sebastian and how he felt. I tried approaching him again a week later. This time, he was standing in the field, facing away from me again. I approached him from behind.

He must have heard me coming because he spoke before I could say anything. “I have to leave, Alisa.”, he said, without turning towards me. “But why? You seem to be doing fine here.”, I said sarcastically. All he’d done was ignore me, which was funny, because I remembered doing that to him. He turned to me and I saw that his face was peaceful. That he had truly come to understand how things were. I wondered what he knew that made him this calm. “I need to go to Alex, she needs me, Alisa.”. I thought for a bit about the fact that I had left Alex in the woods and that Falsa had said that Bastian was going to come for her. Suddenly, I realized something. “I can’t let you go. It’s a trap. It’s got to be. Falsa stayed there and left someone who isn’t her son in charge. I must believe her reasons are sinister. You understand, right?”. But from the looks of things, he didn’t. He looked at me and in the most shocking manner, he replied, “You can’t stop me from going where I need to go, and I don’t need you anymore.”. He started to walk away, at which point I placed my hand on his shoulder. “Bastian, listen to me, I know that you’re hurting, but this is suicide. Falsa knows more about you than you know about yourself. She will use that against you and kill you. I have a nasty feeling I’m right. Please just consider what I’m saying.”. He turned away again, “Alisa, do you know what it’s like for people to tell you that you’re important, but not feel important?”, “I do understand how that feels.”, I answered, thinking about when Falsa told me I’m a seer. “Alisa, I love Alex, and ever since I met her, all I can do is think about her. I can’t be without her anymore.”, “What about Micka? I thought you loved her?”, I said, in another sarcastic tone. Bastian put his face in his hands, “Micka left me behind. She doesn’t care about me anymore. She banned me from ever coming to Dasha specifically because she doesn’t want to see me.”. He shook his head, once again looking off into the distance. Part of me admired his handsomeness, which I found hard to do when he was sulking and feeling sorry for himself. “All because I can’t stop thinking about Alex. Why can’t I stop thinking about her? I’m even having dreams about her. Please, Alisa, you have to let me go.”. It was obvious now. Alex must have the same connection. All those times she became increasingly jealous all made sense now. Watching Bastian spiral out of control over her, was reminding me of Alex and her tantrums. Before Sebastian could throw one, I made up my mind. “Okay, I’ll let you go, but I’m not letting you go alone. Traveling through the Dark Wood is no easy task. You need somebody that’s been. So, I’ll go with you.”. Sebastian looked like he was considering this. “No, I don’t need you, Alisa. Your place is here, with your people, and your parents. I have to make this journey on my own.”, “There are things in the wood that you are not prepared for…”, “Then tell me what I need to know.”. There was no convincing him. He really wanted to go by himself. “How about this? Give yourself some days to prepare at least. I’d hate for you to be caught in the Den.”, “What is that?”. I gave him a ‘see what I mean’ kind of look, which in turn he replied, “Alisa, I never thanked you for saving me and Micka, so thank you, but it’s time I start learning how to be what everyone is telling me.”, “I can see arguing with you isn’t going to get me anywhere, is it? Well if that’s how it’s going to be, then what can I say? All I ask, is that you tell my parents. They’d be excited that you finally accepted something from them.”, “And that would be…?”, Sebastian asked, dragging his last word. “Well, I’d imagine provisions, like food or something.”.

It was early evening, and Sebastian was still in Kindy. Somehow, I had a strange feeling that once he left, something bad was going to happen. I voiced my feelings to Sheena, who in turn responded in a way I least expected, “I think…you should tell your parents.”, “Why the HELL, would I tell them anything? Because of my parent’s carelessness, Wilson is dead. Not to mention the fact that I’m almost positive they have inhaled today and will not be able to take me seriously.”, I said. “Actually, I wouldn’t blame that on your parents. If anything, it’s all my fault.”, Sheena said, with a touch of guilt to her voice. We had had this conversation too many times. “Sheena, it was not your fault. Micka was on our side and you had no way of knowing that she had sided with Falsa. My parents are to blame because they allowed Wilson too much freedom. They didn't have a guard on him when they should have.". As I finished talking, an unlikely person came up from behind me to argue, "You're wrong...", Caprius had shown up and was shaking his head at me. "Oh, do you have something to say?", I asked, irritation rising in my blood, "Who the hell are you to tell me about MY parents? Where the hell do you get off?". Caprius just stood there, still shaking his head at me, "You have no idea the sacrifices your mother has made for you. I only wish I could say the same for mine.", "Please, I would love to hear about the sacrifices. Pretty please?", I said, mocking Caprius' stance on his cane. Sheena let out a soft laugh. "I get it, I really do. You think your mother tried to kill you, but you're wrong. She wasn't trying to kill you, but prepare you.". This was the final straw. "You do not get to come here and start telling me what my parents were trying to do. You of all people should be locked away for everything you've done. I should have you executed. Yet here you are, living it up in my kingdom.". To my surprise, Caprius let a tear roll down his cheek. I hadn't expected big tough Caprius to cry. "If you want to kill me, then do it. I have nothing to lose, and nobody would miss me.". Caprius walked up to me and pointed at my blade. I stood my ground and looked into his eyes. I saw not a frightened man, but truly a man who had nothing to lose. "Look, just don't try and tell me about my parents.". Caprius stepped back, and I noticed Sheena had her hand on her blade and it was half way out. "Why don't you try asking your mother, what my mother once said to her?". And with that, Caprius hobbled away. I wondered what Falsa had told my mother. I didn't even know they had met. This was all so strange. First, the story of the Rapist King trying to kidnap her, and now she's met Falsa? I supposed it was time to talk to her. I made my way up to the King and Queen's Chamber. Upon entering, my mother was there with a handful of servants. "If possible, try to put something with Alisa in it nearby. This will one day be all hers and I want her to feel...", my mother saw me. She started towards me and waved the servants away, "Alisa, what brings you here? I wanted this to be a...". I cut her off, not in the mood to hear anything else, "I need to know the truth about your connection to Falsa and Caprius' father.". She stood and looked at me, then responded, "So, are you really ready for the truth? Because it isn't as simple as you think.", "What did...Caprius mean when he said you weren't trying to kill me that time?". My mother fixed herself up and puffed out her chest, "Before you were born, I was just a villager here. Your father and his mother would often ride into the village and give sweets to the villagers. The first time I saw your father, I was completely smitten with him. This was over twenty years ago.". We both stared at one another. Me trying to determine if my mother was being honest, and my mother looking for hope that we may find peace. "When I first met Falsa, she was traveling with Wilson and two others. They had come from the Dark Wood. Falsa was the Alexandrian princess at the time.", "WAIT!", I shouted, "You knew Falsa was from Alexandria? Why didn't you ever mention this?". My mother watched me with something close to amusement on her face. "Well, let's see, you never want to speak with me, you go all the way out of your way to show how much you hate me every day, and to put things into a worse perspective, you think your father and I are complete dung heads.". This was all true. "But, it's only ever been that way because you tried to kill me.". My mother's amused face turned into a sad sagging face. "Listen, I never tried to kill you, but my plan did work. I wanted you to be the toughest girl there is, and you have become her. I saw what happened to Falsa and never wanted that for my own child. So, to protect you, I let you think that I tried to kill you and that your father saved you. This way, you'd be tough from the experience while keeping your love for the kingdom. And...letting your hate for me fester. What I need you to know, Alisa, is that...I love you.". My mother hadn't said that to me in over thirteen years. I could feel my mouth open, but didn't know how to close it. Mother just sat there, watching me, then continued, "Falsa just stopped off here to bring Wilson, but she left me with a very chilling message, concerning my daughter.", "But, I thought you said this was before I was born?", I asked. "Of course, it was. I hadn't even imagined you when Falsa first mentioned my daughter. She said she'd had a dream about her. She told me that you would be taken from me by a man with a lot of power and influence. She said he would be a king and that I had best take measures to insure your safety. She said she saw you suffering at the hands of an evil man and I knew that to protect you, I would have to push you away. It was the hardest thing I'd ever done in my life.". I was in shock at my mother's words and confused at the same time. Who was this so-called 'king' who was going to take me away? As far as I knew, there were only three. My father King Derek, King Oliver, and the king in the Dark Wood who I never met. There was also the Rapist King, but I was quite sure he was dead, and that Falsa had been the one to kill him. So, if that's the case, why would Falsa warn my mother about a man she knew she'd kill, before he ever got the chance to consider having his way with me? Once again, I felt this was another trap Falsa had set. As crazy as everything was starting to sound, it was obvious Falsa had been planning all of this for years. I knew I would have to try and stop Sebastian from going to the woods. My mother watched me, expecting me to have a response for everything she's told me so far. I had nothing. So, I decided to ask something else that had been bugging me, "Why have you been so nice to Caprius? You do know what he's guilty of?". At these words, my mother's expression had become sterner, "That poor boy has never been properly loved by his mother. Now she has abandoned him. She hates him because of who his father is, and let me ask you, do you think that's fair?". She gave me a condescending look. "Well, what about all the people he's hurt? Are we just going to forget about that?", "His mother told him he could have whatever he wanted. He was raised in an almost lawless kingdom and being the prince, nobody could say a thing to him, for fear that Falsa would execute them. Being a child and growing up in a place like that will make you despicable.", "But, he's only been here a month! How can he have possibly changed?". My mother watched me for a while, then a smile spread across her face, "If you really stop and think about it, respect can go a long way, Alisa, a very long way.".

I thought about what she was saying, but couldn't see what that had to do with Caprius. "When Caprius first got here, I could feel his pain. You know, I've never told you about your grandparents. I think it's time to give you a bit of insight. My mother was raped, and that is how I was born.". I was speechless. "My father was a Dashin villager who was known for being drunk. My mother was a very kind woman who worked in a pub serving drinks. My father would often describe what he wanted from my mother, even call out to her, but my mother always ignored him. One night, when my mother was closing shop, my father came in and he took her innocence. My mother, after that, had fled to Kindy. Here she started a new life but found out she was carrying. It was the hardest thing my mother ever had to do. When my mother gave birth to me, she wouldn't even look at me. When I was six, my father came here on business. He recognized my mother and realized I had to be his child. My father wanted to take me with him, but Mother refused to allow him to be in any part of my life. From then, he would send me gifts. It made me want to at least get to know him, mind you, my mother never told me what he had done to her. When I was seventeen, my mother couldn't stop me from going, and that's when I first traveled to Dasha.". My mother was Dashin. That means I'm part Dashin.". Suddenly, it dawned on me why my mother was so kind to Caprius, "It's because you're Dashin, that's why you are so kind to him.". My mother smiled again, "Yes, that is part of the reason. You must also realize that having an ally such as him could prove to be useful. After all, it might not show on the outside, but, Caprius has something special inside of him. He is part god.", "What do you mean…?", I asked slowly. "Well, his mother is a goddess, right? So, it would make sense that some of Falsa's blood is running through his veins.". I hadn't thought about this. But, Caprius wasn't like Sebastian, so what exactly does that mean? "Anyway, back to my story.", continued my mother, "While I was in Dasha, I saw King Godrick for the first time. He was the son of King Killian who had died a couple years before. He was a handsome man, who I was a bit taken with. When he first laid his eyes on me, my father tried to keep me from him. Eventually, the king took my father and had his head chopped off. Then he tried to kidnap me and force me to live in his castle. But I managed to escape before anything could happen. I made it back to Kindy, where my mother had fallen ill, and I didn't know what to do. Then, Godrick came here looking for me. He said I was a fleeing Dashin who had to be taken back. This was the same day I had truly met your father, and we became quite taken with one another. Your father showed up, asking why the King of Dasha wants to take a Kindy villager. He fought Godrick off, and that was the last I saw of him, and from that point on, I had been with your father. We were married shortly after. My mother, your grandmother, died with tears of joy in her eyes the day you were born. But it was shortly after we had been married when Falsa showed up and told me something about you. She told me that she was traveling to Dasha. I tried warning her about Godrick, but she seemed to think that was perfect.". Of course she did, I thought, because she knew he'd do the same thing he tried to do to my mother. My mother, who I was starting to admire. "I don't understand, why didn't you tell me any of this before?". Mother gave me a look, "I told you, I needed you to hate me. I couldn't allow you to know the truth. I needed you strong, for you to think that I didn't care. This way, you'd become more dependent on yourself.". My father came into the room at this point. He saw that my mother and I were talking to each other and let out a sob, "I…can't believe it, after all this time…", he took out his handkerchief and blew into it. "Oh, Derek, don't be so dramatic. We knew one day we would finally be able to tell her the truth.". My father came up to me and hugged me, "We love you so much, Alisa, so much, and I'm so sorry for never telling you so, can you ever forgive us?". I looked at my parents, who watched me hopefully. "I suppose so… After all Mother went through, and after everything she's done to get me to this point, how can I be mad after learning the truth?". We embraced each other, my mother finally letting the tears roll down her pretty face. "Oh, before I forget…", said my father, "…Bastian is getting ready to leave. I just thought you'd want to see him off.", "Right, thanks, Father.", I said, and then I did something I don't even recall ever doing. I gave him a kiss on his cheek. I walked out of the chamber and made my way to where Sebastian had been sleeping. On my way, I ran into Caprius, who was engaged in conversation with Sheena. "Look, all I'm saying is my mother is not done, and there must be more. She's cunning and dangerous, and it doesn't matter that she was pregnant last time Alisa saw her. There is something in the works, I can feel it.", "I thought you had no idea?". I said, approaching the two of them. "Alisa, when I first came here, I admit I was afraid, but now, I only want to repay your kingdom for taking me in. I believe my mother has been hatching whatever this egg is for a long time. I don't think Sebastian should leave.". For once, Caprius and I agreed. I felt that as soon as he did, something was coming. "But we have no right to stop him based on our personal feelings. If he wants to go, we can't make him stay.", said Sheena. Personally, I knew she was right, but I couldn't go through with letting Bastian leave. "Well I'm going to see him, so let's just cross our fingers.". I finally made it to his room, and he was indeed getting ready to leave. Casian was on top of his bed carrying small things in her mouth and giving them to Bastian to pack. I thought it was cute. Bastian turned and realized I was standing in the doorway. "I'm going, Alisa, I'm sorry.", "It's okay, Bastian, I understand.", I lied. I noticed Casian had become fond of Bastian. She had even spent time with him when he was by himself in the kind fields. Bastian had started to finalize his packing and Casian had jumped into the bag. "So, you're taking Casian? Not a bad idea, she'll come in handy.". Bastian looked to face me, and I saw something in his eyes that I'd never seen before. "Alisa, there are no words for everything that you've done for me.", he said, giving me a hug. He turned to walk out of the room and I had the impulse that I should stop him. "Sebastian. Remember when I said this was most likely a trap? I still think that. Please stay here… Lets plan on things a bit before you go.". Sebastian looked at me for a minute, then turned and walked away. Sheena had walked up, and I asked her to escort him to the gate. She nodded and gestured for Bastian to follow her. I watched as the two of them walked away and I wondered when the next time I'd see Sebastian would be.

MICKA: Dasha had been a mess before I became it's queen. So much seemed to have happened since I had last seen Sebastian. Tisiphone had taken up the mantle of rebuilding Dasha into something better. I walked through the village most days, finding it hard to believe what I was seeing. Most of the cottages had been remodeled to have second and third floors. There were parades quite often to celebrate the change of rule. I wasn't cruel, like Falsa was, but I was very stern. The liquid I had pilfered off Wilson had given me visions I had not expected to have. One vision I had seen, before Sheena punched me, was a vision of a girl. A young girl, who's features were gorgeous. She was purple haired, like me, and seemed to have a look of anger on her face. As the girl had turned to face me, I saw so much of myself in her. She was a goddess. I could feel the energy coming off of her. I awoke one morning to feel that same energy coming from my stomach. It wasn't till a couple months later that I realized I was carrying. Sebastian had given me a child, and I knew it was going to be a girl. Some part of myself prided on the fact that my child would be beautiful and intelligent. But then I had another dream, of another woman, who looked more like Alisa. I thought this was strange, considering everything I knew, two women cannot make a child. I saw that the child had Sebastian's eyes and let out a loud laugh. So, Alisa would fall for Bastian as well. It appeared he had no shortage of women. "Your Highness, there is a girl here to see you. She says that it is an urgent matter.". Tisiphone had entered the room, looking a bit flustered and worn. She had taken to one of the guards, Pietro. "Ah ha. I shall tend to it.". I walked out of my chamber and proceeded down the hall. As I made my way into the royal chamber, the girl who had come to see me had a familiar look to her. She was just standing in one spot, giving me the impression that she was a statue. She finally faced me, and watched, as I circled around her and sat on my throne. "Real comfortable isn't it?", she said, watching me intently. Anyone else would be freaked out by this girl's strangeness, but I was intrigued to know what this familiar feeling was. "Shall we talk somewhere more concealed? Trust me, you want to hear what I have to say, Queen Micka.". I raised an eyebrow, but got up and led her to a room right on the side of the royal chamber. "So, what is this about?", I asked. Just then, the girl turned into a familiar form. Falsa. I almost screamed, but I caught myself, allowing only a tiny gasp to escape from my mouth, and quickly to cover my action, I said, "What are you doing here? I thought you weren't coming back?". She stared for a moment, then answered, "I just wanted to see how my adopted daughter was running my kingdom. I must say, I'm impressed you didn't kill my son.". She was smiling at me, in a scary sort of way. I noticed her stomach was swollen, as if she too was carrying. Her stomach seemed to have a personality. It would often force her to move in different directions and I could have sworn I heard a giggle. I stared at her stomach, then concluded what, of course, I should have known. "You too are carrying Sebastian's child.", I said flatly. "Right you are, my dear. And let me tell you, it is not easy.", she said, with a bit of mirth. Her stomach gave a sudden jolt and she had to grab a wall, "Listen, I don't have much time, I need you to do something for me. Do this for me and I'll never ask for anything else.", "How could I say no to the one who made me a queen? Just speak it and I'll see what I can do.". Falsa smiled a rather nasty smile, and said, "Bastian is on his way towards the Dark Wood. As you know, he'll be passing near, and I just need you to keep him distracted. Long enough for me to have this child.". I wasn't the silly villager girl Falsa had once easily convinced. "What does distracting Bastian do exactly? How does he pose a threat?", "My dear girl, you know what I did to make this child, right? The boy hates me. Despite how much I may love him.", "What are you…?", I had forgotten Falsa's obsession. But in a small way, I knew as much that Bastian would kill her, and this child she carries. “Of course, you love him and all, but I’m just wondering what you’ve got planned for him.”, I said, looking puzzlingly at her. “The less you know about that, my dear, the better. Just tell me you will keep him distracted.”, “Oh, I’ll do it, just promise me something, Falsa. Whatever it is that is coming out of all this, I want no part of it. None of whatever this is, had better touch Dasha.”, “Making threats to me now?”, Falsa said, with a tone of surprise, “I honestly chose the right person. I bet you didn’t think so at the time, did you?”. I didn’t want to tell her this, but it was that green vial I had taken from Wilson. Somehow, I had knowledge that I wouldn’t have believed possible, but I knew there was much more going on now than I cared for. “A lot has changed.”. I replied coldly. I was still upset with her for tricking me into leaving Bastian here. “Well, if you’ve agreed, now it’s time for me to get back to the Dark Wood.”, “That’s where you’ve been?”, I asked, amazed. She hadn’t told me where she was going, and I had no clue that’s where she had run off to while I had traveled to Nasher and Kindy. Of course, I kept it secret what I had taken from King Oliver. “Why, yes, I’ve been in there. It’s where I plan to give birth.”, “Why?”, I asked incredulously. “That is for me to know, my dear.”. Falsa said in a cool dreamy voice. She turned back into the young girl and winked at me. “You two, escort this girl to the gate.”. Two men who were nearby nodded grudgingly and led Falsa to the front gate. I watched as the soldiers and Falsa disappeared into the village. I wondered what Falsa was thinking of the new Dasha. After all, even I was amazed by it. Unfortunately, there were those who felt that going from one queen to another wasn’t what they had in mind. These people secretly missed King Godrick and saw my takeover of the kingdom as an opportunity to put a new man on the throne. Leading this group of idiots was a man named Fod. Fod was a bit of an older gentleman, who I remembered from the day I had exiled Caprius. He seemed most angry and shouted out things like, “Blood is blood!”, and “You’ll never take Dasha from Godrick!”. Godrick was the former king, and Falsa’s former husband. What had happened to him, I had no clue. Falsa never told me what she had done to the king. I remember she said Caprius had killed him, but I was starting to feel that may not have been the truth. I returned to the castle, and found Tisiphone and Pietro embracing one another. I watched until the two had broken apart. Tisiphone noticed me and gathered herself. "I'm sorry, My Queen, I'm just getting off duty and I'm heading home.", she turned to walk away from me, but I called out to her. "Tisiphone, wait a while.". She turned and faced me puzzlingly, but all the while obeyed. Pietro watched in wonder. "I have to ask you to never do that in my castle ever again. If you two want to suck each other's faces off, do it in the village.". Tisiphone looked a bit surprised, but nodded. "Is that all, My Queen?", she asked solemnly. "Yes, you may be on your way.". She turned to leave, and I faced Pietro, "I need you to do something for me, it's very important.", "Just name it, My Queen. I would do anything for you.". I had been receiving this kind of devotion ever since I exiled Caprius. I loved it. I knew eventually I'd have to deal with Fod and his men, and that's when the most glorious plan came to me. One that would help Falsa, and perhaps, aid my own purposes as well. "I need you to seek out the man named Fod, tell him he's to wait outside of the kingdom for a young man who will be traveling nearby. He is to kill this boy. And I want you to aid in the endeavor. Can you do that for me? Will you kill for me?". Pietro had puffed his chest out and smiled from ear to ear, "Yes, My Queen, it would be the greatest honor. May I see Tisiphone before I leave?". What I had planned for this poor boy, it was only fitting to allow him to see his woman for the last time.

SEBASTIAN: Casian was indeed a good travel companion. Ever since I had left Kindy, she had kept me entertained by chasing huge insects and catching them. At night, I would eat the meat of an animal that she killed. I would share the meat with her and she would fall asleep on my chest. Casian belonged to Alex and therefore she was traveling with me. I remembered Alisa telling me that Falsa was carrying my child, and the thought made me sick to my stomach. I didn't want a child with her. Most of all, what I wanted was to see Alex's face again. To feel her lips on mine. It all seemed so far away. Especially the Dark Wood. I wasn't even near it yet. I was barely near Nasher, which I hadn't been to since our grand escape. I could see Oliver's castle in the distance and wondered what was happening there. I decided I'd take a detour and travel into Nasher. It's been almost six months since I've been here, and I remember the blood in the streets, my parents' farm being burned, and my parents…killed before my eyes. The first thing I saw was the old farm. The barn had burned to the ground and all that was left was shapely debris. The outline of the barn was still there, but the top half of the building itself had burned down. The house was still there. I was afraid to go inside, but decided maybe I should. I walked through the front door, and saw the blood was still on the floor, but my parent's bodies were gone. I never got the chance to bury them, because we were in such a rush to escape. I wondered where their bodies had gotten to. I went into my old room. It was the same. It appeared that nothing from that night had changed in the house, except for my parent's bodies not being anywhere near. Casian, who had been riding in my shirt, jumped out and sniffed a certain spot. I bent down to touch the spot, and immediately, I saw Alex. Alex had been here. Her hand had touched where my hand was touching. Casian let out a small cry and jumped into my hands. "Don't worry, girl, we're going to her. We'll be with her soon, I hope.". I looked in my cupboards, to see if I could find some stony, which was just about the only thing King Derek and Queen Shay hadn't managed to give me. Once I felt that I had done everything I could here, I left out the same door, only to be confronted by the least expected person, "Oy, so you've returned, eh? Well I have half a mind to scalp your scalp.". Tig. Another young person who I'd see in the village. Tig was the closest thing that I may have had to a best friend at one point, but he had stopped talking to me when Micka had mentioned what she thought of me. Tig was a light skinned boy, with a lot of freckles and teal colored hair. He stared at me, shaking his head in disbelief. He then saw the shield on my back and looked at Casian in my shirt and realized I was hardly the Bastian he associated himself with. "Bats…", he usually called me for short, "…what's happened to you?". I walked him back into my parent's house, where I told him the full story. It was enjoyable telling the story to Tig. He gasped at all the right parts and got angry when I told him what happened with Falsa. When I told him Falsa was carrying, he nearly fell out of his seat. "So, let me get this straight, Falsa raped you, impregnated herself, and Micka is the Queen of Dasha now? Hell must be gone, because I can't see any of that. You're having fun with me, aren't you?". Tig was giving me a disbelieving look. "I mean come on, Micka leaving you like that, Falsa taking advantage of you like that, you are some kind of god, I mean it all sounds like those stories my father used to tell us.". Tig's father used to tell us stories that we always knew he was making up, they were just good fun. "And that bit about the Alexandrian Queen and you being destined to be together!", at this point, Tig started to laugh. There was a part of me that was kind of having fun. After all, Tig stopped talking to me last year, and now, I'm telling him everything that's happened so far and had to admit how silly it sounded. "Tig, it is rather funny and all, but I'm telling you the truth. Falsa killed my parents, right here, in front of me. Then she shackled me to her and dragged me up to the castle. Tig, what's been happening these past few months? How is Oliver? What's the village like now?". Tig straightened up, "Well, there were a lot of issues at first. People were down right pissed. I mean, families were killed that day. Lucky for me, me and my parents weren't here. We had gone camping. But it was a nightmare when we returned. People were calling for Oliver's dethronement. And at the same time, people were afraid Falsa was coming back.", "Micka said she spoke to Oliver. You didn't see her when she came here did you?", "When Micka came, she didn't talk to anybody. Guards wouldn't leave her alone, would they? I thought they were taking her, but she smiled on her way out. I tried calling out to her, but she didn't hear me.". Tig looked highly disappointed. Tig had really liked Micka, but, of course, she had become taken with me. Tig was upset by this, which is why he stopped talking to me. "Micka… I don't know what her game is, but she is dangerous, Tig.", "Come off it. Our Micka is dangerous now?". Tig's ignorance was starting to grow annoying. "Maybe we can go to the castle. You think Oliver will have an audience with me?", "If he thinks you're a god, I don't see why not.". Tig, Casian, and myself made our way out of my parent's house, and made our way towards the castle. The village had been cleaned. The horror of what happened the last time I was in Nasher had been wiped away. Tig was watching the shield on my back with great interest. "So, you say Falsa gave this thing to you, eh? It's quite neat.". We reached the castle, where two guards who were standing at the door saw what I was carrying and stood aside. Taken back a bit by this, I continued forward. Inside the castle, I remembered running back through here to escape Falsa. Everything seemed like years ago. A man in a red gown came to me, "Lord Sebastian, King Oliver was expecting you, I'll take you to him, but your friend will have to wait here.". Tig looked livid. "It's okay, I'll be back, and I'll tell you everything.", I said, leaving Tig standing with his hands in his pockets, and following the man up to the king's hall, where Alisa first saved me. King Oliver was sitting on his throne, looking depressed. Next to him was a slimy looking man. His hair was black and touched the sides of his face as if they were being pressed down. When Oliver looked up and saw me, he waved the man away. "My boy! I have been expecting you.", he said jovially. He strode across the room and embraced me. "I haven't forgotten how you saved me.", "That was Princess Alisa, not me.", I said modestly. "You said something before she entered. You stood up for your king, even though he barely did anything for you.", Oliver looked a bit down trodden, "But, that's hardly the point. We need to discuss Queen Micka.", "What about her?", "Well, for starters, how exactly does a villager from MY kingdom become the queen of the most lawless place on Plinth?". I considered this for a moment and realized it would take too long to explain, so I gave a short tale, "Well, Falsa, for whatever reason, favored her, so she gave her the kingdom.". Oliver's face had a look of shock and awe. "And that shield, my boy, how did you get that from Falsa?", Oliver asked, with that same look on his face. "Micka gave it to me after…", I trailed off, remembering waking up in sweat and feeling drained. Bits and pieces of my time with Falsa started to creep into my mind. "Listen, I'm glad you're still alive and all, but there is nothing to do about Micka. It's best if we don't try anything.". Oliver looked at me confusedly. "But, my boy, this is our chance. You have the shield, we can take all of Dasha.". I knew what he meant. He wanted vengeance. "What happened when Micka came here?". The king moved uncomfortably, and then looked up into my eyes, "She took something very important from here. Something that belongs to you.". Oliver gave me a look of mirth and pity. "What exactly is this thing she took?". Oliver reached into his cloak and pulled out a parchment which he unfurled. "Not many knew it was here, because we kept it after the first great sacrifice.". On the parchment was a drawing of a ring. It didn't seem like anything special, then, Oliver told me what it is. "It's your protection ring. It's to protect you from yourself.". I was confused when Oliver told me this. Obviously, I didn't feel like I needed protection from myself. It made no sense. When I tried asking Oliver to explain it, he didn't understand either. "Well, what is the great sacrifice? I've never even heard of that.". Oliver eyed me suspiciously. "You've…never heard of it…", Oliver repeated after me. He was now looking at me amusedly. Maybe he thought I was supposed to be all knowing or something, but all I knew was what I had learned. I decided maybe it was my turn to be ahead. Falsa knew more than I did. She was older and wiser than me. But if this really was her game board, then maybe it was time for me to move my piece across the board. "The great sacrifice…was when we…", I could tell he didn't want to say what was on his mind, but he fought this hesitation, "…when we killed a goddess.". I didn't understand right away. "Killed a goddess? I thought I was the sacrifice. That the god was killed and that's what this whole situation is.", "No...", replied Oliver, "...we made a mistake and killed a goddess, hoping that it would bring honor to our land, but we made a huge mistake. A mistake that King Godrick only made worse. It wasn't until Falsa came here and attacked that I realized we are the architects of our own suffering.". I was as lost as when I left Kindy. "When that poor girl was murdered, we thought we had solved a problem, but instead, we created a bigger one.", "I need to know this story.", I said, with a serious tone to my voice. The more I learn about Falsa, the better the chance I'll have to stop her. Oliver sat back in his seat. "Well, this is going to be a long tale.", he said, sitting comfortably to one side and putting his face in his hand. "Well, it begins with my wife, the queen. Who, you may have noticed, is no longer with us. It was twenty years ago, we were very foolish back then. The goddess, who had come from Alexandria, was named Falta. She was beautiful. She was kept secret though. None of the other kingdoms really knew about Alexandria. Until, that poor girl tried to introduce herself. On one hand, you had those who worshipped her. On the other hand, you had those who wanted to destroy her, and everything she represented. If she was a goddess, then that means the god was out there, somewhere, planning his vengeance on the people that killed him. Falta had first come here, then she went to Kindy and Dasha. After she had visited all the kingdoms, it was my wife who called the royal meeting.". A royal meeting is when all the royalty in Plinth come together to make a decision that affects all of the kingdoms. There hadn't been one of those since before I was born, and from the sounds of things, this may have been the last one. "My wife, Penelope, claimed that Falta told her...that she is the one that will bring back the god. Penelope feared what this meant, and she convinced the other kingdoms that we should kill Falta. So, we sent soldiers to find her, and when they did, they brought her back to Dasha. We all traveled there to watch that poor girl be killed.", "But I thought goddesses had a certain strength.", I interrupted. "True, Falsa explained as much to me. But every god and goddess must go on a journey to achieve this strength.

But unfortunately, Falta was stopped mid-journey. I still remember her pleas as the axe came down on her neck.". I felt a tear coming to my eye. The story was sad, and for some reason, made me think of Alex even more. What if it had been Alex that this happened to? How would I have dealt with that? "So, what happened to Penelope?", "Well, after the deed, she disappeared. I sent men searching all over for her, but I couldn't find her, then that's when we got the news about a new goddess. This one came fully grown, with a determination to make us pay. She vowed vengeance on all of Plinth. Now I finally realize that it was Falta's death that started this. Brought you back, but you don't even remember your past. So, we are fools. Falsa will destroy all of Plinth, just to make us pay for what we did to that poor girl, Falta.". Falta, Falsa. Something was familiar about this whole situation. Falta was somehow connected to Falsa. I didn't know how yet, but I could sense it. And, Queen Penelope's disappearance was connected as well. Falsa came fully grown, then around the same time, Alex came as well. Something was there that was being left out. "As for Godrick, nobody has seen him since Falsa was pregnant.". This much I knew. Everyone did, really. What happened to the King of Dasha? As much as I told myself I didn't care for Caprius' father, I once again found myself realizing something that I'd been ignoring. It was me, who was going to put all the pieces together. King Oliver sat back in his chair and leaned his head against the back headrest. Falsa had taken so much, but I didn't realize it went this far back. Even the Queen of Nasher had disappeared, and Falsa had something to do with it. But my question was, what did this mean for Alex? "So, Alex came when Falsa came, right? So that means there are two goddesses here. But that doesn't make sense if only one at a time can be here, right?" "Ah, my boy, now you've reached the main point.", said Oliver, sitting forward again. The man with the greasy hair pressed to each side of his face returned. He whispered something in Oliver's ear, and I watched his face turn scarlet. "When did this happen?", he asked the man. "About ten minutes ago. You want I should...", "No!", Oliver interrupted. "I wish to show the boy here what has become of his parents.". Oliver gestured to me and I followed. We walked a good distance past the castle in the other direction of the village. Oliver was leading me to a part of Nasher I'd never seen before. We walked past roses and what appeared to be treacle trees. Finally, we reached a large treacle tree that stretched far into the sky. The leaves were a dark shade of black, and Oliver finally faced me. "Buried here, are the two people who gave birth to a god.". I looked at the tree and realized something had been carved into it, (HERE LIES NIVEA AND CLADINO, PARENTS OF A GOD). I felt my eyes burn. I could barely remember what my parents sounded like anymore, but I could still see their faces. I placed my hand on the mound of dirt and felt a tear fall from my eye and into the dirt. Oliver was watching me. "I had heard a tale, that there was a young man, who took all the nerve he could muster, to go around trying to convince people that the god was real, and that he'd come back one day. It's sad that young man had to learn his son was that god, in the moment of his own murder.". I looked up at Oliver, puzzled. My parents always believed in the god, and I never thought of them as younger people. "Did you know my mother?". Oliver looked down trodden and even more so, scared. "There is something about your mother that I should tell you, Young Bastian. Your mother…was the daughter of my wife, Penelope.", "But, does that mean…?", "No, I wasn't her father. I married your grandmother after her first husband had died of lilac poison. Your mother…never wanted this life, so she lived with her aunt in the village. When her mother disappeared, she was pregnant with you. But she blamed me for her mother's lack of faith. She also blamed me when her mother disappeared. She was a sweet person.". I had issues with this story. "If this is true, why did my mother act as if she didn't know who you are? Like she'd never seen the king.", "Easy, my boy, it was many years ago. Your mother was only five when I married your grandmother, boy, and she never looked at that life. She was raised in a very devout home. Surely your home was almost the same.". This was true. My mother and father both worshipped. They didn't force it on me, but rather allowed me to worship however I saw fit. Which was usually never. But now I understood. This world was filled with people who stopped believing a long time ago or they never did in the first place. The god chose my mother and father as parents because of their devoutness. Suddenly, I knew what I had to do. Almost like a small voice in my head had decided to convince me this was right. "Thank you, Oliver, for everything.", "It was nothing, my boy. Please come visit anytime you like. This is still your home.". I was always taught that Oliver was a dog. But now I was starting to realize maybe my mother just never got over her own mother abandoning her for the throne. So, technically, I'm supposed to be the Prince of Nasher. But my mother never wanted a privileged lifestyle and I appreciated her for that. I started to leave Nasher. Tig had found me, and demanded I tell him everything. Once I was done, Tig just stared at me, star struck. "So, all this time I was chums with the prince and had no idea?", "I'm not the prince, Tig, I just sort of have a connection to Oliver.", "So, where are you headed?", Tig asked, once again getting his eyes stuck on my shield. "I'm going to get my woman.". Tig bowed to me. "I wish you the best, my friend. All the best.". Tig reached out his hand. I grabbed it and he pulled me into a hug. "I'm always here if you need me, brother.". I nodded and proceeded out of Nasher. Past my parents' burnt-down barn and our old home. I was going to the Dark Wood.

Casian had come out of my bag for some air. The two of us made our way into the woods and found a place to camp. Casian had found a spot to just lay there. I on the other hand was thinking too hard for anything else. Queen Penelope was my grandmother. She ordered Falta be killed. Falsa has some connection to Falta, and Alex is ahead of her time on this planet. Not to mention the ring Micka stole that protects me from myself. I was confused as to what the hell that meant. The next morning, Casian and I started early. When we came around to the Jasmine, we gathered some water and I decided to rest. I watched Casian try to catch fish for us to eat, then

I heard a noise that brought me to my senses. I turned and there were about fifteen men standing behind me. They started circling around me. I realized right away that they were Dashin soldiers. "I have no problem with your queen, so why don't you just go away?". Casian had come out of the water and was standing next to me, hair on end. "Well, funny you should say you have no problem with our queen, because she wants you dead.", said a young man with a proud look on his face. "Let's just kill him and be done with this, Pietro.", said an older looking man. "Now, Fod, I'm just trying to be cordial before we kill him.". This didn't surprise me. I had told Tig that Micka was dangerous. Now, apparently, even though she let me leave Dasha, she's still sending men to kill me. Just then, there was a loud yell, and Tig came out of the trees and slashed at one of the men. I immediately followed suit and took my shield off my back and started swinging. The young man, who seemed to be the leader, came at me and I plunged my shield into his chest. I removed it and his blood splattered the air. He fell to the ground, gasping for breath. The other men had turned tail because Casian had taken out three of them by herself. Tig looked amazed at the creature. The young man lying on the ground, dying, gasped one last word before he died, "Tisiphone...".

CHAPTER 11

The Price For Leaving Dasha

MICKA: There was a large ruckus, then, Fod, and two others were coming towards me. Tisiphone and I stood watching. Tisiphone, obviously looking for Pietro. "You bitch! You set us up!". Fod was yelling. "What the hell are you talking about, and how dare you disrespect your queen like that?", I said, with every syllable vibrating with my anger. "The boy had a Dattur with him. Plus, he wasn't alone, there was another boy!". I considered what he was talking about, but almost as if I could see it in my mind, I knew what had happened. "Tisiphone, can you please go wait in the common? I wish to speak with Fod alone. Take his two men with you as well.". Tisiphone looked confused but obeyed. The two men who had come with Fod looked at me mutinously, but followed Tisiphone out of the room. Fod was watching me with thirst in his eyes. "You think I'm beautiful, don't you, Fod?". Fod eyed me from top to bottom, taking extra time to stare at my hips. "Oh yes, Your Majesty, I do.", Fod said with a certain perverse to his voice. "Well, then explain to me what happened.". Fod looked like he was about to yell. From the look in his eyes, I could tell what he wanted to do, but I wasn't about to let him. "Well, we arrived upon the boy. He was coming from the Nasher direction. When we found him, that little creature was with him, and the other boy came later. Pietro and a few others were killed.". I watched him, still staring at me through perverted eyes. I stood up. "What did this other boy look like?", "He had teal colored hair.". Tig. Him, Sebastian, and myself were once friends. He had a crush on me, but I didn't feel the same for him. Apparently, he's teaming with Sebastian, which means that I had another chance to kill him. "Fod, darling, come to me.". Fod moved towards me and I grabbed his testicles. "If you ever, look at me like how you just were ever again, I will rip these off. Nod if you understand.". Fod gave me a very curt nod, tears forming in his eyes. "I know you don't like the idea of me being a queen, but unfortunately, that is how it is. Now, I need to know, who exactly killed Pietro?". I released Fod, who was holding his middle part and looking sadly at me, "It was the boy you sent us after.", "Okay, good…you may leave now, and send Tisiphone back in.". Fod limped out of my throne room and a few minutes later, Tisiphone came back inside. She was looking anxious and scared. "Mam, they are telling me you told Pietro to kill some boy. They won't tell me where he is.". Part of me felt sorry for Tisiphone. Pietro was her first love. Not to mention everything her father and her have been through. But Pietro was a loving, gullible, fool, and I knew she can do better. "Tisiphone, I'm sorry to say that Fod has informed me that Pietro was struck down.". Tisiphone broke down almost immediately, "No…he can't be…", she was crying. I knelt next to her and put her in my arms. "I'm truly sorry, Tisiphone.", I said, as she continued to cry into my arms. "But, he said he'd be right back. We were meant to have children, and my father liked him… He said he was a sign things are changing here!", she half cried, half yelled. "I feel it's only right you know how he died. He was killed by Sebastian.". Tisiphone looked at me with almost certain hatred. "Why would he do that? Sebastian is no murderer.", "A lot can change, Tisiphone.

He was att…", "YOU SENT THOSE MEN TO ATTACK HIM!", she yelled at me. "Now, let's not forget our place here. Yes, I sent those men to attack him. But you don't understand how dangerous he really is.". Tisiphone stood up now. "May I leave please?". I had almost every reason to tell her no, but decided that if I want to keep her around, it's best I let her get some space. "Return to your father. I won't make you stay here.". She turned to leave. I watched her as she walked out. I sat on the throne and put my face in my hands, "What have I done?", "You did…what you know you needed to do.", said a voice from almost nowhere. I looked around, and there was nothing. Just as I thought I was hearing things, a figure took form. It was Wilson. I screamed a loud scream that made soldiers come running into the room. "I'm fine, I'm fine, I just…thought I saw something. I'm going to my chambers.". I walked out of the room, looking around, still looking for the figure I thought I had just imagined. As I walked into my bedroom, I felt a cold breeze. I turned, and Wilson's ghost was right in front of me, "You stupid, foolish, girl! You have no idea what you've done. Falsa has begun the transition. And soon, you'll see that Dasha, as well as the rest of Plinth are in grave peril.". I fell on my bed, staring up in horror. Not knowing what I should do, I dashed to the other side of the room, where my make-up was sitting, and tried to throw a vial at the apparition, it flew through him. Wilson's ghost watched me impatiently, as I reached for another object, "STOP THIS AND HEAR ME!", Wilson yelled. "What do you want from me?". Wilson glided towards me, "You are the one who will end it. You have the greatest weapon in your possession.". I knew what he was talking about at once, but just to be certain, "The ring. You're talking about the ring, aren't you?". Wilson nodded. "What am I supposed to do with it?", "When the time comes, you will know.". Wilson's ghost disappeared. I laid there on my bed, trying to think, but the only thing I could think about was what I wanted the ring for. Which was, of course, to hold something over Bastian's head. Now I had to rethink what I was going to do. Just then, Fod appeared at my door. "WHAT?!", I barked at him. "Mam, Tisiphone is leaving, mam. She's Leaving Dasha.". In the past, nobody could just leave, but if Tisiphone thought she was going to just leave, she was mistaken. If I let her leave, she'll try to get to Bastian to warn him. Or at least give him some idea of what's happening here. "Fod, you are to intercept her and stop her at all costs. Do not let her leave, and most importantly, DO NOT LET HER MEET SEBASTIAN! If she comes anywhere near him, I'll have your testicles and head mounted in my throne room.". Fod nodded and left the room. I sat on my bed, pondering. I was going to be the hero somehow? I couldn't wait to see how everything turned out.

TISIPHONE: Father and I rode as fast as we could. A few times, he had come close to falling off our horse, but I had managed to keep him up. Fear and anger like I had never known was swelling in my veins. Pietro was the nicest man I'd ever met. He was all Dashin, minus the attitude of ignorance. I had only known him for two months, before Queen Micka sent him to his death. I really did like Queen Micka. She was better than Falsa anyway. Falsa, who would let her son have his way with any woman he chose, which, of course, led my sister to kill herself. Sebastian had been the one to save my father and me. Now, Micka, for whatever reason, wanted him dead. Sebastian is the reincarnation of our creator, and she is disrespecting him in this way. It was simply shameful. Father once told me that we had killed a goddess. He always said Caprius and Falsa were our punishments. But now I was starting to think that perhaps Micka was the real punishment. She came into Dasha like a white princess, looking only to better the kingdom. But really, she uses Dasha to accomplish her own agendas, and kills anyone who goes against her, or that she feels isn't good enough. All we've done is trade one evil for another. As we continued to ride, we saw a group of people ahead of us. Bandits from the looks of them. "Jake, we're starving here.", "Well look, unless you want to raid a kingdom, I'd hush. It's tough enough out here without having to hear your shite.". The bandits were just talking amongst themselves. They turned towards my father and me. "Well, look, boys, a horse and a lass. A good-looking lass.", "Now, be careful, remember what happened before with the Dattur.", an older bandit was saying cautiously. "Please, me and my father are trying to get far from Dasha, please just let us pass.". The bandits took their weapons out, "I don't see no Dattur. I say we kill the old man and take the cunt.". Just as they started moving in towards us, Fod and some other Dashin soldiers arrived. "That's far enough, Tisiphone. Either come back with me or die. Queen's orders.", "FUCK THE QUEEN!", I shouted, jumping off the horse and brandishing my sword. "Tisiphone, no, let's just turn back.", "No, Father. If we go back, Queen Micka will kill us anyway.", "You die if you don't come now…", said Fod, in a really menacing sort of voice. Almost as if he were daring me to not come back. Fod had a perverted look in his eye that said quite clearly what he wanted. Fod and his men took a step towards me and my father, then one of the bandits stepped forward, "I don't think you'll be taking this one, Fod.". It was the man called Jake. He eyed Fod with a look of familiarity and held up his dagger. The rest of the bandits followed suit. "This has nothing to do with you, Jake, so take your merry band and get.", Fod replied. Jake moved closer to me and blocked me and my father. The rest of the bandits did the same. "I'm warning you, Jake, you don't know what you're doing.", "Looks to me like I'm protecting a fellow bandit.". The Dashin soldiers stood there for some time, wondering what they should do. They stared real hard at the bandits. "You are going to regret this, Jake.". Fod turned, and the rest followed. "Why did you protect us?", I asked. "Well, we did have other plans, but seeing that fool, Fod, quake in fear at the thought of failing, was too good to pass up. Plus, like I said, I was protecting a fellow bandit. I'm Jake, the leader of this gang. And you're, Tisiphone, eh? Pretty name.", "So, you aren't going to kill my father and have your with me then?", I asked threateningly. Jake laughed, and the rest of his men put their weapons away and pulled me, my father, and our horse into the group. They introduced themselves and gave us water.

Later, a few of the men had gathered around my father, while my father told stories. I was sitting by the fire, discussing my situation with Jake, "...and so that's my tale. And as far as I know, Sebastian is somewhere out here.", I finished. Jake was what most would consider a miscreant. But in truth, he was really a good guy. What I was surprised to learn is that most of the bandits were. They were men who had been exiled from their kingdoms and were forced to live in the wilderness. There were plenty of tales of women who had been taken and never seen again. The bandits were always held responsible. But this was because they were so angry about the fact that they had been exiled, that they sought out anyway to make the kingdoms pay. Jake had told me the story of when they had cornered the Kindy princess while she was traveling some time ago. She had a Dattur with her. "I'd only heard stories about those. They're real?", "As real as the hair on my face, love. Mad dangerous they are. Took out three of my men without even trying. One bite can go through the bone.". As we sat there resting, we heard a rumble from behind us. Then we heard a shout. We went in the direction of the noise and found Micka, holding a dagger to my father's throat. "No! let him go!", I shouted. Almost as if to mock me, she ran the dagger across my father's throat, opening it. Blood ran all down his neck and chest. I watched, as my father fell to the ground, his eyes never leaving mine. I lost track of what I was doing and stormed at Micka. But before I could reach her, Jake had jumped in front of me, "You take that horse and you go. NOW!". I looked at Micka again, who was watching me and smiling nastily. She pointed at me and I was tempted to put my blade in between her eyes. Jake was still standing in front of me, shielding me, while his men were occupied fighting off Dashin soldiers, they were losing. Micka started walking towards me without the slightest sliver of fear in her face. "You need to GO!", Jake yelled again, and this time I vowed silent vengeance and hopped on the horse. "GET HER!", hissed Micka, as I rode off. I saw Fod riding on a horse and trying to catch me. I rode through the field until I came upon the woods. There was a path that was big enough for my horse. I rode onto the path, checking back only once to see if Fod was still behind me. Finally, I stopped, and fell off the horse. I couldn't think or do anything. All I could think about was the father I just lost. The only family I had left was gone. I let out a scream that was so loud, the mamels, (winged insects the size of an adult man's hand), flew out of the trees. I heard movement and turned and saw two boys coming out of the thick woods. A cute creature following them. The creature's floppy ears stood up and looked like triangular rabbit ears. "Tisiphone?", one of the boys said, eyeing me quite closely. I did not recognize anything at the moment and assumed it was Fod's men coming for me. I swung my blade out of my sheath and brandished it towards my attackers. "Tisiphone, it's me!", "Maybe, she isn't this, Tisiphone, Bats. Maybe you've got the wrong girl.". I started to look at the one who called my name, and relief like it's never seeped through me before, seeped throughout my body. Even when Jake decided to help me and my father, had I never felt such relief as I did now, "SEBASTIAN!", I shouted, and I threw myself into his arms, crying madly.

"Geez, Bats, maybe you were telling the truth about that whole, Micka thing.", the other boy was saying, once I had calmed down enough to tell my story. Sebastian was shaking with anger. "She killed your father...", he kept muttering under his breath, while the other young man just kind of sat in disbelief. "You know, we all grew up together. I just can't think what would turn her into such an evil prat.". I watched the other boy quite closely, "You grew up with Queen Micka? You too, Bastian?", I asked, quite surprised by this info. Micka never mentioned she had a personal connection to Sebastian. It suddenly made sense why she was after him, or at least seemed to want him dead. Sebastian didn't answer me right away, and when he did, he only nodded. "Hey, my name is Tig, by the way,

Tisiphone. Tisiphone, what a pretty name.", Tig was saying, looking at me admirably. His gaze made me think of Pietro and I turned quickly away. "Where are you headed?", I asked Bastian. "Dark Woods. Going to go find Alex.", he grunted. It seemed informing him that Micka had killed my father, stirred some kind of anger in him. For the rest of the day we traveled further away from Dasha. Sebastian keeping to himself all the while. The strange creature who had the floppy ears was resting on Bastian's shoulder, and my curiosity could wait no longer, "Tig…", I chose to ask Tig because I felt that Bastian would have become more irritated, "…what is that thing on Bastian's shoulder?". Tig, who was walking behind me, said, "It's a Dattur. You know, the most vicious animal on Plinth.", "Well, why does Bastian have one? It seems very tamed for a wild animal.", "Ah, this one is from Alexandria. It belongs to the queen, who WE, are going to meet now.". I pondered on this. I had no idea what was going on. I decided it was better to just travel, not talk.

Over the next few days, Bastian had become increasingly distant. He would get far ahead of me and Tig and we would have to hurry to keep up. When we went to sleep, you could often hear Bastian muttering in his sleep. Always calling out the name, Alex. Eventually we had finally come close to the Dark Wood, and almost immediately, I felt we should turn back. "You alright there, Tisiphone?", Tig had asked. I could tell by the look in his eyes, he was thinking the same thing. "Hey uh, Bats, why don't Tisiphone and I wait out here for you to return with your girl, eh? I mean, Casian should be enough protection.", said Tig, with a very hopeful tone in his voice. "You don't have to come with me if you don't want to. You can wait here.". I knew I'd feel bad if we didn't go in with him. So, when Bastian crossed the threshold into the woods, I followed. Tig right behind me. We proceeded down a hill into a thicket of trees. It was very difficult to walk, and you could feel darkness creeping all around you. Trees seemed to snatch at us as we tripped and stumbled through the forest. "Do you even know where we are headed, Bastian?", I asked. But Sebastian did not reply, rather, he continued moving forward like a man possessed.

When we finally came to a clearing, we decided to set up camp for the night. Once Bastian had fallen asleep, Tig and I laid awake. Both of us were finding it difficult to sleep due to the watchful eyes through the trees. "Never thought I'd be here.", said Tig, in a confused sort of tone. "Neither did I, but I'd do just about anything for Bastian. He saved me from Caprius. And he IS our creator's vessel, after all.". Tig looked at me sideways. "You know, growing up with him and all, he did always seem sort of different. But you don't really think much about the stuff, do you? I mean, why would I think my best friend is actually my god?", Tig laughed hard at his own comment. I smiled a bit. "That's the first smile I've seen on that pretty face.". I quickly wiped the smile away. I turned away from Tig, immediately once again thinking about Pietro. Tig had grown quiet. I was quite sure he was starting to notice these actions, and I wasn't ready to talk about Pietro yet. As both of us sat in the darkness, Sebastian let out a scream and was suddenly awake. Tig and I jumped to our feet and rushed towards him. "What's wrong, Bats?", said Tig, placing his hand on Bastian's shoulder. "I…had a dream. You two need to go to Kindy and tell Alisa to come here, now.", "Are you asking us to leave you here?!", I asked incredulously. "YES!", he yelled at us. Then he grabbed his head as if he was in some sort of pain. "Bastian, let us stay here to help you!", I yelled, watching him writhe on the ground. Finally, he stopped, and in great heaving breaths repeated what he said, "Go…get…Alisa.". He jumped to his feet and rushed off into the forest. Tig and I stared at each other for a moment. The eyes that had been watching us started to get a bit closer and we made to move out the woods. We made it to the hill we had gone down upon entering the forest. We could hear strange noises and movements in the trees. When we finally made it out, it wasn't exactly glorious, for Queen Micka was waiting for me.

SEBASTIAN: Nothing was stopping me, I was going to find Alex. In my head, the strange voice I'd hear every time I was near that revealer potion, seemed to be stronger here in the wood. Fear like I had never known was rushing through me and I couldn't explain why. I rushed and rushed through the trees, until, finally, I came to what seemed to be a small village. In the back of the village was a huge building that was basically a giant hut. The smaller huts all around were surrounded by children and green flowers with a glowing green center. The revealer flowers were glowing strongly. Everybody stopped what they were doing to face my direction. Just then, there were running footsteps and as I looked to my left, Casian jumped from my shoulder and ran in the direction of none other than Alex. Casian jumped onto her shoulder, but did not block her from being able to sink herself into my chest, "Oh, Sebastian, I can't believe you're here!". She broke her face apart from my chest, looked me in my eyes, and kissed me. It was the most glorious kiss ever. The two of us finally reunited had brought something out of me. I lifted Alex into the air and spun her around. Her skin began to glow that strange pinkish glow. A young man with long blue hair came towards us, "I am Prince Lab, My Lord. Welcome to the Dark Village. May I show you to your quarters?". Aside from the fact that I didn't know I'd have quarters here, I also didn't expect everyone to know who I was right away. I followed Lab, Alex holding my hand along the way. "So, how are you?", asked Alex in a worried tone. "I feel more alive than I ever have in my entire existence.". Alex beamed weakly. "What's wrong?", I asked her, starting to feel like she wasn't as happy to see me as I was to see her. "I know what happened with Falsa. She's carrying your seed.". Part of me was shocked, but at the same time, not really. I knew she knew because Alisa had told me. Alex stared at me sadly, waiting for me to respond. I responded by pulling her close and kissing her deeply. "I don't want to think about that, I only want to enjoy this moment.". Alex beamed a lot stronger this time and she jumped into my arms, and I carried her up the steps that led to the giant hut at the back of the village. Once inside the building, it was quite nice. The walls were made of branches that had leaves lined along them. The floor had been sewn of quilt leaves(thick leaves that usually people sewed into clothes), and spread throughout the hut. There was a bed, which appeared to be made of a stack of quilt leaves and tuk. Casian had jumped from Alex onto the bed. Alex climbed out of my arms and sat on the bed. She gave me one look and I knew what it meant. Making love to Alex was nothing like making love with Micka. There was this strange sensation the entire time. As we laid there later, Casian sleeping in a corner, I felt this overwhelming urge to look for something. I didn't even know what I wanted to look for, but I had to look. Alex looked worried, "Bastian, if something is bothering you, you can tell me.", "I thought Falsa was here. Where has she gotten to?". Alex looked taken back by this question, "She disappeared from here a few weeks ago. Prince Lab hasn't been able to find her.", "And that's another thing, who is this Prince Lab? Where is the king of this place?". Alex looked at me as if I was a stranger asking these questions. It was almost like the happiness we felt seeing each other, was starting to subside, and was being replaced with regret, "He is the son of the ruler of this place.", "Have you ever seen the ruler?". Alex looked confused at this, "Actually, no. I haven't. I remember when I was a child and I came here for the first time, Lab looked the same as he does now. I suppose I just never really gave his father any thought.". As I was pondering on this, there was a knock, and the voice of Lab was outside. "My Liege, if you aren't too occupied, I was wondering if we can walk.". I got off the bed and looked at Alex, who was looking at me with a very weak smile. "It's okay, Bastian, just go.". I reached down and kissed her. She grabbed my face and kissed me passionately. I walked out of the hut, and Lab was standing there looking amused. "What?", I asked, wondering what he was smirking about. "I just didn't think that you'd turn up like this. People here have been waiting for a long time, and now that you're here, I don't know what I'm supposed to think.". I followed him down the path and into the village. As we walked, some of the people stopped doing what they were doing and followed Lab and I with their eyes. It all seemed quite strange that this place existed. Where did it even come from? Alexandria was once a secret, but now it seemed like it was a reality, as well as this Dark Village. "Lab, where did this place come from?". Lab waited before he answered, "Well, from nowhere. This place sprang into life all on its own. Twenty-five years ago, a voice said that there would be a girl who would come here to learn the ways of the goddess. Said that the flowers were the key. We just listened.", "Yeah, but how did this voice contact you?", "The revealers. We figured out that they have a certain effect the closer you are. No doubt you've noticed that, haven't you?". I did. But it was worse for me. Even now it was calling out to me. I realized Lab was walking us out of the village. "Where are we going?", I asked, starting to feel that same fear I felt earlier. "Oh, don't worry about that. You will be pleased once we get there.". Finally, we came to a strange cave. Inside of the cave, I could sense that something was amiss. I turned my head, and Lab had put on these golden gloves. He punched me, and I fell into the cave. I tried to lift my head, but the gold dust on my skin was doing something to me. "Well, I must admit, I never thought this day would come. The day when our god finally becomes one.". I didn't know what he was talking about. "Becomes one? What the hell do you mean?". I could barely stand, but I turned and realized there was something moving behind me. It seemed to be a lake of some sort, but all the water was black. Just then, the water rose and slowly came out to form a figure, which once the black water had left it, Falsa was standing there. She was no longer pregnant from the looks of things and was standing there in a peaceful state. "Falsa?! What the hell?". I looked at Lab, who was just standing there with a strange smile. Just then, something else came out of the water, but this crawled out. It was a man. It was the most sickening thing I'd seen yet. He looked starved, pale, and barely alive. Upon fully coming out of the water, he retched up and grabbed his sides. He was naked and shivering. He looked up at me and tried to speak but couldn't. He looked over at Falsa, and fear spread across his face. He stood up and looked towards the exit, and tried to run for it, but the water outstretched and grabbed him by the ankles, and he fell to the floor of the cave, hard. "PLEASE, LET ME GO! I CAN'T TAKE ANYMORE!", the man was shouting. Falsa finally made a movement. She bent down and grabbed the man's cheeks with one hand, "Oh, poor, Godrick. Had enough, have you? No. I don't think you have.". She forced him to stand, keeping her hand on his cheeks and pushed him back into the water. For a minute, the man bobbed on the surface like he was drowning. Screaming and thrashing around, the man made to come back on the surface, but the water, which seemed to have a life of its own, snatched him back. If I had felt fear earlier, it was nothing like what I felt now. I was frozen and didn't need the gold dust to keep me in place. The strange black lake started to dry up. As it slowly drained, I could hear the voice in my head shouting. It felt like my head would split open, "SEBASTIAN, ITS TIME! WE WILL BE ONE AGAIN!". Somehow, I found the ability to move again, but I remained on the ground, as the last of the water disappeared. Now there was another figure standing in the middle. He looked like he could be my age. I noticed there were two bodies lying where the black lake had been. One was Godrick, who was breathing heavily. The other was a woman, who had tried to move, but was so weak from being in the lake for so long, she was only able to wave her hand. The figure standing in the center started to walk towards me. "You may go, Lab, I can handle this from here.", I looked in Lab's direction, he bowed and walked out of the cave, without even glancing back. What the hell was going on? Who was this guy? Godrick and the woman stared at one another and made movements with their mouths. "Ah, it feels good to be free!", the young boy was saying, as he continued moving towards me. "Who are you?" I asked, when I finally found my voice. "Why, I'm you.", he replied, smiling all the while. As he moved closer to me, I felt a wave of energy like that of when I kissed Alex for the first time. I tried to push myself up, and kept failing miserably. "Let me help you.", said the boy, and almost at once, I felt myself capable of moving. I stood up and faced the boy. His eyes were like mine, but his face was different. Standing up, I was able to see the woman more clearly, who was now getting to her feet and slowly moving towards the young boy. "You must be so confused. I can see that you don't know all that I know. I remember everything.", the boy whispered into my ear. He looked me in my eyes, and I saw anger. Anger, so fierce, I was afraid to try and do anything against it. The woman had gotten close enough to stab the boy. She did. She stood there, watching, and waiting, but the boy wasn't at all fazed by this. In fact, he laughed, "Oh, Mother, is this what we are reduced to now? Trying to kill me? Perhaps you'd prefer I put you back in your box.". The woman moved away, frightened. She backed away from the boy and moved away from Godrick, who was now standing as well, but too scared to do anything. Falsa was standing to the side, "Desian, you shouldn't waste any more time, kill them, absorb him, and be done with it.", said Falsa, watching the scene impatiently. Then, she fell to the floor gasping for breath. "Don't forget, who has all the power here, my love.". Falsa released her throat, and stared angrily at the boy called Desian, but knew enough not to say anything else. The woman was crying in a corner. "What are you crying about?", asked Desian, "You chose this punishment, didn't you? You alone made the choice to kill a goddess, so you and your friend here…", he nodded towards Godrick, who cowered further into a corner, "…pay the price.". It suddenly dawned on me. "Penelope…", I said, looking in disbelief. She stared at me, giving me a good look over, then recognition spread across her face. In me, she saw her daughter. I immediately thought, how can I get her out of here? But, Desian seemed to be able to read my mind, because as soon as I thought this, he turned his hand towards her and all the black water came rushing from his arm. It engulfed Penelope, who coughed, sputtered, and started to scream and cry. "STOP IT!", I shouted. Desian returned his hand to his side but the water was still engulfing Penelope. "You don't seem to get it, either. How things work that is. You know, this is like one big, happy, family reunion, isn't it?", Desian said, watching me with child-like mirth. I couldn't stand it any longer. I had left my shield back in that hut, but I was done letting this guy torture my grandmother. I punched Desian in the face and he stumbled some, but kept the smile on his face. "Really? You're trying to save these pathetic Plinthinians? Do you even know what they have done?", he asked. "I know what Penelope is guilty of, and I'm sure she's suffered enough.". Desian let out a cold, heartless, laugh that rang throughout the cave, "Penelope should suffer for eternity. She killed a goddess. Surely you agree that nobody on Plinth has that authority.". I wasn't too sure what to believe, and I knew that in some way or another, I was no match for Desian. I started to work my mind furiously, hoping somehow to get out of here with Penelope and myself in one piece. Desian took the water back into him and Penelope fell to the floor, gasping, but still staring at me. Then I noticed Desian with a confused look on his face, "You got lucky.", he snarled. I didn't understand what he meant, but I noticed Godrick signaling for Penelope to get out of here. I decided to give her the distraction she needed. I lunged at Desian. Falsa was too busy watching the scene to notice Penelope had made it to shore and was fifteen feet away from the exit of the cave. Desian struggled with me and he finally overcame me. At that moment, he noticed Penelope, "NO! FALSA, DO NOT LET HER ESCAPE!", he yelled. Falsa noticed, but I jumped up and stopped her from getting to her. "You are going to pay for this.". Desian said, and he quickly turned back into the black lake and engulfed me in the water. I was thrashing about, trying to stay afloat. I saw Falsa run out the cave and then...darkness.

CHAPTER 12

Enter Desian

TISIPHONE: "Well, Tisiphone, I must admit, you gave us an interesting chase, but now, it's over.". Micka had me and Tig cornered. I looked at Tig, who was watching Micka with more interest than fear, "Micka, come on…what is this?", he said. "Tig, you should have stayed in Nasher. No point to you being here.", "Sebastian was the point, wasn't he?", Tig replied, starting to get antsy. I could see him slowly moving his arm towards his blade. Micka noticed as well. She was on Tig quickly and held a dagger to his neck, "I'll give you one chance, Tig. Leave now, and you live, stay to fight, and you die.", "Micka, is this how you treat all your old friends? Shouldn't be surprised since you killed my friend's father. Oh, and I suppose it's true then that you left Bats to be raped. Oh, and you being a queen…is a joke.". I gave Tig a look that quite plainly said to shut his mouth, but whatever the effect he was trying to cause, seemed to be happening. Micka had stepped back from him, looking him over with disgust, "You don't know what you're saying…", she said in a small tone. She looked dazed and confused, like she didn't know what was going on. "I had to do all those things. I don't have to explain myself to you. As a matter of fact, I won't waste any more time.". She took her dagger and stuck it in Tig's chest. "NO!", I shouted, as I watched him fall to the ground. Just then, I heard galloping and I looked and saw a small crowd of people riding up. Jake was one of them but the other two I couldn't quite recognize. As they grew closer, I noticed Caprius was with them. As I felt my heart fall, I saw a girl with long red hair jump off her horse and start attacking the Dashin soldiers. Micka rushed forward and I dropped next to Tig, who, to my surprise, was still breathing. "Tig, try not to move, okay?", I said, propping his head onto the nearest object. As I jumped up to go aid in the battle, the girl with the flaming red hair came to me. "Where is Bastian?", she asked. "He went into the woods to go find some girl.". Without another word, or glance at me, she proceeded into the wood. As for the others, the Dashin soldiers were fleeing. Micka had disappeared and I didn't see her. Caprius rushed forward at the sight of Tig. He stopped when he spotted me and looked at me for a while. I could tell right away that something was different. I allowed him to proceed, and he bent down next to Tig, took the dagger out of his chest, and placed some kind of paste on the wound. Tig let out a small yell, then he laid back and didn't say anything. I was watching Caprius, who I could tell was trying to avoid my eyes. The other girl had come up next to us. "Alisa, did she go after Bastian?", this new girl asked me. "Yes, but who are you people?", "This is Sheena, and I assume you know who he is.", Jake answered me, pointing at Caprius, who was paying attention to Tig and trying to still avoid my eyes. "How did you survive?", I asked Jake, still looking Caprius over. "Well, it wasn't easy. Queen Micka killed a good amount of my men, I managed to tell them to retreat, while I sought out the Kindy Princess to assist you. Once I told her that Micka was after you, this one here said they had to save you, no matter what, and he was the first to hop on a horse and ride to you.", Jake said, once again pointing at Caprius. "Caprius said that you all had to come save me? Caprius? This man is the reason my sister is dead. My father is dead now, too.", I said, hoping to hit Caprius somehow. He finally looked at me and said the last thing I expected to hear, "I'm sorry that I wasn't able to save him.

I've caused so much loss in your life, Tisiphone. Sorry, will never be enough.". I couldn't believe what I was hearing. I didn't know what to say. I looked at the girl named Sheena, who gave me an 'I'm not buying it' sort of look. "Well, it is true that he led us here to save you. He knew who you were.", she said with some difficulty. Caprius stood up, "He'll be fine. Just some rest now.". He looked at me and then walked towards the woods, "My mother is in there somewhere, isn't she?", "Don't know, haven't seen her.", I said, not really thinking about that, "Caprius, I blame you for a lot of things, but not my father. That was all Micka.". Caprius put his face in his hands, "I'm such a fool. Tisiphone, I don't expect forgiveness, but please, let's just try and figure out what my mother is doing.". Jake was already getting ready to leave, "I'm going to meet what's left of my men. I bid you all good luck.". He rode off. The Kindy soldiers who had arrived were cleaning their weapons and talking amongst themselves. "Caprius, could you lead these men back to Kindy? I'm going to wait here for Alisa.", "ALISA?!", I shouted, "That's who Sebastian told me and Tig to go fetch. She's the one who went into the woods? Good.". Caprius turned to me with a frown, "That isn't a good thing. Most likely, Alisa is walking into a very well sprung trap.". As we sat and pondered on his last words, Tig let out a loud snore.

ALISA: As I walked down the hill deeper into the woods, I had no idea what I was going towards. I remember thinking as soon as Bastian left for the Dark Wood, something bad would happen, and sure enough, I could sense Bastian was in major trouble. Seeing as he is our creator reincarnated, I didn't see how he could be harmed. Except, of course, if you throw in the fact that Falsa knew something. Something that we didn't and something she could use. The creatures who usually watch from afar weren't anywhere near. It seemed too quiet. The trees weren't even stirring, which from my last visit, I confirmed they were sentient enough to grab me as I walked. When I could see the small village that was Lab's village, I was immediately met by Alex, who was walking with Casian on her shoulder, which meant Bastian was here. She was also carrying his shield and looking extremely worried. "Alisa!", she shouted when she saw me. She ran up to me and hugged me. It had been two months since we've seen one another, and she was glowing in a totally different way. Her skin was now a faint pink which actually looked really pretty. I found it hard to be jealous of her when I was worried Sebastian was in real trouble. She was too, judging from her look and the fact she had his shield. "Where is Sebastian, Alex?", I asked, giving her a suspicious look. "That's the thing, I don't know. Lab walked away with him some time ago, and I haven't seen either one of them since.". We heard hurrying footsteps and turned to look. A woman wearing a red dress that was torn at certain places, was running towards us. She bumped into Alex, causing Casian to fall to the ground. Alex knelt to help the woman, but I was too busy thinking how random this was. "Excuse me, but how did you get here, mam?", I asked, watching her. She was obviously terrified of something. She was shaking all over and could barely speak. When she finally did, "Grand…my grand…", she was sputtering. "Mam, I need you to try and tell me what is going on.". She grabbed the front of my armor and pulled me down to her, "HE'S GOT HIM! YOU HAVE TO SAVE HIM! PLEASE! YOU HAVE TO!". She seemed hysterical. I looked at Alex, confused about what to do. "Who has him? Who are you talking about? Lab?", Alex asked. The woman turned to her and shook her head, "NO! DESIAN! DESIAN HAS MY GRANDSON!". I noticed the woman was covered in something that appeared to be a black substance. When I touched it, it was only water. "Who is your grandson?", I asked her, starting to get a bit irritated, "And who is Desian?", "MY SON!", the woman said in disgust. She started to cry and whimper. Just then, a very familiar form came from out of the woods. Falsa was moving from behind a tree. "Well, I'll make this simple; I want her.", said Falsa, pointing at the shaking woman. I looked and immediately knew to protect this woman. "No. You want her, you have to go through me and Alex.". Falsa stared from me to Alex and then laughed. "Oh, you two… Do you even know who this is?", she asked, trying to contain her laughter. “Sure, she is someone’s Grandma.”. Falsa began laughing hysterically. “Okay, I’ll tell you the story. Once upon a time, twenty-five years ago to be exact, there was a goddess who was only seventeen years old, and was so in love with what her destined lover had created, she wanted to spread hope throughout the land.”. I was listening, all the while, I could see Alex becoming more desperate. Like me, she was putting pieces together and figuring out that the grandson who this woman was referring to, might just be Bastian. “So, this goddess decided to spread a certain word. She claimed that the god would come back for her, and that she was going to be with him. Oh, she was warned not to go around saying anything. Told that this was meant to be a well-protected secret. But the girl was so good spirited, that she decided that the people of Plinth must be as well. Well this scared some people, specifically, the royalty.”, Falsa said, looking at the poor woman on the ground. “Oh my, is this Queen Penelope?”, I found myself asking. It was a long time ago, when I was only seven, that my mother told me about King Oliver’s wife, who was never seen again. I looked at the woman shaking and holding my leg. “This one…”, Falsa continued, “…decided to bring the kingdoms together for a royal meeting, then proposed that the goddess must die. Ensuring their safety from the god.”, Falsa laughed extremely hard at this. I felt I could guess the rest of the story. “You were that goddess.”. Falsa looked at me hard. “Clever girl, but somewhat wrong. That girl was named Falta. Who incidentally, I happen to be a reincarnation of.”. Suddenly it all made sense. “So, all this…” I said, anger rising, “…was because you wanted vengeance?”, “Yes.”, Falsa said quite simply, “Now, stand aside and allow her to pay for her sins.”, “SHE HAS PAID ENOUGH!”, yelled a naked man now coming out of the woods towards us as well. But I recognized him. I’d seen him every time I was looking at Caprius. This man was Godrick, Caprius’ father. He grabbed Falsa, “You two need to take her and run! NOW!”. Godrick was known as the Rapist King. I always had the impression that he was heartless. And yet, here he was fighting off a powerful being he knows he stands no chance against. "WHY ARE YOU STILL STANDING THERE, GIRL?! GET HER OUT OF HERE!". I decided that I would listen to him, and if he died, I'd tell his son what a hero his father was. We ran back towards the village. When we got there, we headed to the large hut in the back that Lab had brought us to before. We laid Penelope on the bed. She was so weak that she couldn't speak. She continued to shake though, the fear of whatever had happened to her over these years still sorely affecting her. "Penelope…", began Alex softly, "…we need to know where you have been and what's happened. Who is Desian, and where is Sebastian?". Penelope looked way too frightened to answer anyone of those issues. But she tried to sit up and was too weak. Alex gathered some water for her, but she turned it away, looking at it fearfully. "My daughter's son, he came into the cave, I never knew that it would be him. I'm truly being punished.", she said, in a dry cracked voice. She looked at the water again, took it from Alex's hand, and downed it in one gulp. Penelope didn't even look like she had aged. "Where have you been?", I asked again. Penelope began to tell us a story that I could only think of as anybody's worst nightmare. "After we killed the girl, Falta, Oliver and I traveled back towards Nasher. In the middle of the night, something called out to me. I didn't know what it wanted, but I followed the voice. When I found myself walking through the Dark Wood, I ended up in a cave with a mysterious black lake. The lake swallowed me. The next time I was awake, I was watching a girl walk out of the cave. She mocked me and said she wouldn't exist without my blood. Next, I was swallowed by the water again. Then the next time I was awake, I found Godrick had been brought to the cave. The girl, much older now, watched as an unseen force, forced us to sex.". Hearing that she had gone through that, made me realize, Godrick was right, she had suffered enough. She broke down after saying this and it took a while for me and Alex to get her talking again. "The lake swallowed Godrick and I, and we have been there ever since. Being tortured for his amusement…", she trailed off and had another breakdown. "… please, my grandson, please.", she pleaded with me and Alex. "Is your grandson the son of farmers?", I asked, trying to get confirmation that it was Sebastian she was referring to. "He was so handsome…", she said in a dreamy voice, "…he had his mother's face, but his eyes… weren't…his fathers. They're his… My son, Desian.". Penelope told us what transpired in the cave, and all my worst fears were realized. "So, Sebastian is back in this cave, being tortured the same way?", "I don't know.", Penelope answered me, "But what I do know, is that Desian is powerful, but for a moment, he was weak, and Sebastian did that!". She was becoming a bit frantic. "Alex, you stay with her, I'm going to get Bastian.", "No, let me come with you.". Alex was getting up with the shield in her hand. "Falsa is still out there. I doubt Godrick was able to hold her for long.". Alex nodded at this and sat back down. Seeing her hold the shield reminded me of when Falsa had it. As I walked out of the hut, I looked across the way and realized Falsa was already heading this way, which meant there was a possibility she'd killed Godrick. I decided to let Alex deal with her and ran off out of the village. I could only guess the cave was far into the woods, so I headed as far as I could. Finally, I made it to the cave. I went inside and looked around. The black lake was ominously swaying and gave the cave an eerie feeling. Before I could make another move, the lake came to life, rising in the air, and shooting straight for me. I jumped out of the way, but it quickly grabbed my ankle and started pulling me. As I neared the lake, I started to feel fear worse than anything I'd ever felt. I felt helpless, like I was going to die here and there was nothing I could do to stop it, nobody could help me, and my parents, whom I just started to like again, will never see their daughter, who hated them for so long, ever again. Just then, I felt the water release me and start to go towards the center. As the water dissolved, I saw a body in the water. It was Bastian. I moved towards him, shaking him. "Bastian, Bastian, wake up!". He stirred and looked up. When he realized who was shaking him, he quickly became alert, "ALISA, NO! GET OUT OF HERE!", he shouted, while at the same time getting to his feet and leading me out. "But, I came to…", "NO, I DON'T NEED HELP, THIS IS WHERE I

BELONG, GET OUT OF HERE NOW!". As he continued pushing me, there was laughter coming from out of the corner. "She isn't going anywhere.". I watched Bastian get pulled back, and then, I felt a force around my gut pull me back as well. I looked into the eyes of another boy who was standing only a foot from where I had landed. He had an evil smile spread across his face and neat black hair. His face looked a lot like Godrick, but his eyes were the same color as Bastian, golden and silver. Sebastian jumped up and shielded me. "LEAVE HER ALONE, DESIAN! LET HER GO! THIS IS ONLY BETWEEN ME AND YOU!", yelled Bastian. The boy was still wearing that evil smile. I wished he'd stop smiling like he was, because out of everything that scared me about this moment, it was that ugly, scary, smile. "You know as well as I do, Sebastian, that Alisa here has everything to do with us. After all, isn't she the seer?". I sat there, too terrified to move. I didn't even stop to wonder how he knew who I was. I watched Sebastian for some kind of sign, but he was motionless just like me. Then, right when I thought it couldn't get worse, I noticed how he was watching me, how he seemed to see something passed me that made me actually look over my shoulder, but nothing was there. "You like Sebastian, don't you, Alisa? You want him.". I didn't know how to answer this. I was too afraid of Desian. I understood now what had driven Penelope to the brink of insanity. This boy was a nightmare brought to life. The idea of being tortured for seventeen years by this guy would take anybody's mind. I felt my body moving, but I wasn't controlling it. "DESIAN, NO! STOP!", I heard Sebastian shouting, but this didn't stop me from removing my armor. I was standing there in my gown, shivering. Sebastian was watching me, waiting to see whatever it was that I was going to do. I started moving towards him and it dawned on me. Desian was going to do to me and Sebastian, what he had done to Godrick and Penelope. I could see Bastian was frozen and unable to move, just like me. As I sat on Bastian, I felt him enter into me. I felt my body swaying on his. Tears formed in my eyes and I closed them, wishing for this to be over. I'd never felt this kind of pain in my life.

And while I had nightmares about this type of thing happening to me, actually having it happen was beyond any description. I opened my eyes, and everything was still happening. I couldn't even face Sebastian, and standing behind Sebastian was Desian, who looked directly into my eyes. "You like it, admit it.", "NO! PLEASE!", I pleaded. I couldn't ever remember sounding this weak. It was a sign of how terrified I truly was. I felt Sebastian climax, and I fell off of him. I laid there, sprawled across the cave ground, crying. I couldn't even focus or even think about where I was. I had just been raped. And worse, it was unwilling on both ends. I lifted my head just a bit to look at Bastian, who was watching me with a mixture of sadness and pity. He then turned to Desian, who started to laugh, "Even though you prefer women, you just couldn't help that attraction to your god.", Desian said, with an extremely evil laugh. Then at that moment, somebody came flying into the cave. He hit the wall and fell. Falsa walked in after, quickly followed by Alex, who came from behind and hit her with the shield. Falsa yelled and rolled down the hill. As Alex entered the cave, she saw the scene before her. She came to me first. "What happened here?", she asked, even though, in her voice I could hear that she guessed. Desian was eyeing Alex with great interest, "Well, look who it is, my other love.", "What the hell are you…?", Alex started to say, then suddenly stopped. She gave Desian an entire look over, "No…that's impossible. How can this be?". She looked to Falsa, who was getting to her feet. "What have you done?", Alex asked her. "You can see for yourself. He is our god. Sebastian is just a weak imitation of HIM.", Falsa said, pointing towards Desian. Desian moved closer to Alex. Sebastian was trying to stand but was too weak or was being weakened somehow by Desian. I continued crying into the ground, but soon was gaining my anger. Alex raised the shield against Desian, who quickly turned back into the black water and engulfed us all. As we all were swishing back and forth, I felt my consciousness leave my body. I was floating in a room. Sheena was there, and my parents, Alex, Sebastian, Wilson, Casian, and the girl whom I had just met, Tisiphone. There were others, but I couldn't make out their faces. Then looming over me, was Desian. I was too afraid of staring at him. Then I heard his voice speaking to me from what seemed like everywhere, "You like it. You like the taste of it. You know what you are. She hates you…". I covered my ears, but the voice continued, "Your parents don't want you to come back, Sebastian had his way with you, you're no better than a common Dashin slut, you are weak, Alisa, always have been…", "… no…". I wanted this to end. Then it did. Alex was lying in a corner, weakened, and Falsa was standing next to Desian, while Sebastian was helping Godrick, who looked on the verge of collapse, get to his feet. Sebastian moved towards me and helped me stand but I felt too weak and didn't want him touching me. I threw him away from me but didn't know where to run. "Well, that is that. I bid you all a farewell, until later, of course.". Desian was striding out of the cave with Falsa. The two walked out into the light and were gone. I ran to Alex, who I finally realized wasn't glowing at all. Her hair color had turned white instead of pink and blood ran down her mouth. "Alex, please say something.", I said. She coughed and looked at me and started to cry, "THEY TOOK IT!", she shouted. What was she talking about? Took what? As I looked her over, I could tell she was drained and weak. I assumed it was from the black water. Then I saw Sebastian running out of the cave, and Godrick was sitting against a wall heaving. I helped Alex stand and she looked at me again, "I'm sorry I didn't come sooner. As soon as Penelope told me what was here, I rushed. Part of me couldn't believe it.". I still felt a wave of fear washing over me at the thought of what had just happened. "What is Desian, Alex?", "He's Sebastian's wrath, his anger towards the people that executed him five-hundred years ago.".

SEBASTIAN: I rushed out of the cave. Just ahead, I could see Falsa and Desian. "Ah, it feels good to finally be able to walk out of this cave. It's been ages!", Desian was saying. He was carrying a sword that looked like no Plinthinian could have made it. He turned around, "Sebastian, it isn't a good idea to sneak up on me like you were trying to do.". He rushed at me with the sword and slashed, and I quickly blocked his slash with the shield. A huge explosion erupted upon the collision of the sword and shield, and both me and Desian were blown back. I could see him being helped up by Falsa, who whispered something in his ear and then walked away. "It begins then, we shall see who will rule this planet.", said Desian, and he floated into the air and flew away. I laid there on the ground, breathless. Then, Alex came with Alisa, who still didn't want to meet my eyes. I felt so guilty about what happened between us in the cave. I wanted to say something to her but didn't know what I could say. "Where did Desian go?", Alex asked me, and I pointed into the sky. "No… We have to do something, or he will destroy Plinth.". We walked back into the village, where Lab was waiting with most of the men in the village, brandishing weapons. "Well, I believe you know where I stand, Sebastian. I can't let you stop my lord from completing his vengeance.". I rushed forward without thinking, and I slashed at his neck with the shield. His head flew off and I watched with a sort of satisfaction. I looked at Alisa, and our eyes met for a split second, then she looked quickly away, looking towards the ground. I wasn't used to this Alisa. Penelope came wandering out of the back of the village. The other men who were standing there were still staring at Lab's head on the ground. Finally, one man decided to launch himself forward at me, then, Alex stepped in and grabbed him, then, Alisa took her blade out and started slashing. Next thing we knew, we were battling the Dark Village. Penelope was hiding, and Casian, who had been guarding her, stood on top of her head, on guard. There were finally only two men left and we finished them. Slowly the women and children started to come out of the huts and looked at the scene in horror. "MURDERERS!", one woman shouted, and then, one of the children, a girl, picked up a dagger from the floor and went for Alisa. Alex pushed her out of the way and snapped the girl's neck. "We have to kill all of them!", Alex yelled. Alisa and I both looked at her in horror, but soon learned she wasn't wrong. The women started to surround us and the children as well. We had no choice but to fight through them. Finally, the village was empty, except for the revealers which suddenly were no longer green but had turned red.

Alisa grabbed Alex and started moving towards the end of the wood. I helped Penelope, who was looking forlorn. Godrick came and joined us. I gave him some robes, so he wasn't naked anymore. We proceeded towards the exit, and once we arrived, we found Tisiphone, Tig, Caprius, and Sheena all waiting for us. "What was that thing we saw fly out of there? It looked like a man!", Sheena pointed out. We told her what had happened, leaving out what happened between me and Alisa. Alisa was quiet. She didn't seem to want to be involved with what we were discussing. Even when Sheena called out to her to ask what she thought we should do, she just nodded. "Alisa, did you hear me? I said what should we do? Should we head back to Kindy?", "I don't know if Kindy will be so welcoming to this man.", Tisiphone was pointing at Godrick, who was holding Penelope, who was slowly sobbing into his chest. Penelope soon separated herself from Godrick and spoke, "The boy you saw is my son. I can tell you now, he will bring this planet to its knees. Unless…", she looked towards me. I knew what she was going to say. That somehow, I can beat him. But I didn't know how. I looked at Alisa, and for a small moment again, our eyes met, but she quickly looked away. Sheena, who had been watching Alisa, moved towards her to find out what was wrong. Tisiphone was watching Caprius, who was staring at Godrick. Caprius had never met his father and seeing him for the first time, and learning where he's been, made Caprius angrier than before. Tig was eyeing Penelope, and Penelope had approached me and Alex. "So, you too are a goddess, just like Falta.", Penelope stated, watching Alex with mixed interest. "I'm such a fool! Now I know why I lost my daughter. Because she lost me first. But now I have you.". She placed her hands on my face and looked into my eyes. She shuddered some, because I knew me and Desian shared the same eyes. Alex was watching Penelope with interest, "I must ask you, how did Falta become Falsa? She said she used your blood?", Alex inquired. Penelope looked positively afraid to answer, "She came to exist through an ancient ritual that Desian forced me to perform. And before you say anything, I don't know how he was able to control me before he was born or even inside of me.", "So, what does that make her? I mean, she isn't your daughter, right?", Alex asked. "No…", replied Penelope, "…she is something completely different. The water that makes up Desian, is some kind of connection to the other world.". This made a lot of sense. When I had been engulfed by the water, I saw my parents, but for some reason, could hear Desian trying to talk to me. It was there that my mother told me how dangerous he is. She was in the other world, or her spirit is, and she was able to communicate with me. But the real question was, how was I able to block out Desian? Even when I wanted him to stop torturing Penelope, somehow, I made him stop. Whatever that power was, I needed to tap into that. It was obvious my grandmother thought the same thing because she was watching me with high interest. "I DON'T WISH TO TALK ABOUT IT!", yelled Alisa towards Sheena, who was backing away from her, hurt, and confused. I ran over to her and placed my hand on her shoulder, and she punched me. When she looked at me, clear in the eyes, tears formed and ran down her face, "Don't ever touch me…", she said, and she ran away, Sheena running after her. Caprius, who had been watching his father, now faced me and quickly put pieces together. "You've…", he started to say, but Tisiphone kicked him, mouthing not to say anything. Instead he went back to eyeing his father who had finally approached him. It was quite obvious he was frightened of his son. Especially because of who his mother is. Alex had gone after Alisa. I had a feeling she knew exactly what happened.

It wasn't too much later that we had all strolled into Kindy. King Oliver had been alerted of Queen Penelope's rescue and rode to meet her immediately. When we arrived, he had already been waiting for a day. He ran up to her and embraced her before she was even in the kingdom, "MY GOD, YOU HAVEN'T AGED!", he exclaimed, kissing her. I couldn't help but notice the small glances between her and Godrick. Sheena, who was still somewhat upset because Alisa wouldn't talk to her, had gone straight into the castle to check on other things, as she put it. Caprius had led his father away to go find a place perhaps so they could talk. Casian, who was riding on my shoulder, had jumped down and ran towards a little girl with green hair, who too had come to Kindy from Alexandria. "We have a lot of visitors. We never have many visitors in the castle.", King Derek was saying to Tisiphone, who was learning where Caprius' new change had come from. Tisiphone, who had never been outside of Dasha, was amazed at the differences, and like myself had become accustomed to the kind flowers. Tig was hanging around Tisiphone, hoping she would give him some sign that she liked him. Alisa had been somewhere with Alex. Alex seemed to be the only person Alisa would talk to. Even her own mother, who was a bit upset that Godrick had come seeking refuge in Kindy, had not been able to get through to her. I felt completely at fault. I knew it wasn't my place to tell anybody what happened, but Penelope, who too had been a victim of this, knew what must have happened. "I was too weak and hysterical, and perhaps those aren't good reasons, but I should have told her not to go fetch you. Instead I begged her to. If anyone is to blame for what happened between you two, it is me.". I didn't blame her, but I did have a good amount of questions. Where was Desian now? What am I supposed to do to defeat him? Where is Falsa and this child that's ours? Why was Desian able to fly away, and where did he get that sword? Now that I was thinking about it, Alex didn't look the same. Her hair was white, and she had lost her glow. Something strange had happened to her and I'm sure she had only shared this with Alisa. I thought perhaps Desian had his way with her, but she would have said so, or at least been more like Alisa about it. But the more I thought about our grand escape from the Dark

Wood, the more that I remembered what Alex had said about the god sword. So that was the weapon that Desian had, and somehow, he removed it from Alex. If he had the shield he would probably be twice as powerful. The time had come where I knew that I could no longer pretend. Desian was proof of what I am. He knows what I am and has a broader knowledge of everything. How was I supposed to compete with that?

Six days later, things were calm. Caprius and Godrick left Kindy two days ago. Queen Shay had been hinting that she didn't feel comfortable with him around, so Caprius felt that his father had no place here and decided that they were going to run away. Since they had left, Tisiphone had changed her attitude towards Caprius. Even hugging him when he left. Alisa watched from a distance. Once again, I tried to catch her eye. When she noticed, she turned and walked away. I was becoming fed up with her sulky attitude. I felt like I needed somebody, too. Alex, who was still spending a lot of time with her, hadn't even been talking to me that often. Part of me started to think that they both blamed me. I knew that what happened to Alisa was messed up. I understood why she couldn't look at me, but it was unfair. After two days had passed from Caprius' and Godrick's departure, I ran into Alisa in the kind fields. She had never had an interest in being here before, so I was surprised. She looked and saw me coming and made to get up. "Alisa, wait!", I yelled, as she started to pick up the pace. I caught up to her and grabbed her arm. She swung around wildly at me. She continued to throw punches until I had grabbed her and pulled her closer to me. She broke down and started to cry into my chest. "Don't you understand? I just want to be alone…", she moaned into my chest. "Alisa, we really need to talk. I know that it's hard. I know what you're feeling, but avoiding me like this…". She looked up at me and broke away. "I've never had that feeling before. I'd never been with a man, or even really ever wanted to. Desian…he made me feel so…so weak.". She looked down trodden. Saddened by the events. She wasn't at all the same

Alisa. “It hurts when I see you.”, she said, finally looking me in the eyes, “The sight of you, just everything, I can’t. I can’t be around you.”, “Alisa, it hurts me, too. But we’re friends. You can’t let him do this to us.”, “You don’t know what he has done to me.”. She stepped closer, and to my amazement, kissed me on my lips. “He made me want you.”. She walked away without saying another word. I didn’t know what to say. But now it made sense why she had been avoiding me and Sheena.

CHAPTER 13

Godrick's Plight: Caprius Makes A Choice

CAPRIUS: Father and I made our way away from Kindy. Godrick had been kept prisoner for over seventeen years. From everything he told me, I knew I had guessed correctly. Mother had indeed tricked him and led him to the Dark Wood, as soon as she learned she was pregnant with me. I asked my father why she would have me in the first place? "Well, your mother is a twisted person. I was no better, but she had her reasons. Which most of them, made no sense. But I guess it was all about freeing your brother.". A large part of me had forgotten that Desian, the boy my father was forced to sire through Penelope, was my brother. Somehow, this connected me with Sebastian. Desian and Sebastian are the same person, so I questioned if this made him my brother as well. Father quickly shut down this notion by explaining to me, "Desian is his own person. He was born through Penelope and myself, whereas, Sebastian is the son of a farmer and Penelope's daughter. The one strange thing I can say you have in common with that boy, is the fact that Desian is his uncle.". Now it was entirely strange, so I decided to switch the conversation. "Everyone called you the Rapist King. Did you know that?", I asked. I watched his face to see how he would react to this, after all, he gave me his genes. I had unknowingly carried on his tradition of forcing women. He looked at me, then answered, "Son, I just spent the last seventeen years being forced upon someone. What I used to do, I've now become a victim of. I could never imagine ever doing that again.", "And what of Penelope? Did you think nobody noticed you watching her, and her watching you?". My father had been a prisoner alongside Penelope after all. All that time being forced upon one another must have taken effect. "Penelope, is where she belongs.", he said quite simply. I could tell he didn't want to talk about that. It was strange in some small way, my father and I had both learned lessons the hard way. Often, when he thought I wouldn't notice, he would just stare at me. I chalked it up to him just not ever meeting me until now. But I finally understood one day. As we were nearing Nasher, we were accosted by none other than my mother. She had come from out of the woods. She carried with her the baby that Sebastian was father to. My father and I stood rooted to the spot. I hadn't seen her since our last return to Dasha five months ago, when she abandoned me. She stood there with a haughty look on her face and was watching me and Godrick with a kind of amusement. "GO AWAY, WITCH! I JUST WANT TO BE WITH MY SON!", Godrick yelled at her. "Your son? You barely know him. Caprius, come on, I need you to come with me.". It was unbelievable. The nerve this woman had. "I'm never going to go with you.", I said under my breath. "What did you just say to me?", she asked. "You heard what the boy said.", Godrick replied, standing in front of me. "Godrick, you really are that stupid, aren't you?", "Well, I let you in my bed, didn't I? I must be barking.". The baby started to cry, and I could see Falsa was getting impatient. "CAPRIUS, COME WITH ME, OR YOU

WILL NOT HAVE A FATHER ANYMORE!", "I have never had a father because of you!", I yelled. I felt my blood rising and I was ready to attack if need be. I knew now what my mother truly is, and I wasn't about to let her take my father. I stood in front of him and brandished my blade. Falsa started to laugh, "How foolish. Do you really think I'm going to come over there?". Just as she said this, I heard a cracking noise above me and then a boy landed from the sky right behind Godrick. He stuck the sword he was carrying into Godrick and Godrick fell to the ground. "NO!". I slashed my sword, but the boy just blocked my every attack. Then he grabbed my blade with his bare hand and threw it to the side. "You have one choice to make, Brother, either come with me now, or, I kill our father. And unlike you, I've had plenty of time with dear old dad. So if you want to make up for lost time, I suggest you make the right choice.". I watched as Godrick lay dying, "How can you save him?", I asked. "Well, I can easily heal him.". The boy put the sword over Godrick's body, and I watched in amazement as the wound started to close. The blood stains remained, but other than that, now, Father was just asleep from the blood loss. "So, what will you do?", Desian asked, watching me closely to see what I do. "What do you even want from me?", "Well, we all are going to Dasha, where we will be one big happy family.". I didn't know what the hell he was talking about, but then I thought about it and realized that maybe I could help Sebastian somehow. "Okay, I'll come, but you have to let Father go.". Desian looked at Father, then at Falsa, "No… I'm afraid he will be joining us. There is a lot for him to discover about his Dasha. Personally, I want him to meet the girl I left in charge.", said Falsa, taking steps towards Godrick. She kicked him, and he awoke with a jump. He looked around, realized who was still standing over him and started crying, "You're free, what could you possibly still want with me?", "Well, me? Nothing. But Caprius here wants you alive, and I need him to do something for me, so I'm keeping you alive, just long enough.", said Desian. "But, what the hell do you need from me?", I asked. I felt like I had the day Sebastian tricked me. I knew I was in an impossible situation, but I also felt I couldn't let Desian know I felt that way. "Well, that's why you are coming with us to Dasha. Besides, don't you want to see your little sister?". I looked at the baby in Falsa's arms. I felt sick to my stomach just thinking about how that baby was made. When I was a scoundrel, I remembered feeling powerful because nobody could stop me from getting what I wanted. Learning that you aren't that powerful, and that what you've been doing is wrong, can take a large toll on you when you finally come to sense. I followed the strange couple. Desian would often fly ahead and see what was before us, then tell us we could continue. I didn't exactly know what we were hiding from. At night, Father and I would bunch up and we could hear Falsa and Desian having sex from the other side. One night, I didn't want to lay there listening to my brother screwing my mother, so I went for a walk. While I was walking, I heard strange noises. I turned, and standing right in front of me was Micka. She looked like she had been staying in the forest and hadn't returned to Dasha. "What…?", she quickly covered my mouth. "Shh… We don't want them to hear.". She looked around cautiously, then said, "You have to come with me, now. They are going to kill you and Godrick.". I looked at her for some time, trying to determine if she was lying. "How do you know?", "Because, they want you to give the rest of your power to your sister. They intend to exterminate you.". She looked like she could be telling the truth, but considering who she was, I was having a hard time buying it. Not too far away, I could still hear Falsa moaning. "Why didn't you return to Dasha?". Micka raised one eyebrow. "Really? Because they were going to kill me. I'm no fool. Falsa has been using me. But if you come with me, we can defeat the both of them.", "And how the hell is that possible for us?". Micka looked annoyed with me, but reached into her pocket and pulled something out. It was a ring that had a green stone on it. She was also wearing my mother's ring that showed the stars. I wondered if she knew what my mother's ring does. "What is this?", "This will help Sebastian, but I must be the one to give it to him.", "What about Godrick? If I leave him, they will kill him.".

Micka looked in the direction Godrick was laying. She looked like she wanted to say no, but instead, she allowed him to come. We made our way towards him and gently shook him awake. Desian and my mother were still going at it. We quietly snuck away. Part of me had already seen the flaw in this plan. Desian would most likely catch up to us. Then I looked, and not too far away, I saw my baby sister, sleeping. She was smiling in her sleep and it made me realize something. "We have to take her, too.", I whispered, pointing in the baby's direction. "Are you mad? She will alert them. We must leave the baby. Falsa won't hurt her.". I was going to argue but Godrick cut me off, "If we are leaving, then let's go...", he hissed at us. We started to move and suddenly, the noises between Desian and Falsa ceased. We looked at one another, then standing right before us was Desian. Naked and smiling that evil smile he always does. "Going somewhere?", he asked, looking at Micka with great interest. "Micka, you weren't really going to save Caprius and Godrick were you?", he asked. Micka looked lost for a moment. Then she took out a dagger and tried to kill Desian. Desian just dodged her and she fell head first into a bush. When Desian went to the bushes to look for her, she had disappeared. "Hmm, well I suppose you equipped her too well, Falsa.". Falsa was walking towards us, putting her robe back on. She watched the scene for a minute, then found her voice, "I had expected her to act in our interest. I gave her power, so naturally I thought she'd be loyal. I guess she will never truly be over Sebastian.". Falsa looked at me and saw that I was angry. Micka just ditched us, and worst of all, left us in a compromising position. Desian, looking at me, and doing that mind reading thing he always does, spoke the answer to my question, "If you try something like this again, Caprius, I will kill Godrick.", "Why not just kill me and be done then?!", I shouted at them. They both looked at each other. "Caprius, why don't you and I go for a walk?", Desian said, already walking in a different direction. Robes appeared from almost nowhere and wrapped around him. He gestured for me to follow. I looked at my mother, who was staring at me coldly. I followed Desian until we had reached a treacle tree. He pulled one of the leaves off and sniffed at it. "There was a time when I truly did love this planet. You understand that, right?", he said, "I mean, look around. Life is everywhere, and I created all of this life. The real reason I favored this place was... because it was so different.". Desian was walking and admiring everything, "I've been trapped in a cave for over five-hundred years. And the whole time I've been there, all I could think about is what will happen if I make the decision to just destroy it all? What happens when all this is gone? My other creations... I have no idea what is going on with them, and do you know whose fault that is?". I stared at him, waiting for an answer. "Sebastian's. He trapped me in that form. He put me in such a state that all I could do...was bubble. But then, after waiting for over five-hundred years, someone finally arrived who was able to change things. Someone who was able to make me whole again. Your mother was and is my savior. Had it not been for her, I would still be trapped in that cave. She led the people to kill her. Then I forced Penelope to bring her body to me. Then I resurrected your mother. That's when she became Falsa.". I had never heard this much about my mother, and found it quite interesting. I remembered when Sebastian was asking me about whether or not Falsa was a goddess. I remember thinking at that time that he was mad. But now, seeing the fruition of things, brought a whole new perspective. I was afraid. I didn't know where this story was going. What Desian thought telling me all this would accomplish. "You know, I can see really far, Caprius. I can see past the lives people are living now and what is possible.", "Is that why you did what you did to Alisa?", I asked with anger in my voice, "You claim to love life and how you created it, but have no problem making your creations suffer.". Desian watched me for some time. Then he smiled again, "I see, you are jealous.". I couldn't believe him. "Jealous? No... I'm furious with you! You made Sebastian rape her!". I felt my blood boiling. I was becoming angrier with every second. "Is that what you think happened? I didn't do anything to Alisa, that Alisa wasn't going to eventually do herself. You truly believe she doesn't feel anything for Sebastian?". He took out a mirror that almost seemed to come from nowhere. It seemed he had the ability to summon objects. In the mirror was a scene. Alisa was talking to Bastian, and walked up and kissed him, then ran away, leaving Sebastian speechless. The scene disappeared and Desian was watching for my response. "I don't believe that was real.", I said. "Well I can promise that I didn't do anything, Brother. You see, Alisa was going to do it anyway. There is a part of her that has always liked Bastian. But see, Alexandria was in the way. But that isn't a problem now. She too has lost confidence, due to this.". He put the sword in the moonlight and I finally understood. "You took that from Alex…how?". Mother had said that is what this war was about. Now that I knew the truth, I thought that perhaps she had made up the story of Alex possessing the sword. "Well, all I had to do was touch her.". Desian laughed that same evil laugh he always does. "Caprius, I won't kill you. And it isn't because we share the same father, but rather, because I need you to live. I need you to survive.". I couldn't understand what the hell all that meant. "So, then why not let me and Godrick go?". Desian gave me a serious look. "You know I can't, Caprius. It isn't my call.", "So, my mother is in charge after all?". Desian became quite livid, but quickly went back to his demeanor, "No, it's her choice, because Godrick is her right of passage. Godrick must be punished. Perhaps, one day, you will understand. Now come on, lets head back.". He started to walk away. I felt something grab at my leg. I realized Micka was hiding in a bush. She pressed her finger to her lips and then released me and disappeared again.

As the days continued to pass by, we had finally reached Dasha. Upon entering, Fod was coming towards us. When he saw my father, he gave a loud whoop, but quickly subsided back into the crowd when he saw Falsa. Desian was looking everything over and my mother was tickling the baby. Dasha was completely different. Cottages had been stacked up and things looked a bit cleaner. I had never seen Dasha like this before. It had always been dirty and filled with filth. But now it looked more like the streets of Kindy. We made our way into the castle. A soldier had come to greet us. "Good morning! Queen Micka is out of the kingdom now and nobody is allowed in the castle. Yes, that includes you, mam.", the soldier finished, eyeing my mother with deep regret. Desian walked up and the soldier started to choke. He sputtered then coughed up blood. He fell to the floor and took one last breath. Desian stepped over his body and walked into the throne room. The throne room had been decorated purple and red. Desian sat on the throne and Falsa sat on his lap. "Caprius, here's what I want you to do. I want you to make your way towards the center of town and go into our vault that is hidden. Then I want you to take out that goblet that I've had put away for some time. You come back with that, and I'll allow you and your father...", Falsa added with a disgusted look in his direction, "...to walk right out of Dasha.". I knew that it was too good to be true. And as for the goblet she was talking about, I remember it from my childhood. I proceeded to the secret place where we kept certain things hidden. I found the goblet and gave it to my mother. Desian summoned forth a green flower I had never seen before. He took the center of it and crushed it in his hands. He then held his hand over the goblet and some of the nastiest stuff I'd ever seen, dripped down his hand and into the cup. They then raised the cup up to the baby's lips. The baby drank it and suddenly became fully awake. It gave a jolt in Falsa's arms, then disappeared. "WHAT?!", Falsa exclaimed. I knew what had happened almost right away. Walking into the throne room, carrying the now crying baby was Micka. "YOU, GIVE HER BACK, NOW!", "No.", Micka said quite simply. She was staring from Desian to Falsa, with a look of triumph on her face. But even I was a bit worried about what she had planned for the baby. "You see, this child is my ticket. My ticket to making Sebastian trust me again.", "YOU LITTLE WITCH! IF YOU DON'T HAND MY DAUGHTER BACK...", Falsa was standing up. Desian stood up and moved her to the side. "You have one chance, then no matter what I think, I will kill you, Micka.", "What about our child? You'd kill that, too?". What was she talking about? When was she ever with Desian? I knew she couldn't have possibly been with him, and yet, Desian was hesitating. "You see, I put a lot of the puzzle together and concluded that everything that's happened to Bastian, must be the same for you. Meaning, you remember being with me. You remember when we made this child. You also remember what happened when I left you with Falsa. That's how this baby was made. You took over Bastian's conscience and forced this baby on him. Once he sees what you've done to it, he will forgive me for saving his child.". Falsa was staring at Desian with such anger, that I felt her eyes would burn a hole through his head. But he put his arm around Falsa and pulled her close, "What happened during that time, was not regrettable for me. It appears Micka, that you don't know what you want, and at this time I have become impatient. I don't want to harm the child you are growing, but I also will not stand here and allow you to take my other daughter. Caprius! Get the child from her.". I looked at him in disbelief. I didn't know what to do, and I knew that challenging Micka probably would not be the best thing. "Micka…just give the baby back. You said it yourself, Falsa won't hurt it.". Micka continued to stand still, with that same look on her face. "Caprius, if you don't get that child…", Desian snapped his fingers, and large daggers appeared from out of nowhere and pressed hard against Godrick's stomach. I could see some blood coming down and Godrick was looking at me pleadingly. "Micka, please, just stop! What could you gain? You really think Sebastian will just forget all the evil you've done?". Micka looked in Godrick's direction, and Godrick gave a curt nod that seemed forced and he grabbed one of the daggers and jammed it all the way in. "NO!". I rushed to him and held him as he lay dying. He grabbed my hand, and said, "I…will no longer be her puppet, neither should you…". Godrick died. He was staring at me as he went, and a small smile spread across his face. He was finally free. Free from the torture he's had to endure over the last seventeen years. I looked up in rage. Micka rushed forward and grabbed me. We were suddenly in a forest clearing. I recognized it to be right outside of Dasha. "What the hell did you do?", I asked Micka, who was still holding the baby. She handed the baby to me. "I just saved your life, and don't you ever forget that.". Then she disappeared again. Apparently, she knew exactly what mother's ring does. I looked around incredulously, and then I heard the cracking noise in the air and knew I had to hide from Desian. I took the baby into the bushes and hid. She had fallen asleep again. I didn't know what that green liquid did, but I had the feeling that it wasn't poison, so that's good. Now the next phase of everything was a bit jumbled. I thought about taking the baby to Sebastian, but then I thought about it again, and realized what I needed to do. We stayed hidden. Once I was sure Desian had gone back to Dasha to say he couldn't find us, I took the baby and ran as far as I could for as long as I could. Whatever I did, I wasn't going to allow her to be raised by the same woman that had raised me. If I had to, I would raise this baby myself. No matter what, I didn't want her to be a part of this. I wanted her free of gods and goddesses. I knew her life would never be normal, but it would be better without Falsa.

CHAPTER 14

Sebastian Goes Home

SEBASTIAN: Things had become more strained over the next few weeks in Kindy. There was a rumor that Micka was no longer in Dasha and nobody knew where she was. I thought perhaps Desian killed her, but some part of me, the part of me that could feel what was happening with Desian, told me that she was still alive somehow. Alisa had finally calmed down and was now returning to her tough self. She had even started sharing her room again with Sheena, who still didn't know why she was acting strange in the first place. Alisa was still very cautious around me. I believed that she thought that at any point, Desian could take control of me, so she stayed well away from me. Alex had finally started speaking with me again as well. Her hair had become black and the pink glow her skin used to have was completely gone, and now she was left with pale white skin. "Alisa isn't avoiding you...", Alex was explaining to me one day as we laid in the Kind Field, "...she has developed strong feelings towards you and to make them go away, she is keeping a certain distance.", "But she doesn't need to do that. I don't feel for her the way I feel for you.". Alex laughed, "It's funny, women want you, and you know almost nothing about their feelings.". I kissed her on her forehead, "Maybe not, but I do know that I love you.". Alex kissed me passionately, "And I love you, but there is something both I, and Alisa haven't told you yet.", "What is that?", I asked, trying to imagine what in the world could be so big a thing that they would keep it from me. "Well, both Alisa and I are carrying.". I sat up immediately, and Casian, who had been sleeping peacefully on my chest, fell off, growled, and then ran off. No doubt to go find Alexa. "I don't understand. You're both carrying? But…", I trailed off. My mind wandered to the child I already had in this world. The one I hadn't seen yet. I wondered what that child was like and if I would ever see it. There were also rumors stating Caprius had also gone missing, and that Godrick was dead. Penelope, upon hearing this news, wished to be alone for a while. When I found her, she was sitting in the garden of the castle. "You cared for him, didn't you?". She turned towards me with tears in her eyes, "I hated the man, when I first knew him. But over time, he became something much more than I could have ever hoped for. No, I didn't love him the way you might think, but we were very good friends. He defended me the best he could in the worst of moments. I am sad, because I lost a good friend. This planet has lost a good man.". She stood up and faced me with a smile, "I suppose I've overstayed and should be returning to Nasher with Oliver.", "Are you sure you don't need more time?", I asked, half hoping she would stay. It had finally occurred to me that even though I had lost Mom and Dad, my grandmother was still here. "No, I'm quite sure it's time for us to leave. But I leave you with these words; You can defeat Desian. I know it seems overbearingly frightening, but you will overcome this trial, and you will leave this planet, and we will be happy, knowing that once again, you are watching over us.", "But, what about my children?", I found myself asking. Penelope beamed, "To know that I have great-grandchildren is the best blessing I could ask for.". She kissed me on my forehead then took in my features, then smiled, and left the garden. Alexa was nearby playing with Casian. When she noticed I was there, she ran up to me, "Hi, Sebastian!", she shouted at me. "Hello, Alexa. How are you today?", "Well I'd feel better if I wasn't so darn angry with Alex. She hasn't spent any time with me lately. I want to know how her hair changed color!". Thinking about it, it was easy to see why Alex had been avoiding her. Alexa was only twelve, and she was very smart for her age. I spent a good amount of time in the garden with her and Casian. It wasn't until evening that Alex had come and found us. Alexa and Casian were both sleeping in the grass and I was just watching the sun set, trying to imagine how I could create something so beautiful. Alex came and fell on my chest. "Hello, you.", she said, kissing me. We laid there a bit longer and then decided to go ahead and pick up Alexa and Casian and take them to the chambers they had been staying in. On the way to mine and Alex's chamber, we ran into Queen Shay, "Your grandmother and King Oliver have departed. I was hoping to have a quick word with Alex.", she said, with a sort of somber tone in her voice. Alex looked at me a bit confused, but followed her anyway. When I entered our room, it was to find Sheena waiting for me, "We need to talk.". She was standing with her arms crossed and was giving me a sort of accusing look. "Alisa hasn't been the same since you all came out of the wood. Now I don't know what happened, but I deserve the right to know.". She sat on the bed, now looking up at me, and waiting for an answer. "Did you know she has been sick lately?". I swallowed, "No, I didn't know. Is she okay?", "I was hoping you'd tell me that answer.". I knew what she was asking, and I knew it wasn't my place to say. I stared at the ground, not knowing what or how to say the truth. Sheena was obviously getting impatient. "Look, you know something, and nobody will tell me anything, and I'm starting to get angry. I just want to know what is going on!". Alex returned, and next to her was Alisa. Alisa saw the scene and knew that she couldn't put it off any longer. She told the story of what happened in the cave. "That's what you didn't want to tell me…", Sheena said in a sad tone. She tried to hug Alisa, who put her hand up and said, "There is more. I'm…", she looked to Alex for support, who nodded for her to proceed, "…I'm carrying now.". Sheena sort of backed away. She gave me a look and I couldn't even look her in the eyes. She left the room and didn't say anything else. Alisa looked at me, then proceeded after her. Alex and I didn't say anything to each other. We got undressed and climbed into the bed. We laid there for some time, holding each other. Finally, Alex spoke, "It's not your fault, you know that, right?". I didn't answer. I didn't know how to say it wasn't. Even now, I could feel Desian in my head. He was with Falsa. They were lying in bed, and Falsa was crying, while Desian stroked her.

Suddenly, I was wide awake. Alex sat up with me. I jumped out the bed and started to pace. "What is it?", Alex asked, standing up, and wrapping her robe around her. "Desian, I just had a dream, or I don't think it was.". Alex was watching me with a confused look, "What are you talking about, Bastian?", "I saw Falsa and Desian. Falsa is upset about something. But, I don't know if it's true. I think Caprius took the baby.". Alex just watched me for a minute, then finally said, "If he did, it doesn't surprise me.", "But, it's mine! I want to see my child!". I didn't know where this feeling was coming from suddenly. For the longest after Falsa had her way with me, I didn't want to see that child at all. I had no interest. But now, somehow, I can sense she isn't with Falsa. Wait. How did I know it's a girl? What was happening? I fell to my knees and grabbed my head. "Sebastian, you're channeling Desian. You're thinking too much. His thoughts are infecting your mind.". I stood up and realized that me and Alex had to leave, "We can't stay here. We may be putting everyone in danger. We have to go.", "Okay, I know where we can go. We'll go to Alexandria.", "I've never been there. I don't want…". Alex cut me off, "You are the King of Alexandria, so we will go to your kingdom, and there we will wait.", "King? What are you talking about? I'm not a king, Alex.", "After everything that's happened, you still doubt yourself?". I thought about it, "Are you saying I'm king, because we're together, or because of something else I don't know?",

"To tell the truth, I don't really know, but you created Alexandria, and I think when you get there you'll see what I mean.". I decided it would be the best place to go. As we packed and gathered things, we had decided it best not to wake anyone, but almost as if she sensed it, Alisa was waiting by the exit. Two guards are always stationed at the exit and several others throughout the village at night. We were known as royal visitors, so most of the soldiers didn't find it strange that we were walking around at night. "Where are you two going?". She looked as if she had been crying and I could also see she was somewhat pale. "We're leaving, headed towards Alexandria. Alisa, it's for the best…", replied Alex. "For whom I wonder?", Alisa seemed to be growing angry, "So, you're just going to leave me here? No words of bye or anything? And you're leaving Alexa and Casian as well?", "They will be safer here. Bastian is dangerous to be around, so I'm taking him where he can't hurt anyone.". Alisa walked up to Alex and got in her face, "YOU KNOW WHY I DON'T WANT YOU TWO TO LEAVE!", she yelled at Alex. Alex just took a step back and answered calmly, "Alisa, I understand, but you have to see things from this point; If we stay, Desian will be able to see what we do through Sebastian, we just learned this now.". Alisa was still fuming but was starting to calm down somewhat, "How did you learn this?". Alex told the story. Alisa looked down trodden, "I don't want you to leave…but I understand the danger.". She hugged Alex and came to me. "I'm sorry, for everything.", she said, hugging me and…planting a kiss on my cheek. "I hope I get to see you again, Sebastian.", "Alisa, how is Sheena?", I felt compelled to ask. "She's sleeping. We will figure it out, Bastian, don't worry. It isn't your fault. Not really anyway.". She beamed at us, then told her soldiers to let us pass. On the outside, Tisiphone and Tig were already waiting for us. "Alisa woke us when she had a feeling you two might try something like this.", said Tig. "You don't have to come. It could be your lives.", I said. Both Tig and Tisiphone looked at one another, then, Tisiphone said, "Micka killed my father, I have nothing left to fight for, if I'm not fighting for you, Sebastian.", "And I can't believe I'm saying this, but I'd rather be fighting at your side then know that you're fighting and I'm just tending to hay.". It made me feel good to know there were people on my side. We all departed together.

As the first day away from Kindy was passing, Tisiphone and Alex had gotten ahead of me and Tig. "So, I heard a little something before we left. I heard that Alisa is carrying. I heard it's yours.". Tig had obviously been wanting to bring this up for some time. "You lucky dog, you. I thought she only liked women.", "Tig, the child she carries wasn't put into her willingly.". Tig became quiet for some time after this. The next time that he spoke, it was when we had all gathered around a fire to cook some meat off a bird that Tig and I had managed to catch. "You know, Bats, it's a bit weird you being a king. Do kings usually hunt turkey themselves? Or even sit around a fire? I just pictured you in your castle, sitting at your throne eating turkey.", "Well, you two just wait till you see my home. It's beautiful beyond description.", said Alex. "I personally can't wait. I've never left Dasha till now, and things have been amazing so far. Kindy was really pretty.", said Tisiphone, as she took a leg off the fire. We ate, laughed, and talked about our past. "So, there was this one time, Sebastian thought to steal some apples. I asked him, why would he want to steal what he already has at home? You'll never be able to guess what he told me.", "That it was all for the thrill.", said Alex, answering for Tig. "Well, actually, yes. How did you know?", "Because I told her this story.", I said, trying to contain my laughter. "Oh, well, I guess… Why didn't you mention that sooner?", "Because, you are an excellent storyteller.". We all laughed. Tig turned red. Tisiphone was looking at the ground. Tig was watching her. At one-point, Alex said, "Why don't you guys go collect some more wood for in the morning and let us ladies clean up?". So, Tig and I went on our way to go find wood. While we were walking, Tig finally explained what was going on between him and Tisiphone, "…you see, since Micka killed her first love, now she's afraid if she gives me a chance, there is a chance she will lose me as well. I keep trying to convince her, you must take chances. But she is so afraid of losing me.", "Has she said she wants to be with you? Or at least given you some kind of sign?", "Yes! Loads. She obviously is onto me, but she won't give us that chance. Sebastian, what should I do?". Considering that Tig never calls me by my full name, I knew he was dead serious. "Look, I can't make her choose you or force her, but at the same time, maybe all she needs is patience.", "Yeah, but you and Alex have something proper, mate. She doesn't even mind the whole, Alisa thing.". This was the second time Tig had brought this up and I wasn't annoyed by it. To be honest, I was worried. I left a pregnant Alisa. I was scared, but at the same time, Alex was carrying as well. I didn't know exactly what I was going to do, but the way my grandma had put it, was that I would return to Heaven. I didn't even know what that meant or where it was. I didn't respond to Tig after he had mentioned Alisa again, and so he asked me something else, "So, what are you going to do, Bats? I mean about this, Desian character. Is there any truth to what they are saying about him? Is he some kind of…monster?". I didn't know how to answer. "I heard he's…I don't know how to put it…he's you or something like that. Didn't make a lick of sense to me.". At this point, it was obvious that he just wanted to know. I haven't really explained because I was still learning myself. So, I told him about the cave in the Dark Wood and how me and Desian are connected. I told him why me and Alex decided to leave without telling anyone. Finally, Tig was speechless and didn't say another word. Most likely, he was totally scared out of his mind.

As we started to make our way back to camp, there was a low breathing sound. When we went to investigate, we found Caprius. He was sound asleep, and in his arms was…, "MY CHILD!", I realized I had shouted this. Caprius awoke and the baby started to cry. Impulsively, I picked her up and held her. She immediately stopped crying. Her eyes were so beautiful, they were an enticing crimson with the same gold markings me and Desian had around our eyes. She smiled, and I impulsively pulled her close. I held her close to my chest. She started to fall back to sleep. Caprius just looked at me, trying to determine what he should do. Finally, he held his arms out, "Give her back, Bastian, it's for her own good.", "WHO ARE YOU TO DECIDE WHAT'S GOOD FOR MY DAUGHTER?!", I yelled, having no idea why my blood was starting to boil. Then I thought about why, and realized right away, "Here...", I said, handing her over. As she left my hands, she started to reach back for me and cry, "...get her out of here! Desian knows you're here. GO!", Caprius took the baby and ran off, further into the forest. I looked at Tig, "You need to run now, too! Go! I'll meet with you guys later!". Tig took off towards the girls and I ran off in the other direction. I could hear a whistling noise above me, and then, as I looked up, I knew before I saw him. He landed right in front of me. I hated thinking about it, but it was kind of cool. "Where is she?", he asked, anger in his voice. I stood transfixed. I realized I wasn't scared of him anymore. "She's gone, and I'm going to make sure you never see my daughter.", "OUR daughter, you mean.", he said, moving closer to me. He reached his arm out and the god sword started to materialize in his hand. "There is no point to this fight, Bastian. We both want the same thing. Caprius has kidnapped our daughter, and we both want her to be safe.", "She's safe, where she is.", I said, trying to keep myself tough looking. I took the shield off my back and placed it in front of me. We stood staring at each other. Then he swung the sword, and once again I blocked it with the shield. There was once again a huge explosion, and we were blown apart. As we both climbed to our feet, Desian dropped the sword and punched me. I grabbed his fist before he could land another one and I punched him. We went back and forth for some time, until, finally, he put both hands in the air, "You know what? I'm done here. Keep the child hidden if you like. One day, I will have all my children together. This includes, Alisa's and Micka's.". I was lost, "Micka...she can't be...", "Oh, but she is, Bastian. She is carrying as well. Funny you didn't know till now. The little bitch used our child against me. She knew I wouldn't kill our child.". It was weird listening to him describe my situation, like it belonged to both of us, but then, of course, with the connection I felt with him, it made sense that he was feeling what I was. The sword flew to his hand, "The next time we meet, Bastian, I will kill you by absorbing you.", "You don't know how to do that, though, do you?", I asked, finally understanding. Falsa had told him to do so and he didn't. "You don't know how to merge with me. You have all those memories I can't remember, but you don't know how to merge and become one with me. That's why you haven't done it yet!". Desian looked livid, "THAT DOESN'T MATTER! I WILL LEARN!", he shouted. "Well, I have a feeling I'll learn before you do, then I'll truly take over YOUR mind. Perhaps, even get my memories back.". At this, Desian swung the sword at me again but I had left the shield on the ground. I put my hands up to block and when the sword connected, something strange happened.

I was in a strange cell I'd never seen. I looked around me and nobody was there. I saw a strange light at the end of a hallway and out of the light came a man wearing what looked like royal robes. He stood in front of my cell. "So, I'm only going to ask you one time, and one time only. Are you telling the truth?". I didn't know how to answer this. I didn't even know what he was referring to. I opened my mouth to answer, and just as I did, a beautiful woman came in. She, too, was wearing a royal robe. "Has he answered you? Has he said anything about who he is?", "No… Now he's suddenly quiet. Where is all that loud boasting you were doing? You said you were our god, yet you sit here in this cell, looking like a man who has lost. God wouldn't look like a man who has lost, don't you agree, dear?". The woman nodded. Just then, the light at the end of the hallway shined again, and this time, the unmistakable sound of battle was flowing into the dungeon. The king and queen ran off. Soon, another man was standing in front of my cell. A familiar looking man. It was Prince Lab. "ARE YOU OKAY, MY LORD?!". As he asked me this, I looked down at my body and realized I was covered in scars. Recent ones, because the blood was still fresh. Lab opened my cell and put my arm around his neck. None of this was making any sense. He carried me out of the dungeons, and I saw that we were in Nasher. Interestingly, there were a lot of differences. Things looked sort of newer. At the same time, there was this overwhelming feeling of dread I had felt. I didn't know where this feeling was coming from. As Lab carried me, I looked around and there were people fighting all over. We were in the middle of a battlefield. Somehow, I was in the past. It took me some time to finally work that out. I tried to figure out just where in the past I was, when another familiar face popped up. "You've got our Lord? Excellent!". The familiar face was a man who looked somewhat like my father. Then as I was being pulled into a small cottage, there were people inside who had taken a very bad beating, and were being patched up. This was an infirmary. "LOOK AT THE STATE OF HIM!", I heard someone yell. Just then, the door was ripped open, and more soldiers came in. The men inside tried to fight but were quickly subdued. Once the men had been captured or killed, I had been taken again. This time, a man was standing before me that looked somewhat like he could be related to Caprius. He had the same smug face and was wearing purple royal robes. "THIS IMPOSTER, CLAIMS TO BE OUR CREATOR! NOW I DON'T KNOW FOR ALL OF YOU, BUT I FEEL THAT I SPEAK FOR ALL OF PLINTH WHEN I SAY, THIS BLASPHEMY CANNOT CONTINUE!". There were shouts and applause at this. I felt someone behind me. When I turned to see who it was, the man's face was covered, and he wielded a huge sword. It reminded me of the one Tisiphone carried. It didn't take much deduction to realize I was being executed. This was five-hundred years ago. I looked around and saw that the castle was barely being built and that all the people seemed to be more unorderly. "...SO, I SAY WE KILL THIS BLASPHEMER, AND BE DONE WITH IT! EXECUTIONER, PLEASE!". The last thing I remembered seeing...was the man who looked somewhat like my father in tears. I realized this must be one of his ancestors. The sword entered my back and I was ripped from my body. I was flowing through the stars and then I saw the most beautiful thing I ever saw, but was suddenly jaunted into my present.

Desian had somehow become frozen and was halted in mid-air holding my sword. Micka was standing next to him transfixed, but then noticed I was looking at her. She was indeed carrying. Unlike Alisa, she was way more noticeable. "What have you done to him?", she asked me. "Nothing, I don't even know what happened.". She touched him, and he started to unfreeze. "Uh-oh, time to go.". She gave me one look and then she disappeared right in front of me. I didn't have time to process how she gained this ability, because Desian had already awakened. "What the hell did you do…?", he asked weakly. I had somehow drained him, and in the process, gained a memory. Desian looked for the first time, not so confident. He gave me an angry look, then flew into the air. I waited till he flew far away to go and meet the others. When I found Alex, Tig, and Tisiphone, they were all waiting for me to return. Alex ran up to me and wrapped her arms around me. Before she could ask me what happened, I started to tell them everything. Alex was in such a state of shock that she had become very quiet for some time, deep in thought. Tig was just waiting for more. Tisiphone was sitting with a sort of angry look on her face, "Why didn't you kill Micka? She was right there in front of you!", "It wasn't that simple. She disappeared as soon as Desian started to awake.", "Yes, but you had the time!", she yelled, starting to stand. "Listen, I know you're angry about your father, but I couldn't kill her, even if I really wanted to.", "WHY?!", she exclaimed. I hesitated a bit with my answer, "Because she is carrying my child as well.". Tig dropped his turkey leg, and Alex looked up. "I had a feeling. This is not a good thing. My child, Falsa's, Alisa's, and Micka's all have god blood in them. But purer because it's yours.". At this point, whenever Alex said stuff like this, I just nodded and acted like I understood. I totally didn't. I mean, what the hell? Last year, I was barely a kid myself, and now, I've got one child in the world, and three others on the way? Plus, they'll be different? I couldn't believe most of this. For a while, I just wanted to be alone. I walked through the woods, thinking. Once again, I ran into Micka. She was just sitting down, watching me from a stump. “Well, let’s try this again.”, she said, and she reached up and was showing me something. It was a ring with a green stone on top of it. “What is that?”, I asked, trying to contain the urge to choke her to death. “It is the one thing that will save you from Desian. Something to help your transition.”. She stood up and walked towards me. I took a step back and a small twinge passed over her face, “There was a time when you loved me. Do you remember that time, Bastian? Now I carry our child. Don’t you care about that?”, “Sure, I care about my child. Not so much the witch that carries it.”. At these words, Micka looked dreadfully hurt, “Bastian, I can’t ask you to forgive me, but I need you to trust me. This ring will save you. You need this. Take it, please.”. I took the ring out of her hand and immediately the same thing I felt earlier was now creeping up on me again. The feeling of being transported somewhere else.

I awoke with a start and found myself in a strange place. Outside, were what appeared to be rocks, but they were floating past at incredible speeds. As I looked around, taking everything in, I saw that I was inside of a palace the likes of which could only be described as the size of Plinth. All around was gold, but I didn’t feel weakened by it. There was a strange noise, sort of like a buzzing sound. I started to move through this strange place. The gold all around was surrounded by a milky white substance. When I touched it, it felt sort of slimy, but it didn’t get onto my hands. There were strange contraptions making noises and puffing smoke. There were five globes in the center of the area. I went and looked at them. In one, I could see a strange green colored man playing with his children. The one next to it showed a woman who was holding what appeared to be a dead body. She was crying over it. The things in the globe gave me the suggestion that this wasn’t happening on Plinth. The next one was even more strange, as it was blank and not showing any picture. The fourth one had children playing in a field of flowers. One of the children looked almost directly at me and waved. I waved back, and the child positively beamed and continued playing. Next to this one was the last globe, which was split into two different screens. On one, I saw Desian. He was by himself in the woods near Dasha, walking. He was obviously deep in thought. On the other half, I saw myself. Standing in the same place, watching the globes. Where in the world was I? As I continued to stare at the globe, I had this strange feeling I was being watched. I turned and saw a man who looked a lot like me. He was decked out in diamond encrusted armor and was just watching me with great interest. "I wondered which of you would be the first to get here. Should have known it would be you.". He walked towards me and the buzzing noise I had been hearing was getting louder. Images were popping in my head, but I didn't understand them. "Just relax, it'll all settle in.". I tried to relax, but I was not settling in. Somewhere in the distance, I could hear my name being called. But now, all I could focus on was this guy in front of me. The images started to slow, and I found myself sitting in a comfortable chair. I felt like I could melt into the cushion. "Are you ready to talk?", the man asked me. "Yes.", I answered without thinking. "You...are the part of me that I value the most. The part of me that loves, cares, and over all, wants everyone to live their lives for others. Desian only wants one thing; Payback. He doesn't care who he hurts in the process. But he IS you. Ultimately, he wants the same things, but believes his way of achieving it is the best way. He would cast the world into darkness to suit his own needs.". I was listening but still didn't understand. "Where am I?". The man looked at me with a certain, 'isn't it obvious?', sort of glance. "This is our home. This is Heaven.". I took in my surroundings more and couldn't believe it. When I looked out of the window again, I saw gigantic rocks circling around a giant glowing orb. "What is that thing out there?". The man was looking highly amused. "I didn't realize I'd be this much of a child.", he said with a laugh, "The things you see out there are the stars and the planets.", "Planets? You mean like Plinth?". I looked out the window again, and saw that the giant rocks were far apart from one another. I imagined being on one of them and what things would look like from far away. “This is the most amazing thing I’ve ever seen.”, “This is where you and Alex will live once this war is over. You’ll see your other creations. Plinth isn’t the only one.”, “So, I WAS viewing other worlds!”, I found myself shouting. “Yes. They are your children as well. Not in the sense of what you’re thinking.”. I was thinking about my three children who have not been born yet. “So, what am I supposed to do? How am I supposed to defeat Desian?”, “You have all the answers here, but you aren’t seeking them. You must think carefully about what you want.”. I closed my eyes, and then I saw something familiar. Something that I hadn’t seen in a long time. The dream I used to have. The nightmare was before me. Suddenly it dawned on me. This was me and Desian. I found myself ripped apart. I found myself being reborn again. There was something else as well. Desian was alive. He was in that cave. The Dark Wood was his prison. He lived there, trapped in a form he couldn’t control. But somehow, he managed to call to something greater than even us. The goddesses. I watched as they would come and die. It took some time to realize they were dying of misery. Because they never found the god they were sent here for. Five-hundred years passed, and Falta finally arrived. I watched as she grew up in Alexandria. Watched, as her curiosity made her leave. Watched as she campaigned around Plinth. Watched, as Penelope, and the rest, murdered her the same way I had been killed. I watched as Penelope was possessed to bring her body to the Dark Wood. Watched, as Desian resurrected her, and she took on the same look Alex has now of black hair and pale skin. As if she too had lost a great power. I watched her abandon my grandmother to her hell of seventeen years. Watched as Godrick, too, was lured into the cave. Watched as Desian was created. I watched him grow up. Never able to leave the cave because he needed me to get closer. I came to realize, this was all planned out by Desian. But even though he planned all this, he didn’t know certain things. I could see now what I had to do. Because now, I did know. I knew way more. I watched the globe again, showing me and Desian. Desian was returning to Dasha, but still looked unsure of the situation. Falsa was standing outside of the gates, waiting for him. I saw him slap her and walk past. I watched him, as he made his way to the throne room and sat there. He was obviously thinking about what just happened. Trying to put it all together. Desian had the mind of a being who has lived many centuries, and yet was outsmarted by a seventeen year old boy. I could feel his anger. I watched as Falsa came to him and tried to comfort him. He grabbed her by her hair and stood up. He then led her to the balcony. I could hear what he was yelling, "HERE IS YOUR WOULD-BE QUEEN PEOPLE OF DASHA! THE ONE WHO DIDN'T GIVE A SHIT ABOUT YOU OR YOUR LOVED ONES! WHAT HAPPENS NEXT, IS ON HER!". He lifted her into the air. "DESIAN, PLEASE!? I'M SORRY! I JUST WANT MY DAUGHTER! PLEASE?!", Falsa was pleading. It was a sickening sight. Although I didn't like Falsa, seeing her suffer at Desian's hands like this was painful. He lunged her off the balcony. I yelled. She landed, but she didn't land on the ground. She landed in my arms. Confused as to how I got here, I looked up and saw an angry Desian looking down on me.

CHAPTER 15

Alisa Meets Amana

SEBASTIAN: I stared around me, and the crowd was watching me and Desian with the interest of wolves circling prey. Desian floated down from the balcony and landed right in front of me. Falsa, climbed from my arms and looked frightful. She then ran away, tears falling from her face. "You. I am so tired of YOU.", Desian said to me, as I was still trying to figure out how I got here. He raised his fist and swung at me. The hit connected on my chin and I flew back a good seven feet. The crowd was dispersing. Some were running into their homes, while others were licking their lips and howling. One old gentleman, who I slightly recognized, came up to Desian, bowing, and handing him a blade. "Thank you, Fod. Now, let's see if a regular blade will work, since attacking you with the sword doesn't.". Desian came at me with a blade that I knew right away wasn't going to work. He swung it down on me and it shattered into pieces. "NO!", he yelled, unable to contain his anger. He lunged at me and we struggled. Finally, he stood up. The crowd that had stayed to watch were now eyeing Desian with pity. When he realized this, he lunged at the crowd with the god sword. One swing and he killed ten people that had been standing behind us. "YOU MURDERER!", I yelled, as I lunged forward to stop him. I wrapped my arms around him to stop him from hurting anyone else, "RUN!", I shouted, and the people listened. Desian was squirming in my arms to get free. I could feel him starting to drain energy. He flew into the air, me holding onto him. We flew so high, that I recalled asking myself what it would be like to be on a different planet. "Go ahead. Keep holding on, Sebastian.". Desian was trying to go higher, but I could feel him falter. This was his limit. I had no idea how high up we were. He grabbed me with one arm and held me in the air. "I've hated you since you were born! Now I must deal with this! Why couldn't you have just let me rule?! You don't know how to rule a planet! You're just a stupid BOY!", "No, actually, I'm you.". As I said this, the shield somehow materialized in my hand, and I uppercutted Desian. He dropped me. I felt myself falling. I didn't know what would happen when I landed. But I was looking forward to the next time me and Desian met.

ALISA: "Alisa, I'm going to the garden with Alexa and Casian.", Sheena was telling me. Despite what I had said prior to Sebastian and Alex's departure, I still couldn't stop thinking about Bastian. Even at night, I would have dreams about what happened in the cave. In the dreams, Sebastian would come to me and I would gladly remove my coverings and make love to him. Every time I had this dream, I would wake up in a cold sweat, with regret and shame on my mind. Sheena had gotten so tired of my behavior, that she wouldn't even talk to me. She would only tell me what she was going to do. One night I had called out Bastian's name and Sheena had left the room angry. That next morning, we argued so loud that my parents had to come in and separate us. I felt so bad for what I was putting Sheena through, but it was Desian. He did this to me. But somehow...I could sense it wasn't fully his fault, either. And now, I was going to have a baby. My parents were overjoyed. This, of course, only made Sheena angrier. Then, one day, one of my messengers returned with a strange message. "Queen Micka has returned to Dasha, and Desian and Falsa are long gone.", "How did this happen?", Sheena asked, as I just listened. "Well, Desian was going to kill Falsa, then out of nowhere, Sir Sebastian appeared. Last we saw, Desian flew off with him and never came back.", "I need you to go find Sebastian.", I said, getting to my feet. I was feeling the baby inside of me. At times, I would still get sick, but at other times, I just felt completely nauseous. The man nodded and went on his way. Then, some other visitors I wasn't expecting arrived, "Tig? Tisiphone? What are you doing here? You're supposed to be with Bastian and Alex!", I exclaimed, looking them over in disbelief. But looking again at their faces, I saw that both had been crying. Tisiphone came up to me and placed her face in my chest, "HE'S DEAD! SEBASTIAN IS DEAD!". I felt there had to be some kind of mistake, "HOW?! He can't be!". Tig looked me in the eye and told me how they were all sitting and waiting for him, but he never came back. Told me he had some kind of encounter with Desian and Micka, and that when he had walked off, he wanted to be alone. The next thing they knew, something landed from out of the sky. When they went to investigate, it was to find a bloody mess in a crater. Upon looking closer, it was Bastian. They checked to see if he was breathing, but there was no breath. "Well, if this is true, then where is Alex?". They both looked worryingly at each other before Tig replied, "She's gone after Desian herself. She was so broken and angry, I didn't know what to say. I tried to stop her but...", "BUT WHAT?! YOU WERE TOO WEAK TO STOP HER?!", I yelled. "Well actually, yes. I tried to grab her, and she threw me. I hit a tree.". Tig turned around to show me where his head and the tree connected. Being that I had been on the receiving end of Alex's wrath as well, I knew I couldn't hold this against him. I turned to look at Sheena, who was lost for words. She kept opening her mouth and closing it. "What do you think we should do? How do we move forward if Sebastian is dead?", Sheena asked. "I need some time to think about this.". I walked away from everyone and proceeded to the garden.

Sitting there, I started to remember when I had first met Bastian. I thought about how I'd never see him again. Or even get the chance to really tell him how I saw him. I felt my eyes burn. He was always innocent. Sure, he killed, but just to protect innocents, right? He was lost after he lost his parents. But the strength in which he made it this far, fighting against something as impossible as Desian, is tribute enough for him. As I found myself crying into my hands, I remembered that time in the cave. How it felt to have him inside of me. I caressed myself. I looked up and tried to scream, but couldn't. Desian was in front of me. He held out his hand and I found myself rooted to the spot. "Where is he? You're hiding him here! I know it!". Desian looked confused. Mad even. And was staring at me with a face of such screwed up anger, I was afraid of what he'd do if I answered wrong. "HE'S DEAD! YOU KILLED HIM!". He backed away and started to laugh, "He is not dead. I would know if he was dead. But I can see you don't know. Which means I have no reason now, to keep you alive.". He swung the blade down and right when he did, I felt no pain, and a bright light had engulfed me. Desian began to shout. Suddenly, I was in a different place.

I had no idea where I was. I looked around and saw Alexandrian memory sheets all over the walls in what appeared to be frames. They contained a young woman who looked just like…, "Yes, the resemblance is very uncanny.". I turned around and saw a woman. She had flaming red hair like myself. Her face was a lot like my mother's but she had a gash across the right side of her face, and she had Sebastian's eyes. Except where there was silver in Sebastian's eyes, there was a red line with the golden center. She wore a leather outfit that looked like it may be military. She watched me with a kind of reminiscent look on her face. "Who...?", "I am Amana Tia. And yes, I am indeed your daughter.". I just stood there. How could I be talking to my daughter? It made no sense. "MY daughter hasn't been born yet, so I don't know who you are, but you can't possibly be...", the woman moved towards me and grabbed my hand. She placed it on her face. The feeling of her face was very soft. She looked me in the eyes and I saw, "You are my child.". I fell back onto a seat. She continued watching me. "I called you here for a very important reason. Soon, you will meet the girl in that picture. I need you to give her a message.". I was still taking everything in. I looked out the window and saw buildings that rose higher than castle turrets into the air, a lot of them. I saw down below, people moving about, their clothing was different. "Where am I?". Amana looked like she wasn't too sure on how to answer this question. But she took a deep breath, and answered, "The future, three-thousand years from your time.". I felt my jaw drop but couldn't find the strength to pick it back up. "But, but, but...", I sputtered. I looked around more and saw that there were contraptions I'd never seen before. One square item that I was highly interested in, turned on by itself. I screamed, and Amana reached underneath me and took something that she pointed at the strange mirror and cut it off. "Relax, you only accidentally sat on the remote.". I didn't know what to think. Everything was completely different, and the only thing keeping me sane, was the girl who looked a lot like my mother sitting across from me, watching me. She looked half amused and was trying to find the words to speak to me. "I get it, coming and seeing this much of the future can be overwhelming. You aren't the first time-traveler. But what I will tell you is this, you will meet Emillie. When you meet her, you must convince her that she doesn't have to move on. That she can come back. That...", she looked somewhat downtrodden, "...I need her. We need her. Please. You have to tell her this, Mom.". I flinched some when she called me mom. But as I looked at her, "You've lost somebody.". I could see it in her face. It was easy to spot, considering that we had just lost Sebastian. "Yes, I lost you. A long time ago. Many years ago. But

I had to call you here. I knew I probably shouldn't, and I know it makes me a hypocrite, but…", "You don't have to explain yourself. You needed your mother. I get it. For a long time, I hated mine, but now I know the truth, I've never been happier to have my mother.". Amana smiled a sad smile, "Listen, you and I will have a lot of time together. We will also have another war, but don't worry about that one. I'll take care of it.", "What do you mean…?", "Like I said, don't worry about that war. I will handle it. In the meantime, it's probably a good idea to send you back.", "Wait! If this is the future, what happens to Desian?". I knew I had to ask. After all, where I just came from, Sebastian is dead. Even though Desian said he wasn't, he didn't seem so sure. "Desian? You mean Father?". Hearing her refer to Desian as father, was even more scary. "Oh! I know what you mean. Of course. Well don't worry too much. Something good will happen. I can't tell you too much, I'm sure you understand.". I didn't understand. "It's time. I love you, Mother.". I woke up and found myself on the ground.

Desian was standing over me, unable to move from the looks of things. I rushed off the ground and looked into his eyes. Just as I was moving away from him, Alex came from behind me and tried to stab Desian, who at that moment was able to move and flew away. "COME BACK, COWARD! COME BACK HERE!", Alex yelled, running after him. "Alex, he's gone. Just come back.". Alex looked hurt and angry. Tears were running down her pretty face. "I just want…", she started to say, but she trailed off and fell to the ground crying. "Alex, is Sebastian truly gone?". Alex looked up at me and nodded. "I saw him. I can't…", she got up and ran away. I knew I should go after her, but I couldn't find the strength. My legs had become frozen. Then I remembered my daughter. I thought about if I should tell Alex what she said. I knew if Bastian was really dead, then this war was over and Desian had won. But if somehow my daughter was right, we were going to win anyway. Tig, Tisiphone, and Sheena came out of the castle. "Did you see Alex? Where did she get to?", asked Tisiphone. I pointed in the direction she ran. Sheena noticed I was sort of shaken and came to me. She placed her hand on my shoulder and asked, "What's happened to you? Is it Bastian?". I told Sheena about meeting my daughter. "But, how? She isn't even born? Are you sure it wasn't just some trick Desian played?". I thought about this and had already made up my mind, "If it were, he would have just killed me. No, I think I really met my daughter. I think that the future of this planet is set. Desian won't win. I'm sure that somehow, it was Bastian who saved me.", "But he's dead. Alex saw with her own eyes!", "But we don't really know! I mean he's our god! We don't know that he truly died. Look, all I'm saying is, I saw the future. I don't think that the world would have been what I saw, if Desian won this war!". Sheena nodded, "Listen, I'm sorry for how I've been. I should have tried to understand more. The truth is, at this point, I just want us to move on. If you can.". I nodded. In truth, I wanted nothing more, but first, I had to make Desian pay. That was the second time he made me feel weak. I was sick of it. Alex had returned, "We need to have a meeting.". We went to the meeting room inside the castle. Me, Alex, Tig, Sheena, and Tisiphone, all sat around a huge round table. I told them what happened when Desian attacked me. Alex, who was deep in thought once I finished, was the first to speak up, "I have a theory. Your daughter sensed your danger and saved you. Even if it was a different moment in time, she was able to sense her own danger. Therefore, she was able to save you.". This theory didn't make sense. And it had holes. "Well, I don't think so, Alex. It didn't feel coincidental. More like right on the spot, something knew to put me there. I think…", I hesitated before answering, "…it was Bastian.". This had the exact reaction I imagined. Alex gave a yell, Tisiphone put her face in her hands. Tig threw up. Sheena was supportive and nodded. "WE SAW HIM DEAD!", yelled Alex, as tears started reforming in her eyes. Just then, at that moment, Caprius joined us, "Sorry, I've only arrived. I've heard about Bastian.". He was holding Falsa and Bastian's child, who was sound asleep in his arms. "Listen, I know things seem bleak, but there is a way to defeat Desian.". We all became quiet. "And how is that?", asked Tisiphone, who still had a hard spot when it came to Caprius. "Well, Micka tried to give this to Bastian.". He held up a ring that had a strange green glowing stone that reminded me of the revealer flowers from the Dark Wood. Alex's jaw dropped. "This is why he is dead!", I didn't understand. Caprius looked confused. "What do you mean? How is this the reason that Bastian is dead?", asked Tig. "Well, for one, this ring would have opened him up for Desian.", "Funny, Micka claimed it does the complete opposite. She said it would help him control Desian. So, which is it?". A part of me had come to accept that Alex doesn't always know. I'm sure that whatever she had been told about this ring, had most likely been a lie. Which brought up another question, "Alex, where did you learn what this ring would do?", "Lab…", she started to say, then she realized what I was thinking, "You might be right, Alisa. Perhaps this was a lie. But even so, we can't put that ring on Sebastian if he is dead.", "Well, we need to figure out what we are going to do, because Desian is getting bolder if he came here to kill Alisa!", shouted Caprius, "If this rage that he is casting continues, Plinth will go down.". This was true, and with Bastian gone, there was no theory of defeating Desian.

I tried to remember everything Amana had told me over the next couple of days. Fear was spreading throughout the land. Desian was terrorizing everyone trying to find Bastian. He just wouldn't accept that he was dead. Rumors were that he had already killed several people and was now headed towards Nasher. Out of the fear I felt, I sent Tig, Tisiphone, and Sheena with a clutch of soldiers, to try and stop him. Alex volunteered, but I said I needed her here. "Alex, we have to figure this out. We can't let this situation continue.". Micka, who was the last person I had expected to see, showed up four days after Sheena and the group had left. "What are you doing here?", I asked her. She looked like she was ready to spit her baby out. "Well, considering that Desian is just killing people for fun at this point, I think we need to come together, don't you?", "WE, are trying to figure out how to stop him. We don't need your help.", "Are you quite sure of that? I believe you believe Bastian is dead. Well what if I told you I know where he is, and he isn't dead.", I hesitated. The thought of seeing Bastian again was such a joyous feeling. Remembering who's telling me where to find him, immediately doused my hopes. "Where is he?", "He's here in this room with us. He asked that I come here. He told me to give Caprius the ring. And he told me what to do after.", "And when did he tell you all this?". I felt my blood starting to boil. Now I knew how Alex felt when I said that Bastian saved me. "No...you don't get it. Let me help you see...", she started to walk towards me with her hand outstretched. When she touched me, I saw two things behind her. They weren't easy to make out at first. But it was Wilson. The other figure was too phased out for me to see who he was. When Micka took her hand from me, I realized that she wasn't crazy. She truly was being guided. We couldn't see it, though. "Do you see now? I'm telling the truth. Bastian is here, and he's telling me to tell you to trust me. The ring will work.". I looked at the ring sitting on the table. I went and picked it up. There was a certain energy around it, but other than that, I didn't fully understand. When I turned around to ask Micka what was going on, she was gone. I pondered over the ring. I kept asking myself, what I was supposed to do with it? Bastian's body had finally made it here. When I went and looked, it was the most horrible thing to see. Sebastian's body was all mangled and broken. The look on his face was one of peace. He seemed to be smiling. I couldn't imagine what he was smiling about. How damaged he was, the blood all over... I just wanted to hear him say my name. I placed my face on his chest, not caring about the blood. There was no heartbeat. He truly was dead. I cried softly into his chest.

CHAPTER 16

Falsa's Sacrifice

MICKA: It had finally dawned on me that I didn't need everyone else's forgiveness, I had Bastian's forgiveness. Wilson was with me all the time. Telling me what I should do. When Bastian's ghost first appeared, I thought Desian was playing a trick on me. Then, Bastian told me he was dead, but not really. I didn't know what that meant at first, until I saw it. The shield that Bastian had left behind. It took a lot out of me to do what I knew I needed to do, but with him gone, Alex was the only one who could possibly defeat Desian. Sure, he was strong, but he was getting weaker. This was obvious based on the fact that he was on his murderous rampage. Just using the excuse he can't find Sebastian to kill as many Plinthinians as he can. When Alex entered the garden in Kindy, I came up from behind her. Bastian was telling me in my head, because he couldn't speak to me like Wilson, that I had to act this way. Alex didn't like me, and most likely would kill me on sight. Funny how so long ago I hated her. She turned around, surprised by my presence, but none the less, gaped at the shield. I handed it to her. She looked at it admiringly. Feeling my job was done, I departed back to Dasha. I materialized into the throne room and found Desian waiting for me. "Tell me, Micka, where is he?". I hesitated. Although Wilson and Bastian were here, they weren't physically here and could not protect me from Desian. "TELL ME WHERE THE HELL HE IS!". I felt terrified, but then remembered something, "YOU WON'T KILL YOUR CHILD!", "I don't need to kill my child, I have other ways of hurting you.". He raised his hand and I felt pain in my brain, so violent, I fell to the floor. I could feel myself shaking and sweating. When the pain stopped, Desian was stroking my face, "Now, tell me where he is, and I don't want to hear he's dead. If you don't start telling me, I will destroy Dasha. Do you understand that?". Dasha wasn't my home. It was given to me by Falsa. Falsa, who chose this moment to spring into action. She dashed into the throne room and gave Desian a sharp blow that made him hit the wall. "COME NOW, GIRL, WE HAVE TO LEAVE!". Falsa held out her hand for me, but soon, the blade had pierced her. "FALSA!", I screamed. Desian, seeing the pain in my face, twisted the blade, making more blood squirt out. I fell next to her and looked up pleadingly. He removed the blade. "This is only the beginning. Tell me where the hell my other half is.", "YOU SHOULD KNOW!", "ALL I KNOW IS HE ISN'T DEAD!", Desian yelled madly. He flew out of the throne room. I held the bleeding, dying Falsa in my arms. "He...he's going...going to kill...", she was sputtering but couldn't finish her sentence. "Sorry...Micka. Sorry for...father.". she died. The life had left her eyes. She turned into black liquid and dissolved. I laid there for some time, mourning over a woman a large part of me hated, yet she called me her daughter and hardly ever once did she betray me. And she apologized for my father. Desian had taken something from me I had never known, he had taken my mother. I picked up a sword and rushed outside to what can only be described as a massacre. This day will forever be marked the Dasha Massacre. People were being thrown from the buildings, and some were stabbing themselves. Desian was killing anyone he saw. His eyes had this strange glow, and I realized he was controlling everyone. "DESIAN, STOP THIS! PLEASE?!", "TOO LATE!". I tried to swing the sword at him, but he was deflecting all my attempts. The baby was weighing me down. Then, as if on cue, Alex arrived. I had no idea how she got here or where she came from, but she hit Desian with the shield and they began to clash. I watched as god, fought, goddess. Eventually, Alex overpowered him, and he fled. People all around were coming to and realizing what they had done. The time had come finally. I had seen enough. Desian was the worst thing to happen to Plinth. "How did you get here? I left you all the way in Kindy. Do you have one of these?", I asked, holding up the ring Falsa had given me. "The shield. It brought me here.". I realized it was probably always capable of this, but Sebastian never knew. "So, what are you going to do now?", I asked Alex. "Now, I'm going after him. This is going to end. Now.".

CHAPTER 17

The Final Battle

TISIPHONE: It was quiet when we arrived in Nasher. Everything seemed to be the same everywhere. Tension filling the air all over Plinth. Nasher was being remodeled from the look of things, and everywhere you looked, children were somber and there were sad faces. Tig had seen his parents and had gone to them. Sheena and I had stationed soldiers on the outside, while we went up to the castle to check up on Oliver and Penelope. Penelope was first to greet us. She informed us that Oliver wasn't feeling well at the moment. When we had told her about Desian trying to kill Alisa, Penelope put her face in her hands. We were careful not to mention Sebastian, but of course, that was foolish. "Where is my grandson? Surely he put a stop to it.". We looked at each other. I couldn't help myself. I started to cry almost immediately. "What has happened?", she asked, getting to her feet. "Desian has killed Sebastian. But he is going around trying to find him. His body should be in the kingdom of Kindy now, mam.", said Sheena. Penelope just stood frozen. Then she replied, "If, Desian believes he is not dead, then truly he must be alive.". She walked away after she said this. We remained in Nasher for the next three days. Then, Alex turned up with Bastian's shield. "This is it! I'm going after him once and for all! He must die!", Alex was saying, as she riled up a group of soldiers, "...he will kill your families, he will destroy everything you know! He's already taken one person from this world that I loved, I will lose no one else!". The soldiers were cheering her on. "I never knew she had that kind of ability. She usually kept to herself. I have to admit, I like this Alex.", Sheena was saying, as we listened to her speech. Then, there was a loud scream. Looking in the direction of the scream, there was a skeletal looking body. It was stabbing people with a sword and making its way through the crowd. "Oy!", yelled Sheena, as she rushed into the crowd. I looked up and saw Desian flying towards the castle. As I headed that way, more undead soldiers appeared. Some of the undead appeared to be regular villagers. One I recognized as a bandit, "JAKE!". Jake waddled towards me, eyes looking in every direction. He slashed his sword without aiming it and I had seen enough. I stabbed him through the heart. But he was still alive. I noticed Sheena too was having trouble, "They won't stay down!", she yelled. Tig had joined the fray but got overrun quickly. "TIG!", I found myself yelling, as I rushed to his aid without thinking. I jumped into the hoard, swinging my blade. I finally had cleared enough of them to pull Tig from their clutches. "I knew you cared.". Annoyed, I took his hand and tried to head towards the castle, but more undead blocked our way. Suddenly, I realized they were everywhere. They were attacking villagers and anything that was just there. No matter how much we fought them, they seemed to not want to go down. I looked and saw Alex headed towards the castle.

ALEX: I ran into the castle. First thing I saw was a dead Oliver. His head had been twisted. Then I saw Penelope, gasping, her neck in Desian's hands. "You may have birthed me, but I was alive way before I created this vessel. Now I know you are hiding Sebastian, so bring him HERE!", "LET HER GO!", I yelled. Desian dropped her and

I rushed forward. "Alex, you of all people cannot defeat me! So why don't you…?", before he could finish his sentence, I had slashed open his face with the shield. He looked up at me and grabbed my throat. "Now, Alex, I am going to…", but whatever he was going to do never happened. He burned the moment he touched me. He dropped me, backing away, somewhat frightened, "TRINITY?!", he shouted, and he flew away again. I rushed outside to see the army of undead that he had brought along with him were following him out of Nasher. I went back into the village. It was horrible. There were dead people in the streets, and a large number of people looking for lost loved ones. As I made my way through the crowd, I found Sheena and a clutch of Kindy soldiers. I also found Tig and Tisiphone. Tig had a large cut on his side that a nearby doctor was patching up, while Tisiphone kissed him all over his face, "I promise if you live, I will make love to you every day! Just please say something!". Tig was still bleeding pretty badly but managed to say, "…promise?". As I looked around, anger like never before was settling over me. I knew that I had to hurry after Desian. I started to think about where he might be headed now and found myself in Kindy. I had appeared right next to Alisa in the Kind Field. When she noticed I was here, she said, "Remember this place was Bastian's favorite place? He would just sit out here and think for large amounts of time. I know, he was only depressed after what Falsa did to him, but he was such a good person. I hate that I didn't see that until it was too late.", she said, her voice starting to crack. She looked at me, with her flaming red hair covering parts of her face, "Alex, what are we going to do?", she asked me helplessly. I told her about how Desian had attacked Dasha and killed Falsa. "So, Falsa gave her life for Micka's? I can't believe it. What is Micka doing now?", "I'm here to help fight.". Micka was standing next to me. She had Falsa's ring, but was in no condition to fight. "Micka, I think you need to sit this one out. You, too, Alisa. Let me handle it.", "You're carrying the same as us. Why should you be allowed to fight?", Micka asked me with a face full of tears. "Because I'm not Plinthinian. I'm a goddess.". They both considered this for a minute, then nodded. "This is going to be the final battle. I'm going to bring reinforcements.".

ALISA: Alex disappeared, leaving me and Micka. Micka was still crying. "All these tears for Falsa? Really?". Micka looked up at me, "YOU DON'T UNDERSTAND! So...don't try to.". She stood up and walked to the other side of the field. I followed her. Alexa, who had been nearby with Casian, rushed forward, "Did I see Alex? Where did she go?", she exclaimed. "Alexa, it's time to return to Alexandria.". Alexa looked angry, but Casian licked her face. This was her way of saying she agreed. She could sense what was coming. Micka had waited for me. "Where is the ring? Is it safe?", I didn't know why she was still asking about that ring. Then I remembered she could hear the dead. "Has Bastian said anything else to you?". She gave me a sad sort of look, bit her lip, then answered, "He isn't with me anymore. I don't know what happened. Wilson is gone as well.". I didn't know if this was good or bad. Then, Alex appeared again. She had brought the entire Dashin army with her. Micka was staring, jaw dropped. "I never would have guessed she was this powerful!", said Micka. I thought to myself the same thing. I'd seen Alex fight plenty of times and knew she was a skilled hand to hand combatant. But what I didn't know is she contained this other worldly power to teleport large armies, and even fight Desian. Then I realized maybe the shield was giving her this strength. If only it had given some of that to Bastian.

I watched as Alex disappeared on the spot again. My mother and father both came to my side, "Alisa, how are you? How is our grandchild?". Before I could answer, my father cut me off, "Your mother and I both agreed that you are not to fight. You are to remain in the castle under heavy guard.", "It's okay, Alex has already forbidden me to fight.". I said, in a regrettable tone. "Sebastian, bless her. Please guide us in this time of trial.", my parents prayed.

We made our way back to the castle, where Alexa had come with a packed bag and Casian riding in it. "Casian, you are to guard her, understand?". Casian licked my finger tip and rubbed her face in my hand. Alex appeared next to us, the shield glittering on her back. "BIG SISTER! I WANT TO STAY!", "You can't. I'm taking you back home. It'll be safe there.", "NO!", yelled Alexa. Alex patiently placed her hands on the crying girl's shoulders. "I ALREADY LOST SEBASTIAN! I DON'T WANT TO LOSE YOU, TOO!", "You won't lose me! I'll be home with you before you know it!", Alex replied, tears forming in her eyes as well. Caprius had shown up with the baby in his arms, "Probably a good idea if I go as well.", he said. Alex nodded and gestured for him to come closer. "Good luck, everyone.", Caprius said, as he, Alexa, Casian, the baby, and Alex all disappeared. Tisiphone came into the room now and was holding onto something. "Tig asked me to give this to you. He said, since he can't fight, he was wondering if you'll wear it.". It was a blue shawl. It had three kids on there. Micka came forward and grabbed it. "I'll wear it. Seeing as how it belongs to me.", "What are you talking about?", asked Tisiphone, who was just realizing Micka was here. Seeing the look in her eye, "Tisiphone, let's talk out there, shall we?". I led her outside. "I know the anger you have towards Micka, but don't forget she is carrying Bastian's child.". Tisiphone locked livid. "THAT WITCH KILLED MY FATHER!", "And Falsa killed hers. But do you know what the last thing Falsa did was? She sacrificed herself for Micka. Think about that.". Tisiphone was looking at me through confused eyes. "Falsa... She really did that? But I always thought...", she trailed off. Micka was still admiring the shawl. "What is that to you?", I asked her. "I made this when Bastian, Tig, and myself were children.", she said with a slight tear in her eye. Alex had reappeared outside with the Nashin army now. Queen Penelope was amongst them. She turned and was headed in the direction of the castle. There was a loud boom. I realized right away what the sound was. Desian had arrived. The Dashin and Nashin soldiers were fighting his army of undead. Alex had rushed to meet Desian head on. I sat down, wishing I could join.

CAPRIUS: Upon arriving in Alexandria, there was a small bit of urine that exited out of me. I had never seen the like. When Alex had breathed on the stone that flew us to the floating kingdom, I remembered when mother had come here and stolen the shield. But I never got to see this place. Mother had come here on her own. She took no soldiers. Now I understood why. This was definitely a secret my mother would want to keep. The castle rose all the way to the sky and I saw gold and white all over the walls. There were pictures of other goddesses, and one large picture that had a man in diamond armor, and a pink glittering girl holding onto him. Alexa watched me, as I moved through the castle in amazement. "Can I hold her?", Alexa asked me, as I stared transfixed at one of the strange realistic paintings. "Yes. Here you go.". Alexa took Ko-e out of my hands. I looked at the picture closer and realized the glittering woman in the picture was my mother. I tried to imagine what she must have been like before all the evil. Then, as Alexa had walked off and left me alone, I felt a presence near me. When I turned to look, it was my mother. But she wasn't fully there, "My son, I'm so sorry for failing you.". I looked at her in shock. I didn't know what to say. "Where are you?", I asked her. She gave me a sad smile, "Desian has killed me.", "But you're here!", I exclaimed. How was she dead if I was talking to her? "Caprius, I don't have much time, so let me say what I have to say. It may have never seemed like it, but I did love you. I was wrong to abandon you. I was so fixed on my vengeance, that I couldn't see straight. Desian warped my mind into believing that there was no choice but to make people suffer. And the worst one to suffer was you. I miss you already!", she said, reaching towards me, but her hands just passed through me. It was extremely cold. Tears were falling down her ghostly face. "But, I don't understand. How did Desian kill you?", "He killed me, to punish Micka. The poor girl has lost two mothers now. But I ask you to take good care of your sister. I understand why you kept her from me. You may have been like your father before, but now, you are the young man I had hoped for. I regret that I realize that now, when it is too late. I love you, My Son, and never forget that.". Falsa started to fade. "WAIT, I HAVE MORE QUESTIONS! MOTHER!", but it was too late, she was gone. I felt this hole in my heart. I was angry with her. We didn't part on good terms. Perhaps that's why her spirit came to me. But then, I remembered something from my childhood. When I was five, I was very attached to my mother. But my mother was hardly attached to me. She was always leaving for long periods of time and then returning only for short spells. Once, when she had returned, I wanted to surprise her. So, I planned a whole party. I had the servants help me. They were delighted to help, mainly because they thought that would change my mother's attitude. But they were madly wrong. When Mother returned and saw the decorations, she destroyed it all and flogged the helpers. When I cried to her that it was me who came up with the idea, she slapped me and beat me. "I NEVER WANT TO EVER SEE THIS UPON MY RETURN AGAIN! DO YOU UNDERSTAND?!". After that, I had grown distant from my mother. I wished I had anyone else but her. But there was something I had noticed that same night. My mother was crying. "Why? Why did I do that to my son? He didn't deserve it. He's still just a baby after all. He loves me! Why can't I appreciate that?! Why do I need this anger?!". At the time, I didn't understand. Now I do. Desian had made her this way. I knew I had to remain with my baby sister, Ko-e, but Desian was going to pay. I didn't care what it took. Desian had to go.

ALISA: The shouts were all over the kingdom. Desian was in the air, lording over the situation. Or he was scared of Alex. Alex was in the crowd fighting the undead. She seemed to be the only one who could make them stay down. "DESIAN! GET DOWN HERE NOW, YOU COWARD!", Alex was shouting. Tisiphone and Sheena were partnered up, fighting and watching each other's backs. Micka, who was still sitting with me, was getting antsy. "That's it, I'm going out there.", "Micka, you are going to stay here! We must wait. We don't know what's going to happen. Plus, I will not let you endanger that baby.". I still didn't fully trust her. "Give me the ring, Micka.". Micka rubbed her stomach and sat back down. She looked at me for a second, then slowly slid the strange ring off her finger and gave it to me. The battle seemed to just keep going, with the undead getting back to their feet or being knocked down by Alex and staying down. The Dashin and Nashin soldiers were doing the best they could, but the undead were everywhere and more seemed to keep popping up. Finally, Alex had catapulted herself off one of the undead's chests, and flew at Desian. Desian caught her and the two fell out of the sky and landed. The fight was getting worse. Finally, I saw Tisiphone leading a group of men who had been injured away from the battle. Sheena was still in the crowd waiting to see what was happening with Desian and Alex. Alex and Desian were throwing blows at one another.

ALEX: "I've already killed one goddess, I'll have no issue killing another. Even if you are carrying my child!", Desian shouted at me, but I didn't care. I fought with every ounce of my being. Him swinging his sword and me blocking with the shield. I remember Sebastian telling me that the sword and shield wouldn't go against each other, so I thought it was strange that it seemed to be functioning differently for me. I noticed that the god sword had become different somehow. Before I could feel its energy. But now, it seemed drained somehow. Desian took another swing of his sword that I managed to deflect, but he tricked me and pulled out a dagger, which he moved in an upward motion and cut my chest open. I fell to the ground bleeding. "ALEX!", I heard someone yelling. Then I saw Alisa, holding the shield and standing up to Desian. She had taken Micka's ring and teleported onto the battlefield. "STUPID GIRL!", Desian had yelled. Then, there was a huge burst of energy and I saw Alisa on the ground, gasping. Desian moving towards her. "You are the most foolish person I've ever had the displeasure of creating. Now I will show both…", he cut off. As he reached his sword up to stab Alisa, a loud boom echoed throughout the field. Then a large light came from the sky. It engulfed everything and gave off a warm feeling. In that light, I felt things were going to be okay. Just then, I saw a figure putting something on his hand. He stroked Alisa's face and looked up. I couldn't believe what I was seeing, "SEBASTIAN!". He was alive. He picked up the shield and then held out his right arm. "THE SWORD?! BUT…", he turned and winked at me. Desian stood there in shock. He looked at the sword in his hand then at the one Sebastian was holding. He opened then closed his mouth. "Desian, lets finish this. No more collateral. Just you and me.". Desian licked his lips. Then, Sebastian walked up to Desian. "I knew it. I knew you weren't dead! Where the hell have you been hiding?", "I went home. I hope that's okay with you.". Desian looked livid and started swinging his sword. Upon touching Bastian's sword though, it shattered. Desian had a shocked look on his face. He was in such a shock that he didn't immediately react. Once he gained his senses again, he started throwing punches. This too was a waste, because Sebastian just caught all his punches. Now with both fists clenched in Bastian's, Desian rose into the air. They went so high up I couldn't see them. But then, Sebastian landed cat-like on his feet, while Desian landed sort of hard. "What the hell is happening?!", Desian said. Bastian walked up to him and touched him with the ring Micka had given Caprius. Desian started to fade. "NO! I'VE WAITED FIVE-HUNDRED YEARS! IT WON'T END LIKE THIS! I WON'T LET IT!". Desian broke away from Bastian and flew away. Bastian flew after him.

SEBASTIAN: It was over and Desian knew it was. He was trying to escape. We flew across Plinth at speeds that would probably kill any normal Plinthinian. When I finally realized where we were flying, a small chuckle left my mouth. He was seeking the sanctuary of the cave. The cave I trapped him in. When I saw him touch down in the woods, I landed as well, just in time to see him running towards the cave. I entered the cave and saw a broken Desian. "What happened to my essence? It was here! What the hell happened?!". He was digging where all the black water used to be. "It's gone, Desian. The last of it was gone right when you killed Falsa. Should have thought that through a bit more, huh?". I decided to pull my armor on. I watched Desian's face go from confusion to horror. Then, he smiled, "So, this is how it ends. You, taking me?". He started to laugh, "No matter what, Bastian, I'll always be a part of you! So, you'll never kill me! You hear that? YOU WILL NEVER BE RID OF ME!". I walked up to him and pressed the ring to him. This time he was stuck and couldn't move. He allowed me to absorb him. He faded with that same insane nasty smile he always wore. At once, there was a conflict within me. I felt the anger rush, then I felt pain, then I felt…nothing. Desian and I had melded. I felt his feelings but had control over them. Desian and Sebastian were no longer two people, we were one. I flew back to Kindy, where the battle had subsided. The undead, unable to function without Desian, fell to the ground. There was a large mass of dead bodies all over the Kind Field. I landed to find Alisa recuperating with Sheena sitting next to her. Tisiphone was aiding the wounded. King Derek was walking amongst the men, while Queen Shay was aiding Tisiphone with the wounded. Micka was there as well and she was patching up Alex. It was strange to see, but I understood. Desian had united everyone. When Alex saw me, she pushed Micka away, and rushed to me. She jumped on me, wrapping her legs and arms around me, and kissed me. Alex refused to let me go. "I thought you were dead! We all thought you were dead! I saw your body!". I calmly pushed her away from me. "Well, it's kind of a long story, but I really was dead. But when I died, I didn't die. I woke up like this. It took me a long time to learn how to operate this body. After all, this is only my Plinthinian vessel. Are you ready to go to our real home?", I asked Alex, who beamed positively brightly. Alisa walked up to me next and hugged me tightly, "I thought I'd never see you again!", she exclaimed. She kissed me on my cheek. Then the king and queen came to me. Next thing I knew, I was surrounded. People were trying to kiss my boots or just get near enough to touch me. That night hosted a huge party the likes of which hadn't been seen in centuries. Tig had arrived with his parents and Tisiphone helped him move around. I noticed that the two of them were finally together, because Tisiphone was kissing all over Tig, any chance she got. Alisa and Sheena were dancing. Caprius, who had returned from Alexandria via teleportation with my shield, was dancing with his baby sister, Ko-e, in his arms. Alexa was watching them with interest. Alex was drinking with Queen Shay. "I've…never seen anything like what you did today! I believe you are the true hero today.", "No, I believe that would be Alisa. She saved my life.". Alisa, who was dancing so hard, didn't notice Alex tipping her cup towards her. Casian was on the dance floor as well, jumping up and down. Micka was sitting by herself in a corner. I decided to walk towards her. "Hello, Micka.", "Sebastian, I can hardly believe this war is over. Seems like yesterday we were escaping Nasher and making love.". Micka had a cup in her hand, so I knew she was under the influence of spirits, "But, you know what? I am the Queen of Dasha.". She started to laugh. Then she pointed at Alisa. "At the last second, she convinced me to give her my ring.", "Well, if you hadn't, Alex would be dead.", I said flatly. Micka turned around, considering my words. Just then, Queen Penelope approached me. She took in my armor and smiled, "This is amazing. Is it all diamond? It is glorious. You are simply amazing.". She gave me a hug and kissed me on my cheek. We walked away, and I looked back at Micka, who didn't seem too interested in joining the festivities. I, of course, knew why. Falsa was something she never had. And now that she has lost her, she is lost again, alone. But that isn't true. For now, I see my own great design. She will see it, too. "I want you to know how proud your mother would be.". I didn't want to be rude, but I knew exactly how proud she would be, because I can hear her spirit. "Thank you, Grandma. It means a lot to me.", "You're leaving though after this? Aren't you? You're going to your real home? Desian would mock us and tell us how beautiful Heaven is.", she let out a small sob, "I'm sorry, it's just that I've lost my husband, and now I'm losing my grandson.". She sobbed into her hand. I pulled her into a hug. "I have an idea. Why don't you come with me and Alex to Alexandria? You can stay there with Caprius, Alexa, and your great-grandchild, Ko-e.". Penelope looked up and I saw her smile brightly, "Well, who would take over Nasher as its ruler?", "I have a solution to that as well.". She hugged me. "Now go on, and enjoy the party. There is something I have to do.". Penelope walked away and joined Micka in her dark corner. I found Alex and gestured for her to come with me. We stepped outside, where in the distance, you could hear people in the village celebrating as well. "So, why did you bring me out here?", Alex asked me, wrapping her arms around my chest. "I wanted some alone time. Is that an issue?", "Not at all.". I flew us into the air. We kissed, and I flew even higher. We flew around for some time, just enjoying the night air around us. "We will go to Alexandria tomorrow, get our affairs in order, then, we depart for Heaven.". Alex didn't say anything, so I landed. We were in a clearing near the Willet. "What's wrong?", I asked. "All my life I've dreamed of this. Exactly this. And now it's here and I don't know. Leaving the planet, when I've been here all my life. Leaving behind all the people I've come to know as my friends. Leaving Alisa or Alexa? I don't know if I can.". I wasn't too surprised to hear this. There was a huge part of me that felt the same way. "Alex, wait until you see it. I guarantee you'll feel differently. Please, just come with me. I need you. I love you. You are my queen.". Alex blushed, "I feel so embarrassed. You've never spoken to me like that.", "There are plenty more words I have for you. Come with me and you'll see, we won't ever be apart from our friends.". Alex reached up and kissed me. We fell where we were and made love.

When the sun had come up, we went to Kindy to say our goodbyes and take everyone to their proper homes. Caprius agreed to watch over Alexandria, realizing what a huge deal that was. Alexa was his partner and was to aid him. Penelope would go with them to help as well, and keep watch over Ko-e. Tig, who was barely waking up, woke up to me throwing water in his face. He had been lying next to Tisiphone, who I had woke up and convinced to go use the restroom. "Wazza hellBats?", he slurred as he was jumping to his feet and I roared with laughter. "I'm leaving soon for my real home.". Tig tensed up at these words, and then he hugged me. "Hey, I'm leaving you with a great gift, though. I'm leaving you in charge of Nasher. In other words, hail, King Tig and Queen Tisiphone.". Tig's jaw dropped. "Are you serious, Bats? What about, Penelope?", "She is going to Alexandria.". Tig grabbed my hand, "THANKS, MATE! I can't believe it! I'm the king! What will my parents say to me? My dad thought I wasn't worth anything. Wonder what he'll say now…". Alisa was sitting in her room with Sheena. When I arrived, Sheena hugged me and kissed me on my cheek, "Don't worry about your daughter, I'll make sure she is always loved.", she whispered in my ear, then left the room. Alisa smiled at me. She was really beautiful and was the brightest, bravest, person I knew. I didn't know what to say to her. But the look we were giving each other were words enough. We had been through a lot. Alisa stood up and grabbed my hand. She placed it on her stomach. "Even though you're leaving, I know that a huge part of you, will always be with me.". She kissed me on my lips, passionately, and then left the room. I felt that was all she could muster to do. King Derek and Queen Shay greeted me. We spoke for some time about how things were going to be now that things were peaceful. Tisiphone came into the room, "TIG'S ONLY JUST TOLD ME! YOU'VE MADE ME A QUEEN!", she was shouting, and she planted a kiss on my cheek. The day was filled with happiness and sadness. But eventually the time had come. Alex and I left Kindy, after saying a few more goodbyes. We arrived in Alexandria, where Parnim had prepared a great feast. We feasted with Penelope, Caprius, Alexa, Casian and a few other important people within the kingdom. After the feast, Alex and I headed to the top of the castle. "Well, this is it. Are you ready?". Alex nodded. I called on the force that would take us to Heaven, and the light glowed brightly. Alex's eyes never left mine, and she embraced me, as we ascended into the Heavens.

CHAPTER 18

The Story Of Amana And Calypsa

ALISA: Five years had passed since Sebastian and Alex left us. It had been a hard five years. Amana was born and my whole life changed. Dealing with a baby was something I had never truly prepared for. She pooped, and puked, and urinated on me enough times for me to consider putting her in the yard, and leaving her for whatever creature decided it wanted her. Sheena had the worst of it so far. She had been throwing her into the air and catching her, when she had to go poop. Unfortunately, Sheena hadn't realized when she caught her. It was like a poop bomb had gone off. Sheena was covered in it. I sent letters to Penelope, often asking if she had similar issues with Ko-e. Apparently, this had to do with the fact that they were goddesses. They had stronger metabolisms. This was true, because I know for a fact, Amana could eat. I remember the first day I gave her milk. She just kept crying and crying for more. I remember praying to Sebastian to just take his daughter. Micka never said anything about what was going on with her daughter. But like most royalty, it wasn't easy to hide. Micka's daughter was named Calypsa. She, from what I could tell, was just as much a handful as Amana or Ko-e. Micka was forcing all the servants in the castle to help out, so, talk got out. After the baby phase, Amana was four and a genius. She, like myself when I was younger, was very good at mixing potions and chemicals. At the age of four, she developed a much stronger kind flower elixir. This one not only eliminated the symptoms before a soldier's shift, but also gave an energy boost so that the soldier wasn't too groggy. She loved having Sheena take her into the kingdom to see all the people and all the happenings. I saw a lot of myself in her. But I also saw Sebastian. The red rim around her eyes was a sign she was Sebastian's daughter. The gold in her eyes was her goddess sign. One night, while I was sleeping, Alex came to me in a dream. She told me to make sure that the girls never know that they're father is a god. There could be dire consequences. When I awoke, I decided to listen to her.

Plinth had been a peaceful place ever since Sebastian had left. I couldn't imagine if it had become worse than it was. We did business with all the kingdoms. We enjoyed the peacefulness of it all. Just being able to relax and not having to worry about anything. On Amana's fifth birthday, we had a huge party in the castle. We invited the other children from within the village and had set up booths where they could play. The kids played all day and ate ice cream and cake. After a long day, once the parents were shuffling their children back towards the village, I was with Amana. "Mother, I have a question.". I waited to hear what her question was. "One of the games involved having your father put you on his shoulders and spin around. The idea of the game was to not get too dizzy and keep your balance. I wanted to play, and Sheena offered to put me on her shoulders, but...", she hesitated, "...I felt it wouldn't be fair because

Sheena isn't my father. Who is my father?". I feared she would ask this one day. But I knew I couldn't tell her, her father is a god. "Your father was a brave soldier named Bats. He fought hard beside me in the last war.", "Did you love him like you love Sheena?". As always, Amana was very perceptive. This wasn't entirely a good thing for me as it was for her. I had to think on the spot. Part of me saw where this conversation was going, "Well, not exactly. Things just sort of happened. Whatever the case, why don't we...?", "Yes, but don't you have to make love to make a child? How do you make love, Mother?". Now I was completely at a loss. "Amana, these are things you should worry about when you're older.", "But...I really want to know about my father.". She looked sad. "He's dead. I'm sorry. I never thought I'd have to tell you that. But he's dead.". Amana looked sadder. "Hey, why don't we go get some ice cream? That will cheer you up.". But it didn't cheer her up. She continued to brood, as me, her, and Sheena ate the ice cream. My parents, who had waited for all the other children to leave, came to see her. But even my parents couldn't make her feel better. The next morning, I woke up and went to check on her, "Amana, time to wake...", there was nobody here, but I found a note;

Dear mother,

I love you, but I really need to know about my father. I think about what he must be like all the time. I know you told me he is dead, but forgive me for not believing you. Please try to see things from my perspective. I know that you would probably do the same. I promise I'll return.

-Love, Amana Tia

While I was, of course, in shock, I acted immediately. I sent out scout's, soldiers, and anyone who volunteered to try and find Amana. Nobody knew where she was. By the end of the day, I was in tears, worried where she was. I still remembered that I had met her future version, but that didn't stop me from worrying about if she was hurt or not. The next morning, I found myself waking up to a wet soggy pillow, and I was in Amana's chambers. I had never felt more lost. I was more lost now than when me and Alex had gone into the Dark Wood. I kept thinking about Amana. Was she hurt? Did some bandit find her? Was she in another kingdom wandering around lost, unable to find her way back here? Finally, a scout had returned, but with no new news of Amana's whereabouts. I became completely distraught, and right when I felt like things weren't going to get any better, they got much worse. A horse was riding down the path. Sheena had come and fetched me. It appeared to be two young girls. One looked like she could be badly injured. The girl who wasn't injured had long purple hair that was in waves. Her eyes, even from this distance, had a great glow to them. I realized right away who she was. "I'm sorry I couldn't have gotten here sooner! It wasn't easy riding with the both of us.". She climbed down off the horse. Sure enough, the injured girl was Amana. She was bleeding from her head and was unconscious. "WHAT HAPPENED?!", Sheena exclaimed, taking Amana into her arms. "We met two days ago, and we went on an adventure!", the girl said, as if this was some game she was playing, "You see, when we first met, I was running away, too. And we had so many similarities that we thought we might be sisters.". It was scary to think that she didn't realize how correct they both were. "We were on our way back here because Amana thought I should meet her mum!". The spunkiness in her reminded me so much of Sebastian, that I was brought to my senses. "Princess Calypsa, right?", "How do you know who I am?", she asked with her jaw dropped. "Thank you for bringing back my daughter, but you are to return to your kingdom at once, and never seek Amana out, ever again.". She looked hurt. I felt bad telling her that. "But, she is my sister. We should be together all the time!". Another horse was making its way down the path. This horse was pulling what appeared to be some kind of moving house. Calypsa turned to see what we were gaping at, and horror spread on her face. "PLEASE DON'T MAKE ME GO

BACK WITH MY MOM! PLEASE?!", she started to plead. As the strange vehicle came to a stop, Micka stepped out of it, "CALYPSA! I HAVE BEEN SEARCHING FOR YOU! COME!". Calypsa looked at me with tears in her eyes. "Micka, it's been a while.". Micka just looked at me as if she didn't have time for such things as friendly greetings. "Alisa.", she said nodding, "Calypsa, lets go. Now.", "I DON'T WANT TO! I DON'T WANT TO BE A PRINCESS ANYMORE!", she shouted, "I just want to live with my sister.", "YOU DO NOT HAVE A SISTER!", Micka yelled at her. "But... Amana is...", "The princess to Kindy. So just like you, she has her own responsibilities. So, stop this foolishness.". Amana was waking up, "I'm sorry. I fell off the horse and hit my head. Please don't yell at Calypsa.". Micka turned in her direction. She eyed her for some time, "This isn't about you getting hurt, it's about my daughter running away from her responsibilities. Now, Calypsa, I will not ask you again, get in the carriage.". I looked at the thing called a carriage and immediately thought of buying one. "Micka, perhaps we can let the girls play...", "NO!", Micka shouted, "Alisa, I mean, you know.". Alex had come to her as well. I bowed my head and looked into Calypsa's eyes. They were so much like Bastian's. "I'm sorry, Calypsa, but you must do as your mother says.". Amana jumped up and ran to Calypsa, hugging her, "MOM, PLEASE?! I WANT HER TO STAY WITH US!", "AMANA, PLEASE DON'T MAKE THIS HARDER, NOW MOVE! SHE ISN'T YOUR SISTER!". Amana looked at me with pain and hate in her eyes, but ran away towards the castle. Micka was pulling Calypsa into the carriage. I noticed the look that she had given me. She hated me. I hated myself. The last thing I expected was for Amana to bring home one of her sisters. Let alone the one I hadn't even seen yet. This to me was proof that things were going to be more difficult than I imagined. If this is what it was like to deal with them as children, what will they be like when they are older? I shuddered at the thought.

www.ingramcontent.com/pod-product-compliance
Lightning Source LLC
Chambersburg PA
CBHW021549310726
48972CB00003B/741
9781963883138